A SONG TO TAKE THE WORLD APART

A SONG
TO TAKE THE
WORLD
APART

ZAN ROMANOFF

ALFRED A. KNOPF

NEW YORK

THIS IS A BORZOI BOOK PUBLISHED BY ALFRED A. KNOPF

Grateful acknowledgment is made to the following for permission to reprint previously published material:
Hal Leonard Corporation: Excerpt from "Lorelei," words and music by Philip Chevron, copyright © 1989 Wardlaw Banks Ltd. Administered by Downtown DLJ Songs. All rights reserved. Reprinted by permission of Hal Leonard Corporation.
Wixen Music Publishing, Inc: Excerpt from "Mercedes Benz," by Janis Joplin, Michael McClure, and Bob Neuwirth, copyright © 1970 Strong Arm Music (ASCAP). Administered by Wixen Music Publishing Inc. All rights reserved. Used by permission.

Visit us on the Web! randomhouseteens.com

Educators and librarians, for a variety of teaching tools, visit us at RHTeachersLibrarians.com

Library of Congress Cataloging-in-Publication Data
Names: Romanoff, Zan, author.
Title: A song to take the world apart / Zan Romanoff.
Description: First edition. | New York : Alfred A. Knopf, [2016] | Summary: "Lorelei has the power to change hearts and minds, just by singing, but it comes at a terrible cost." —Provided by publisher
Identifiers: LCCN 2015043446 | ISBN 978-1-101-93879-9 (trade) | ISBN 978-1-101-93881-2 (ebook)
Subjects: | CYAC: Singing—Fiction. | Sirens (Mythology)—Fiction. | Love—Fiction. | BISAC: JUVENILE FICTION / Social Issues / Dating & Sex. | JUVENILE FICTION / Legends, Myths, Fables / General. | JUVENILE FICTION / Girls & Women.
Classification: LCC PZ7.1.R6683 So 2016 | DDC [Fic]—dc23

The text of this book is set in 12-point Caslon.

Printed in the United States of America
September 2016
10 9 8 7 6 5 4 3 2 1

First Edition

In memory of Amelia Izquierdo and Anne Evans
For Mom, Dad, and Tiny, of course

the only thing I'll ever ask of you
you gotta promise not to stop when I say when

— FOO FIGHTERS, *"Everlong"*

1

LORELEI AND ZOE LIE about going to the see the band.

It is, as usual, Zoe's idea. She's the one who pulls a flyer down on her way to geometry, and slips it to Lorelei as she walks up the aisle to her seat. When Lorelei unfolds it, she recognizes it right away: she's been seeing the posters and ignoring them for weeks.

This one is printed on salmon-colored copy paper. On it, two figures lean against one another in silhouette. Their heads are thrown back and their guitars are raised ecstatically. They're surrounded by lazy hand-drawn doodles of stars and spirals and peace signs and pot leaves. *THE TROUBLE at the ROXY,* it says. Zoe has scrawled across the back: *We're totally going. And I will make you talk to him!!*

Zoe's parents are less strict than Lorelei's, but they're unpredictable, and the girls have never done anything like this before. Lying will make everything easier, Zoe says. They'll say they're going to a movie. Her mom will drop them off. They'll walk to the Roxy, and back again when it's over. No one will ever have to know.

Anxiety tugs at Lorelei on the drive over, up until they get out of the car and Mrs. Soroush drives away, turning a corner and falling out of sight. It's only as she and Zoe start walking toward the venue that her worry blossoms into something sweet-centered and sharp-edged with thrill.

Los Angeles is too big to navigate all together; instead, Lorelei has learned it as a network of neighborhoods, like stepping-stones that lead from one to the next. They started out miles west of here, in Venice, where the air is heavy with ocean water and everything is crusted in a fine layer of salt. Mrs. Soroush took the 405 to the 10 and then La Cienega north for miles, all of it flashing by too fast and black to see. Now Sunset Boulevard is wide and grungy, illuminated mostly by neon signs and white marquee lights. Lorelei likes how strange it is: dark and then shining, like a mouth full of unfamiliar, gleaming teeth.

It's a hot September and the air smells like diesel and exhaust, mineral and dry.

The bigness of the night makes her skin feel small, so Lorelei tries to take up space. She stands up straight and throws her shoulders back. Even her clothes are asking her to play a part tonight, her floral print baby-doll dress soft as it moves against the tops of her thighs. Her hair is loose and long against her neck and shoulders, a shifting cascade of honey blond. Zoe let her borrow a beat-up leather jacket, which makes her feel tough, and safe.

The pair of enormous, sour-faced bouncers at the entrance to the venue cross the backs of the girls' hands with thick black *X*'s to mark that they aren't even trying to pretend they're twenty-one, and they get drink tickets in exchange for a ten-dollar cover. The first thing they do when they get inside is sneak into the bathroom to scrub off the *X*'s and put on their faces.

Zoe holds Lorelei's chin and pencils a thick, confident line at the arced rim of her eyelid. Then she turns Lorelei's head to admire the effect. "You're going to look so *tough*," she breathes. Lorelei widens her eyes and rolls them upward, letting Zoe work on her lower lashes. "He'll never recognize you like this."

"Isn't that a bad thing?" Lorelei asks. She licks her lips and tastes the thick wax of Crimson Glow lipstick. "I mean, if he only likes how I look tonight."

It's not like she's ever really talked to Chris, a senior, and lead singer of The Trouble. She's a sophomore. That he remembers her—and wants to see her again—is too much to hope for. She loves Zoe's optimism, but that doesn't mean she trusts it.

"Not necessarily." Zoe has an older sister, which means a closetful of hand-me-downs that smell faintly of clove cigarettes, a working knowledge of the last ten years in pop music, and this particular brand of mysterious wisdom. Lorelei's older brothers have never given her much more than chin-jerk nods when she passes them in the hallways at school.

"Tonight's the night he *sees* you, you know, that he realizes who you really are. Then when you run into each other at school, and you're all shy and stuff, you'll seem extra mysterious. Like, *Who's that girl with the secret life? What kind of cool shit does she do on weekends that I don't know about?*"

"I don't do anything on weekends," Lorelei says. She kicks a Converse against the bathroom wall. "Unless hanging out with Oma counts as *mysterious*." Mentioning her grandmother seems like a bad omen, like it might conjure her, somehow.

"*He* doesn't have to know that," Zoe reminds her. She turns away to put on lipstick, a hot-pink shade that brings out the yellow undertones of her olive skin. It looks weird on purpose, cool and easy and knowing. Lorelei regards her own baby face in the mirror, focusing on the round curves of her cheeks. The makeup makes her features stand out cartoonishly. She looks like she's just a little girl playing dress-up. She wraps one arm around Zoe's waist and leans her head onto her bony shoulder.

Zoe smells like rose oil and Secret baby powder deodorant. Her warm skin is almost masked, but not quite.

"Look at us," Zoe says with triumphant satisfaction, butting her chin against the top of Lorelei's head. "We look, like, at least eighteen."

∼⟨⟩∼

Lorelei first tripped over Chris in the hallway at school. It was the second week of the semester, and she was getting lost trying to find a class. The halls were especially crowded those first weeks because of the wildfires raging around the city, which made strange, dark clouds of smoke and ash, and turned the whole sky orange.

No one wanted to be out under it, so instead of sprawling across campus, almost the entire student body was crammed inside with the windows shut. The closeness of the air and the echoes of high-pitched chatter were driving Lorelei insane.

She was so intent on shouldering her way through the crowd that she didn't realize what had happened at first: all she understood was space reorienting, forward becoming down. She fell before she knew she was falling. Her hands shot out instinctively to catch her weight.

It was over before she could name it, and it took her a minute to reassemble herself: palms against the linoleum, a spreading ache in her knees and elbows. The boy she'd stumbled over came to her last: Chris Paulson, though she wouldn't know his name until Zoe found it out for her.

At first all she could see of him was the crown of his curly head. He had a guitar in his lap, and he'd bent forward to protect it from her fall. As he unfolded, she saw his face, and registered that he was handsome, and older. The summer's surf tan was still brown on his wrists and forearms.

Lorelei had never been so close to a boy who wasn't one of her brothers before. She was consumed by the details. His T-shirt looked like it had been bigger on him when he bought it: now it strained across his shoulders, and the sleeves rode up to show a slim strip of pale, untouched skin. She watched that tender half-moon move as he reached out to put a hand on her shoulder.

"Sorry about that," he said. "I should have been paying attention. You okay?"

"Yeah," she said. Her voice was thick in her throat. "Fine." Standing up seemed like it might be a challenge. She folded her legs carefully so that she was sitting, facing him, like she'd meant to end up there all along.

"Cool." He leaned back, and shifted and resettled the guitar in his lap. His right arm slid lower, fingers strumming idly at the strings. The sound they made was warm and sweet and unexpected, just a ripple of notes. It was the only nice thing Lorelei had heard all day, and it felt like someone stroking down her spine, making her bones go liquid. Her eyes closed without her permission.

"That's nice," she said without meaning to.

"Yeah," Chris said. "I know, right. I shouldn't just, like, sit here, but sometimes it feels like it's the only way to get through the day." He gave her a sliver of a smile and ducked his head again, picking out something deliberate, a melody that hung together with its own gravity.

The tune made everything else around her turn down to a bearable level. It was like he had found a hook-and-eye fastening somewhere on her and tugged just right, undoing her all at once: the sound was golden in her ears and warm on her skin, and she drifted toward the pull of the notes.

"What is that?" she asked. "Is it, like—"

"You really don't recognize it?" The crowd around them was thinning as passing period ended, but Lorelei couldn't make herself move. "My god, what are they teaching you children these days?"

Lorelei flushed, and knew it only made her look younger.

"Dave Grohl was in Nirvana," Chris went on. "So I would think his—" He caught the blankness on her face and shook his head at her, smiling. "Jesus, girl."

He laid the guitar on the ground next to him. Lorelei liked to watch him do it: he was careful, and sure. He handled it like it was a holy object, but one he knew well and had gotten used to being in charge of. "You've got a lot of listening to do," he said.

Chris got up and dusted himself off and she did the same, trying to keep anything in her mind long enough to stick. She couldn't, though: her ears buzzed with the absence of music, and her fingers twitched toward the guitar. Even lying there quietly it was full of the promise of sound, its curved body and hollow belly waiting for a single finger to tug a string so it could hum a song. Lorelei didn't know whether she liked the boy or the guitar more. They both disappeared down the hallway before she could say anything else.

In class she couldn't stop thinking about him. Boys had wanted her attention before, once or twice, and they'd gone about getting it clumsily, sometimes angry when she didn't jump at their advances, and especially when she didn't feel the same way. She wasn't sure whether that was her fault or not, not knowing how to respond to something she'd never asked for in the first place. She liked the quiet contrast of Chris, the way he settled down in the hallway and made himself space. She thought all through the period about his hands on the guitar, steady. The images came to her, unbidden, of those same hands on her skin instead, notes rippling up out of her own throat.

She didn't recognize the gentle lick of warmth in her belly as want. She only knew that it was unfamiliar, the way the sensation lit her up. That was the day she discovered why they call it longing: because desire is full of distance and unfilled space. She felt like the empty center of the guitar, waiting for someone to pluck a string and fill her up with sound.

2

THE ROXY'S SINGLE ROOM is dim and crowded, with pre-recorded music blaring from crappy speakers. Lorelei's ears prick toward it, but the sound is so bad there's no way to distinguish any kind of melody. The air is at least half echo and static. It's just the thump of beat and bass that she picks up on, backbone sounds like a spine to the noisy chaos.

She checks the impulse to slam her hands over her ears. It's never made sense to her, the way people play music to fill in quiet and then ignore it—as if anyone could ignore it. But then not everyone grew up the way she did, accustomed to long stretches of domestic silence, in a house where no one ever plays music or even talks much at all.

She and Zoe spend their first drink tickets on Cokes and suck them down quickly. Lorelei is starting to sweat in her borrowed jacket in the humid room. The space already seems impossibly full, and it's packed even tighter as they move up toward the front. They're just wriggling through a bunch of disorganized bodies until something shifts, and there's a stir that is the mass becoming a crowd, moving in unison.

When Lorelei looks up, the band is making its way on-stage.

Chris, lead singer, lead guitarist, is front and center. He's wearing tight black jeans and a faded black T-shirt with a pink and green *D.A.R.E.* logo peeling patchily off the front. His hair is still growing out from its September trim, and his tan is turning milkier, more golden, but he's still just as heart-stopping as he was the first time she saw him.

The boyishness of his curls sets him apart from the other band members, who are all blandly good-looking, with spiky hair and blank, bored eyes. Lorelei recognizes the bassist, Jackson, from school, but the guy behind the drum kit is unfamiliar.

Lorelei catches Chris's eye and panics, looks away.

"It's not weird that we're here, right?" she says to Zoe. "Like. Pathetic. Or something."

"You worry too much," Zoe says.

Lorelei doesn't know whether to believe her or not. She's so far out of her depth that she has no way of guessing whether Zoe is also out of hers. The house Lorelei grew up in isn't just devoid of music: it's quiet in a way she's only just beginning to understand, covered by a hard-edged daily silence that sits over a deeper absence, something she's not yet able to name. The crowd moves like a crowd. She isn't sure yet whether she belongs inside it.

But then the music starts.

Lorelei is glad that it's too loud to talk, too loud to do

anything but dance. She probably wouldn't be able to say anything anyway. She has no words for the sound of the music and the way it makes her feel.

Later, Chris will tell her what he calls it: California skate-rock, ska-inflected, maybe a little bit punk. She'll learn to recognize the bands that influenced them, Green Day and Sublime, those godfathers of their lazy LA vibe. She'll learn how to talk about music the way that people do, which is in proper nouns, without ever trying to describe the luminous, impossible fact of actual sound.

That night what Lorelei responds to is the bright, high wail of a horn playing when a boy from the marching band steps in to add a trumpet blast or two, the fuzz of the guitar, and the clear kick and thrust of the drummer's beat. She's never been surrounded by so much at once before, listening to a song someone made up because he felt like it.

Her skin prickles and burns, and gets tight and dry over her bones. Her throat wells up with choked-back notes. Her body wants to open itself up from the center, turn itself inside out to touch everything at once. The thrum of her pulse falls into the rhythm of each song, like her body recognizes the beat.

Chris stands tall in the spotlight. He sweats and spits and swaggers. The press of bodies all around her crowds Lorelei too closely, and she wants to jump up next to him and take up space the way he does. Chris and the band demand things: the stage floor, and the people to watch them, and the very air in the room, which they fill to bursting with the vibrations of their voices.

Lorelei is small. She's been small. The music makes her want to be bigger.

She's dizzy and light-headed afterward, when they finally stop, bereft in the sudden hugeness of the silence.

"Oh man, I can't hear *shit*," Zoe says, beaming, sticking a pinkie right in her ear.

Lorelei almost can't understand her. She's still listening for the last echo of the last song, trying to get the melody back in her mind.

A few minutes and a second cold Coke bring Lorelei back to herself. Now that she's used to the noise and the people, she can start to pick out groups of her classmates in the crowd. A handful of tables crammed into a corner on the far side of the room seems to be the gathering spot: she recognizes Jackson the bassist's girlfriend, Angela, and her crew of friends. They're all draped on each other, laughing and drinking from dark glass bottles with the labels peeled off.

The boys are starting to load out, pulling equipment offstage, but they pause to say hi to those girls. Jackson tugs Angela off her feet and spins her around in a circle. Lorelei looks at Chris again and tries to look like she's not looking. He moves around easily, like he's used to this chaos. There are so many girls so much closer to his orbit.

He greets them all evenly, though, weaving his way through them like he has somewhere else to be. Lorelei watches Chris as he comes up behind one of the chairs at the far side of the group.

A middle-aged woman is sitting in it, her ankles neatly crossed and her handbag in her lap. Her dark hair is pulled back from her face, which is bare. Lorelei must have seen her and managed not to notice, before. The woman doesn't look like she wants to be noticed. There's something shrunken about her, trembling, like she's only barely clutching herself together.

Chris drops a kiss on the top of her forehead. For one wild, hysterical second Lorelei thinks, *That cannot be his girlfriend,* and then it comes to her, sharp and clear: that's his *mother,* at his gig, his *mother* is here, keeping an eye on him.

The upside of having two overworked parents and being raised by her no-nonsense grandmother is that no one has ever shadowed Lorelei. No one hung around to make sure she felt okay on playdates or sleepovers, or on the first day of school. Lately she watches other girls get pink and flustered when their parents show up on campus or drop them off at parties. It's funny to see her friends trying to navigate between the well-behaved girls they've always been and the independence they're just starting to claim. It's like watching the tide pulling away from the shore only to come rushing right back.

Lorelei has never felt that particular pull. Her mother let her go when she was a baby, first to Oma, and then, later, to the school system and her classmates' parents. She's always been able to separate herself from her family.

Chris's mother stands and smiles at him, and for just a

moment it undoes the primness of her face. She wraps her arms around his broad shoulders and musses his hair. He smiles back, radiant. Lorelei looks away from them. It seems private. When she turns back, Mrs. Paulson is shouldering her way through the crowd, and her mouth is set in a long, firm line again, and Chris is looking past her. This time, Lorelei meets his gaze without being able to stop herself.

It takes a few minutes before he finds a way to drift over. He makes it look casual.

"I feel like I know you," he says.

It's just a line. Lorelei is disappointed to realize that he doesn't remember her, but why would he? It was five minutes, one time. She pretends like she doesn't remember him, either, and tries to play it cool.

"I know," she says.

"Do you, um, do you go to Venice?"

"Yeah," she says. "I'm a sophomore."

"Cool." Chris rocks back on his heels and smiles at her. "I'm a senior there. What did you think of the show?"

"It was *great*," Lorelei says. She wonders if she's being too enthusiastic, and bites down hard on her lower lip to keep it from trembling, or from smiling too widely. "I mean, you know. You guys sounded—um—really good."

"Good or great?"

Zoe elbows her in the ribs. "I'm Zoe, by the way," she says.

"Lorelei," Lorelei offers.

"Laurie?"

"*Lorelei*," she says again. She can hear her voice getting lost in the room.

"Okay," he says. She isn't sure he's gotten it at all. "Chris."

"Cool," Zoe says. "I'm gonna get one more drink—you guys want anything?"

"Nah." Chris holds up a water bottle. "I'm cool."

"Uh, me too," Lorelei agrees. Panic lances through her, and she frowns hard at Zoe's retreating back. She has no idea what to say to Chris, how to talk to boys or how to talk about music, and she can't talk about *school*.

"Have you seen us play before?"

"No," Lorelei admits.

"Probably for the best. We're, uh, well . . . This is for sure our best show to date. Bean—our drummer—he's new, he's great."

"Yeah," Lorelei agrees. "Where did you guys pick him up?"

"Harvard-Westlake, if you can believe it." Chris shakes his head. That makes Bean a private-school kid, an alien from the other side of the city. Lorelei has only just learned to recognize the names of these places, which uproot people from their neighborhoods and gather them into little rich-kid knots. "But he's talented, so whatever."

"Yeah."

There's a silence. Lorelei feels the gap in their conversation like a physical thing.

"You guys gotta head out soon? Catching a ride?" Chris asks. Lorelei flushes and then flushes harder, embarrassed, even though she knows that it's invisible, under her makeup, in the blue and purple light. It's so careful, *catching a ride,* so that neither of them has to admit that someone's parents will be picking her up.

"In a minute." Soon, actually. The show ran late and the movie they're supposed to be watching ends in half an hour. It will take them fifteen minutes at least to hike back to the theater to meet Zoe's mom.

"I gotta load out," Chris says. "And, uh, I guess I wouldn't ask you to help carry equipment, anyway."

"I'm tough," Lorelei tells him, puffing up under the worn leather of her borrowed jacket.

"Sure," he says, laughing. "But I'll see you at school, maybe? Say hi in the halls?"

"For sure," Lorelei says. She likes the shape of the words in her mouth, the way she can mimic Chris's loose native drawl when she says them. He kind of leans against her arm for a second, and then lopes back to the band. There are layers and layers between them but Lorelei touches the jacket anyway, where he brushed up against her. She rubs her fingertips together and looks at them, like she might actually be able to see sparks there.

She finds Zoe flirting with a serious-looking man at the bar, a twenty-something with a neatly trimmed beard and a solemn, intense gaze. She's trying to talk him into buying her a real drink.

"C'mon," Lorelei says. She used up all of her boldness talking to Chris; now, under this stranger's eyes, she can barely look up from her shoes. She doesn't want to ruin her friend's fun, but she doesn't like the look of this all that much. "Zo, whatever, we've gotta go."

"It's no fun here, anyway," Zoe says. She throws a challenging look over her shoulder as they walk away. The man doesn't respond. "Oh shit, we've gotta get this stuff off," she says then, to Lorelei, rubbing a thumb against her blush-bright cheek. "Bathroom, c'mon."

"Sorry to hassle you," Lorelei says, shouldering the door open.

"It's fine," Zoe says. She pulls makeup wipes out of her bag and passes them over.

"I mean, you came here for me and—"

"L," Zoe says. "Seriously." She keeps wiping at her face, mouth open in a distracted, uneven O.

"Okay." Lorelei starts with her mascara. The sting of chemicals makes her eyes water. She watches Zoe's reflection in the mirror, her vision blurred by reflexive tears, as her friend's face slowly becomes its familiar self again. This is the girl she knows, soft and private. "Thanks," she says when they're done. "For everything."

"I had fun too," Zoe says. "And. You know. Thanks for trying to keep me out of trouble."

"Yeah," Lorelei says. That's the balance of them, the way they work: if Lorelei needs Zoe to tell her it's okay to be loud, to lie to someone's parents and flirt with a boy, Zoe needs Lorelei to keep her at anchor. The flip side of her boldness is that it gets heedless, sometimes. It can skid into reckless. Zoe doesn't like being told what to do, mostly, but she trusts Lorelei to tell her when to stop.

The man at the bar is lost to the crowd by the time they leave.

Outside, the boys are loading equipment into someone's station wagon, Jackson and Bean the drummer slowly losing a complicated game of real-world Tetris. Chris is there too, laughing and not helping, sitting against the side of the building with his legs stretched out across the sidewalk.

He's strumming the unplugged strings of his guitar and singing while everyone else works. Lorelei recognizes the tune: it's from one of the records that Zoe's sister Carina always played when she was still living at home. It's a short song, a woman singing throaty and full over nothing more than handclaps and the cheers of a crowd. *Oh lord, won't you buy me a Mercedes Benz? My friends all drive Porsches, I must make amends.*

"You have a goddamn Mercedes!" Bean yells out. "Come help us deal with this Volvo."

"Worked hard all my lifetime, no help from my friends," Chris rejoins.

The spirit comes over Lorelei: she can hear the next words in her head. She looks at Chris sitting on the sidewalk and thinks, *Of course you're what I want.* She sings out, "Oh lord, won't you buy me a Mercedes Benz?" finishing his verse as she skips nimbly over his ankles.

She doesn't look back, after. She doesn't think about whether anyone heard her over the street sounds, other voices, passing traffic. She just lets her voice ring out behind her, resonant in the dry, clean desert air. It's the first time she's ever sung out so boldly, and the vibration of it rings through her like a bell, high, sharp, and clear.

She doesn't see—though she will later imagine it, over and over again—the moment when Chris hears her for the first time, when he sits up and stares after her. She'll imagine but never know what he must have looked like, called and compelled: wide-eyed, drawn out of himself, being pulled by something elemental and held in thrall. She doesn't see him opening toward her, brilliant in his unfolding, like a flower bursting suddenly into bloom.

Back at Zoe's, Lorelei is grateful to strip off the jacket and dress and wash the last traces of makeup from her face. She likes the costume but it's nice to feel her own skin again, plain and clean. She packed pink and white pajamas but wears Zoe's clothes instead, running shorts and an old T-shirt worn soft with age.

They curl up in Zoe's bed together, the last whiff of the Roxy's stale smoke and booze and sweat swallowed up by soap and lotion and detergent, and the minty tang of toothpaste. They're old enough to go out and young enough to fit two to a twin.

"So that went well," Zoe says.

"Mmmm," Lorelei agrees, touching again the spot on her shoulder that Chris leaned against.

"I've never heard you sing before," Zoe goes on. "Not really. You have a nice voice." The words are broken by a yawn. "Pretty."

"Thanks."

"You should sing with him sometime," Zoe murmurs. "Chris."

Lorelei flinches instinctively. Her grandmother is weird about singing, and about her singing, specifically. There's a rule against it that she's never questioned and never understood. Not doing it is such a deeply ingrained habit that she hasn't thought about it consciously in years, and she's surprised when she runs up against it, a barrier she's almost forgotten was there. "I don't know," she says, but Zoe is already drifting to sleep, jaw falling slack and breath coming soft and easy.

Whatever madness overcame her on the sidewalk pulls away now. *I didn't mean to do it,* Lorelei thinks. *I won't do it again.* She's never gotten caught up like that before. In the dark in Zoe's bed it's hard to imagine what could have compelled her not just to break but to forget about the rules.

3

THAT NIGHT SHE DREAMS about it, though it isn't anything like a dream: just a memory that she ghosts through in her sleep.

Lorelei's parents emigrated from Germany along with her grandmother when her mother got pregnant with the twins. It was almost eighteen years ago, now. She's never known exactly why they left, only that when they did, they meant it. They've never gone back, not even to visit. Her parents threw themselves into the work of their American lives when they got here, and left Oma to raise the children. So it was Oma who sat her down the night before she started kindergarten and told her that it was time for Lorelei to learn a secret.

"Do you know what music is?" she asks in the dream, running her fingers through Lorelei's tangled blond curls. Lorelei's grown-up mind is dimly aware of the smallness of her skull against her grandmother's hand.

"Yes," Lorelei says. She knows she's heard it: snatches of pop songs at the grocery store, and melody blasting out of boom boxes and through open car windows on the board-walk, near the beach. There are whole communities of German émigrés in other parts of Los Angeles, but her family lives in Venice. Her mother wants to be near the shore.

"You know that we don't have music in this house," Oma says. She gathers Lorelei's hair into sections and starts to work them into a tight braid.

"Yes," Lorelei agrees again.

She's never had cause to doubt her grandmother, or question her: this is the woman whose hands keep the family fed and her own hair neat. Oma sorts the bills that come in and pays what needs to be paid. Lorelei's parents work outside the house; Oma is in charge of what happens inside it. In the smallness of this world, Oma is the voice of authority and source of all wisdom.

"It was music that got your mother in trouble," Oma says. "It was singing that ruined her, because I never taught her how."

Lorelei doesn't understand how anyone could not know how to sing. She does it all the time, in the quiet under her covers, making up songs about the sea and shore, the sand and sky. She does it to comfort herself when the nights are long and she can't sleep, or when her pulse pounds too hard. Most days her heart beats softly, but sometimes, too late or too early, it thrums up and gets loud and distracting. She feels it, heavy, moving, in her chest. Then it's only song that helps, pulling the frantic flutter up and out of her throat and bleeding off tension into the air around her.

"So I'm going to teach you," Oma says. "I'm going to teach you how to be careful with your voice."

It isn't so hard. Her natural register is high and clear. Oma has her sing at the low end of it, where the sound comes out rough with work. "It's okay to sing like this in front of people," Oma instructs. "In groups, for school. That's fine. But the high notes: never."

"I like the high notes," Lorelei says. She sings an anxious little trill to demonstrate.

"Just like that," Oma tells her. "That exactly is what you never do."

Lorelei wakes with her mouth closed so tightly that her jaw aches.

4

ZOE'S MOM DRIVES HER home in the morning. Lorelei sits
in the passenger seat and fiddles with the straps on her backpack, which seems to get heavier as block after block unfolds
through the windshield. In the pale Sunday-morning sunlight she's weighted down by the dirty clothes and unfin-
ished homework she's dragging. The pit of her stomach gets
heavy and cold when they pull up in front of her house.

The neighborhood has changed around them since her
parents bought the place in the early nineties, and up and
down the block people have razed the old structures to put
up new, modern ones, square slabs of concrete and glass.
Against them, her family's beach cottage looks even older
and dingier than it is, with its wooden porch and peaked
roof.

The grass out front is sparse and sere after a long, hot
summer. The backyard is lush with Oma's well-tended
kitchen garden, but there are no signs of life in the front.
Other yards have bicycles and surfboards, or pinwheels
stuck in their lawns, Tibetan prayer flags and fairy lights

strung across their gardens. The Felsons have a plain brown welcome mat on which Lorelei very carefully wipes her feet before taking a deep breath and walking inside.

She doesn't know when this started seeming strange to her. It must have been a gradual awakening: the slow realization that there are different kinds of quiet in the world. Now when the door clicks shut behind her, Lorelei feels the familiar sensation of coming home, and ducking her head underwater. Even the sound of her own footfalls against the wooden floor is muted and faraway when she walks. She goes through the dining room and into the kitchen, to the family room. No one is home.

The second floor is covered in carpets that muffle everything further, dusty things her parents brought over when they moved. Lorelei drops her backpack in her room, kicks off her shoes, digs her toes into the thick rug, and slides her feet back and forth, finding friction.

She spins in a circle and takes it all in, the clean floor and bare walls. There are a handful of photos of her and Zoe and their friends tacked up over her desk, but otherwise: blankness. She takes the little ticket stub from the Roxy and tapes it up next to the pictures. Evidence of one more night outside, and away.

Lorelei takes advantage of no one being home to indulge in a long shower. The ancient water heater warms up slowly, so she runs the water in the tub while she strips off her clothes and brushes her hair. The bathroom fills with pale, thick steam, obscuring her body in the mirror. It's like being surrounded by cottony clouds, high up in the sky. She breathes in deep lungfuls of it: almost as much water as air.

She takes twenty luxurious minutes to wash her hair and deep-condition it. She shaves her legs, working slowly over the knobs and valleys of her knees and ankles. She sings while she does it, humming tunes from last night and a song Zoe played while they were getting dressed this morning. It's an old, absent habit, but last night's dream makes her conscious of it. She wonders if she hums like this at Zoe's or at school and doesn't realize it; she wonders whether humming counts, or if Oma only meant real singing.

Lorelei is curious, now. Something just under her skin makes itself known, like an itch, but a pleasant one. Oma's prohibition was explicitly about singing around other people, and she's all alone in an empty house. There's no reason not to sing, now. Lorelei feels the itch resolve itself in the back of her throat, at the seat of her voice. She decides to let it rip.

It feels *good*, like the vibration of the sound is relaxing each of her muscles in turn. Melody runs hot in her veins and when she sings up high, up into her nose, her whole head buzzes with the resonance of her breath. Lorelei turns off the water and steps out of the shower. She wraps herself in a towel and turns one quick, dramatic twirl, getting really into the belt of a song she half remembers. *Why haven't I ever done this before?* she thinks.

When she opens the bathroom door, her father is standing outside it, glassy-eyed.

"Petra?" he asks.

"No," Lorelei says. "No, Dad, it's—Lorelei, it's just me."

Lorelei doesn't look enough like her mother for the mistake to make sense. She wonders if something is seriously wrong with him. He's pale and clammy and confused, white except where he's flushed red. She's never seen him like this before. His displays of deep feeling are usually reserved for her mother, who responds by keeping a cool distance. Now he looks possessed.

"I heard Petra," he says again. "I heard her singing. I heard her singing for me."

"That was just me, Dad." Lorelei has never heard her mother sing. It's impossible to imagine anything as lush and sweet as music coming from her mother's mouth.

"Petra," he insists, coming in a step closer. He reaches out a hand and his fingertips brush against her collarbone, the top of her shoulder. They don't find what they're looking for. He starts to look past her, like her mother is there, hidden in the bathroom's steamy air.

Oma appears behind him in the hallway. She seems taller, somehow, all of her authority gathered up and held out in front of her. "Henry," she says. Lorelei has never heard this tone from her grandmother before. It's rough and low and primal. Her father blinks once, twice, and steps back. "It isn't her."

He turns to Oma. He looks like a child: helpless and exhausted. "I know," he says.

Henry and Oma regard each other.

"Lorelei, get dressed," Oma says. She still sounds commanding, but whatever bone-deep power infused her words a moment ago is gone, and she sounds only as bossy as she usually does. Which is still plenty. "Henry—"

"Okay," he says. "Okay."

Oma disappears down the hall, but her father doesn't

move. He turns to face Lorelei. His eyes find hers and then flinch away.

"I'm sorry," he says. "You sounded—"

"Like Mom," Lorelei says. Water drips from her damp hair down her neck and the line of her spine. She shivers against the cool air and clutches her towel closer. "You said."

"I didn't mean—" He stops and frowns. He's staring fiercely at his shoes. "It's been a long time since she sang for me."

"She used to, though?"

"She did," he says. He smiles. The mention of her mother's voice instantly has him distant again. "She— All the time." The memory stretches, extends itself, and captures him. Then it turns painful, and his expression turns dark. "I thought Oma talked to you about this," he says. "About not doing that."

"She did," Lorelei says. "She just said not in front of people. And no one was home when I got here, so I thought—"

"You have to be more careful than that," he says. There's something burning behind his eyes, the embers of a fire kept banked for years. For the first time in her life, Lorelei is frightened of him.

"*Okay,*" she huffs, and turns toward her room. "I have to go get dressed."

"Lorelei."

She turns back. He looks small, still, standing in the long hallway with his arms at his sides, palms turned up like he's begging.

"Don't go messing with things you don't understand," he says finally. "Please just—don't."

"I won't," Lorelei promises. Her father rarely asks for anything. He wouldn't now if it wasn't important. Right? "I won't sing anymore," she says again.

Instantly, though, she can feel that her promise is a lie. Last night she was wreathed in the band's songs, crowned by them. Chris came over to talk to her and he looked at her like he was thinking about her—only her. And singing just now felt like letting something long dormant inside herself put down roots and send up a stalk, a tendril, a bud. If music is magic, she wants to fall under its spell. She wants it so badly that it's easy to pretend the wanting is all that matters.

Lorelei passes her mother's little office on the way to her room. Petra does the accounting for a fashion conglomerate headquartered nearby; she works long hours in Century City and brings the paperwork home with her. Her door is usually closed.

Today, however, her mother is sitting in the middle of the room in her straight-backed wooden chair, the door half open, ajar as if forgotten. She catches Lorelei's eye as she goes by. If her father looked blank and hollow, furious and then pleading, her mother is stricken, touched by an emotion too deep to name. She shakes her head just once as Lorelei passes, and draws a hand across her mouth, and presses there to keep it closed.

◦◦◦

Lorelei goes to Oma's room as soon as she's dressed. "Hey," she says. She stands in the doorway, waiting to be invited in. Oma is sitting in an armchair by the dark window, knitting.

The click of her needles doesn't pause when she nods for Lorelei to enter. "Is Dad okay?"

"You upset him," Oma says.

Lorelei doesn't sound angry, but being blamed sets off something hot in her chest. "I didn't know you were home," she says. "I wasn't *trying* to be rude or disruptive, or anything."

"I know you weren't," Oma says. She keeps at her work.

The numbness Lorelei felt while it was happening is starting to wear off, and now adrenaline is kicking in. "What just *happened*, then?" she asks. "What even was that?"

"Do you really want to talk about it?" Oma looks up from her knitting, finally, and sets it down in her lap.

"I want to know why Dad was acting like—whatever that was. I don't even know! I thought he was having a stroke."

"I told you not to sing."

"That was, like, years ago."

"Don't tell me you've forgotten." It's not a question, exactly. The shadows on her face deepen. Oma looks hunted when she says it.

"No," Lorelei admits. "I just—I don't know, I never really wanted to, so I never thought about why. Or whether I could, or should. And I definitely didn't think it would be because of anything like that."

"I don't suppose you'll forget about it now," Oma says. She sits back against her chair and puts her knitting on the table so that her lap is free. Lorelei wants to crawl into it like she did when she was little, when she still fit comfortably into her grandmother's embrace.

"Uh, yeah, probably not."

"Tell me why you were singing, then. Why you wanted to, all of a sudden."

Lorelei recognizes the opportunity to tell the truth, and doesn't take it. There's no need to add trouble to the trouble she's in. "I like it," she tries instead. "I was just— It's fun, you know?"

"Fun isn't always the point," Oma says.

"Maybe in *Germany*."

"It has nothing to do with Germany. It's everything to do with being young."

"I'm not so young."

"Talk to me in fifty years," Oma says. She still doesn't sound angry, or even upset. "Twenty, even. You will change your mind about how young you are, and about the singing, about whatever boy you think is worth singing for."

"What boy?" Lorelei says, too fast. She's proud that at least her voice doesn't shake. There's no *way* Oma could know about Chris, but then again her grandmother has always been terrifyingly good at guessing. Almost as good as she is at steering conversations away from things she doesn't want to talk about.

"Whoever he is," Oma says. "There's always a boy. That's always how it starts. Your mother—" But she cuts herself off, biting down on the words. "There is always a boy," she says again instead. "You think you're in love. You think you want to keep him. That he wants to stay with you. You sing about how happy you are, right, Lorelei? Your father said you were singing about love."

"It's just a song."

"You have to be careful," Oma says. "I know we talked about this when you were young, but it changes, of course it does. I had forgotten." She rubs a hand over her eyes. "It isn't enough, I suppose, simply to tell you that you aren't to do it ever again."

"I just don't understand why," Lorelei says. "If it's because I'm *good*, you shouldn't worry—I don't want to drop out of school and become the next Taylor Swift or anything. I just want to sing in the shower, to join the chorus, maybe, I want—"

"*No*," Oma says.

Lorelei feels the word like a flash of lightning, like a grip at the base of her throat. The itch that's been crawling under her skin, waiting for another chance to make itself known, flinches and disappears.

"I know you grew up here, but let me tell you: what you want doesn't always matter. There are things you don't know about our family, things you don't understand, things—" There's a long pause. "Things you wouldn't want to know. Trust me, Lorelei."

"I just feel like I should get to make that decision for myself."

"And I disagree."

Lorelei shrugs. Oma's reserve is a long, high wall. There's no point in throwing herself against it.

"Dad said Mom used to sing for him," she says, trying another tactic. "Is it— I don't know, is it because of Mom?" It would make sense. Petra has never done anything but screw up all of their lives, anyway.

"Not exactly," Oma says.

"Oh my god, it is! Look, whatever she did, I won't do it. You know I'm more responsible than she is." *Responsible* isn't the right word, exactly, but Lorelei certainly isn't going to get pregnant at seventeen and make her whole family move to another country because she's embarrassed. Maybe her parents met at a concert, and Oma is, like, traumatized by live music now?

"I used to perform, actually. I don't know if you know this," Oma says. "When I was young. Until I was thirteen, maybe fourteen. And then my mother made me stop."

"Great, so this is about *your* mother. That's so not fair."

"She had her reasons, just as I have mine."

Lorelei tries to imagine what the reasons could possibly be, but she's distracted by the thought of her grandmother as a young singer, standing in a white-hot spotlight and enthralling a crowd. She didn't know this about Oma, actually. Her family's life before emigration is contained in a couple of old photo albums she's paged through dozens of times. There are no pictures of Oma singing in any of them.

There are many things, it seems, no one has ever bothered to tell her before.

"Was it worse?" Lorelei asks finally. "Losing it, after being able to, for so long?"

"Like losing a limb," Oma says. "Like losing someone I loved."

Lorelei has always known her grandmother as a widow: her husband died a year or two before Petra got pregnant with the twins. She's always assumed that this was the loss that governed Oma's strictness. Her grandmother had watched chaos whirl up at her and decided that from then on, she was going to keep it at bay through sheer force of will.

Now, though, Lorelei sees that there might be something deeper, something she lost long before Papa. Her grandmother wanted something for herself, a space and a voice, and had it taken away from her. She misses it and refuses to want it back. That's Oma, for sure, resigning herself gracefully to whatever there is to resign herself to, and putting a good face on it, and writing a thank-you card for the good parts as soon as she gets home.

Downstairs they can hear the twins coming in, tumbling over each other, hushing their voices after a morning spent outside.

Lorelei asks, "Do you miss it?"

"Every day," Oma says. "But it was worth it. It was the right thing, in the end."

"Will you ever tell me why?"

"I hope I don't have to. I hope you will find something else to do with yourself."

"But if I keep at the low end," Lorelei says. "Like we practiced when I was little. If I don't—"

"It's better that you don't," Oma says. "It's better if you leave it alone. Let it go."

"Let it go," Lorelei repeats.

"You're very young," Oma says again. "Start early. It's easier."

Everyone acts normal at dinner. Lorelei is surprised, and then not: her family specializes in acting like weird things are normal. Plus, the twins don't know about what happened this afternoon, and now they're too busy trying to get permission for something to notice any leftover tension.

"Jens and I might miss dinner on Friday," Nik says.

"If that's okay," Jens adds. He's carefully not looking at any of the adults in particular: Petra won't say anything, so there's no point, but Oma will always find a reason to refuse. The trick is to get their father to agree before that can happen, without letting him know that he's the easiest mark at the table.

"What's so important that you have to miss a family dinner?" Oma asks.

"Soccer team bonding," Nik says. "Ollie is having some of the guys over—"

"Jens isn't on the team."

Jens says, "Ollie's a good friend of mine from elementary school, though. Dad, do you remember when he had that birthday party at Chuck E. Cheese's?"

Henry nods vaguely.

Jens says, "Where he threw up in the ball pit?"

"Sure. Of course." Lorelei can't tell whether her dad is lying or not. "Be sure to tell his mom I said hi."

Jens and Nik exchange a glance that's basically an invisible high five.

Petra's phone starts ringing. She pulls it out of her pocket and doesn't apologize. "Work," she says. "I have to take this." She gets up from the table. Lorelei can hear her starting to argue with someone as she goes up the stairs.

Oma turns to the twins. "You'll want to get some studying done tonight, if you're going out this weekend."

"Absolutely," Jens says.

"You can get started on that," Henry says. "I've got the
dishes."

Oma says, "Lorelei, help your father."

Henry looks startled to be reminded that he has a
daughter. His whole genial absentminded-professor thing
falls away in the face of having to spend fifteen minutes with
her, standing at the sink. He looks like a trapped animal.

"No," he says. "No, it's fine. I've got it." He grabs a few
plates and hurries into the kitchen before Oma can object.
Lorelei pulls her shoulders together and imagines shrink-
ing down and down, so small that no one would have to
see her or even think about her. She's used to her parents
basically ignoring her; actively avoiding her is new, and she's
surprised by how much it hurts. She really didn't mean to
screw anything up.

Oma looks at all the empty chairs around her and folds
her hands in her lap. She leans her head back and closes
her eyes. Lorelei almost never sees her grandmother resting;
she's always moving, tending the garden or making food,
cleaning the house, paying bills, knitting blankets. Oma
comes off as spry and vital, but her hands are liver-spotted
with age and her skin is almost transparent, tissue-thin.

"I'll clear, at least," Lorelei says. She can't disappear, but
she can grease the wheels of the household's working: be
good and easy and helpful. That she knows how to do.

Oma doesn't say anything.

Lorelei brings a stack of dishes to her father in the

kitchen. The roar of the faucet makes saying anything impossible. When she passes back through the dining room, Oma's eyes are still closed, and the expression on her face is one she would hide if she knew anyone was watching. Her grandmother looks exhausted, drawn and drained.

She looks like my mother, Lorelei thinks, recognizing for the first time the way each of their lovely faces is marked, indelibly, by the signs of grief and loss.

5

LORELEI'S PLAN IS TO avoid Chris at school, where there is no music or nighttime magic and she's just another sophomore. He might not even recognize her without makeup, wearing boring jeans and a T-shirt and blinking through pale eyelashes.

She could dress up if she wanted to. She has a closet full of nicer stuff, mostly the dresses her mom brings home from work, samples or factory rejects with uneven hemlines and missing buttons, problems Oma could fix in a few minutes. But Lorelei never puts them on. She doesn't like the air of petty bribery that accompanies them, these things her mother gives her instead of affection and attention. They hang in her closet like artifacts on display.

Still, Lorelei borrows Zoe's lip gloss after lunch on Monday. She's glad she did when Chris lopes up next to her in the hall a couple of hours later, sleepy-eyed even though it's well after noon. He nudges her with the tip of his shoulder as they fall into step. "Here you are," he says. "I've been looking for you."

"Here I am," Lorelei agrees. *Of course I'm here*, she thinks. It's two p.m. on a weekday and she's walking from English to history, her last class of the day.

"It's weird, right?" He walks so close at her side that their hands brush occasionally, his knuckles against the skin of her wrist. He keeps turning to look at her too, not even shy about it. "Seeing people in different contexts." Lorelei flashes back to his mother in the dark club, serene and distant.

"I've seen you around before," she admits. "I think of you as being, like, a creature of the halls."

"A creature of the halls!" he repeats, delighted. "I mean, *no*, but that's—that's great, I like that, a creature of the halls."

She doesn't ask if he's ever noticed her. Pretty blond girls are a dime a dozen at Venice and all across west Los Angeles. She's part of the scenery here: there are palm trees and ocean views and blondes.

"Are you going to class?" she asks as he follows her around a turn.

"Nah," he says. "Maybe that's why you see me in the halls so often. That's mostly where I am."

"You don't get in trouble?"

"I don't."

"How—"

"I've got a system." His mouth turns sly. "I can show you, if you want."

"Um." Lorelei ducks her head. "That's, uh, really cool of you."

"But you're going to class."

They've pulled up outside the classroom door. Lorelei fiddles with the strap on her backpack and examines the bright blue polish chipping off her nails. She has never ditched in her life.

"Yeah."

"S'cool."

She twists her mouth to hide a smile of relief that he won't try to convince her, and that he doesn't care if she doesn't want to be bad.

"Come find me after school, though, okay? My car's in the shop, so Jackson's supposed to drive me to practice, but he and Angela always have, like, at least a half hour of making out somewhere between last bell and us leaving, so I should be findable." He raises an eyebrow at her and rises up onto his toes, drifting farther into her space. "Assuming you know where to look."

I don't, Lorelei wants to say, but she does, and he knows it. He turns on his heel and disappears down the hall.

She walks into class still flushed, her cheeks warm with high, bright color. Mrs. Whitlock asks her a question, and when she answers it, the attention of the room shifts her way. Boys lean over their desks toward her like flowers tilting toward sunlight. Some of the girls do too.

Lorelei notices it and she doesn't. High school is always a sea of bodies reacting to one another, pushed and pulled by chemical change and a lot of loose talk. She never feels like she understands it completely. Anyway, everyone drifts back into place after a minute or two.

Lorelei's mind is elsewhere. She's pleased to have gotten

the answer to Mrs. Whitlock's question right, and that she's had her turn in the spotlight already. She spends the rest of the period thinking about Chris.

※ ◎ ※

As promised, he isn't hard to find. Lorelei tries to look casual as she walks out, chatting with Taylor, who sits next to her in class, but as soon as they walk through the school's front door, she spots him. He's sitting on a bench with his guitar in his lap. Jackson and Angela are sitting next to him, and they are, in fact, making out, so she has to pause awkwardly in front of their trio.

"Oh," Taylor says. "Um. Bye?"

"Yeah," Lorelei says. "Bye!"

Taylor gives her a little side eye as she leaves, surprised at the company Lorelei is keeping. Not just seniors: seniors in a band.

Chris smiles up at her. "You found me!"

"I looked."

"Sit." Chris bumps a hip against Jackson, who scootches over and lets Angela crawl into his lap.

Lorelei is no stranger to PDA. She's not *innocent,* not exactly. She's seen movies, educational screenings put on by Carina in the Soroushes' living room late at night. But she's never been this close to live making out before, the wet slurps of mouths and tongues, even their breath getting sloppy and loud. She watches Angela's hand disappear up the front of Jackson's shirt as she folds herself into the space next to Chris.

"Sorry about them," he says. "J's parents are super strict, and Angela's folks are . . . Jehovah's Witnesses?"

"Regular old evangelicals." Angela pulls away long enough to correct Chris. Jackson is still kissing her neck.

"Anyway. Not into, uh, alone time for these two." He waggles his eyebrows indelicately at her. "So they get it where they can."

"I don't mind," Lorelei says. "What are you playing?"

"No-thing." Chris strums a few big, loose chords. She watches his callused fingers working the strings, and her own fingertips itch. She can't tell whether she wants to touch him or the guitar, each of them smooth and shining in the sunlight. "I was trying to, like, make something up, but it all just sounds goofy."

"Sounded all right to me."

"I mean, it doesn't sound *bad*," he says. He plucks stray notes while he talks. Lorelei envies the ease of his body making music without him noticing. "It just doesn't sound like a song yet, you know? I can make sound, but I'm having trouble making music. I was thinking about you, actually. I've been thinking about you singing with me."

They're sitting in warm September sunlight, but Lorelei can't help her shiver.

"Shuuuut uuuup," Jackson groans. He disengages himself from Angela and swivels around to address Chris directly. "Can this artistic bullshit, please, dude, I am begging you." He notices Lorelei for the first time and tilts his head in her direction. "Don't listen to him, little freshman," he says. "Chris is one hundred percent full of shit."

Before Lorelei has time to correct him—she's a

sophomore—Chris cuffs him on the shoulder and Jackson shoves him back. They're clumsy and familiar with each other, tumbling off the bench so they can wrestle on the grass.

This leaves Angela and Lorelei sitting at opposite ends of the bench, watching. Angela very deliberately straightens out her skirt and her tank top, runs her fingers through her hair, and checks her makeup in a silver heart-shaped compact mirror. She doesn't look at Lorelei. "Boys," she says eventually. *"Boys."*

Jackson has Chris haphazardly pinned. He beams up at Angela. "Look what I did for you, baby," he says. "I caught you a Chris."

"Not interested."

Jackson knees Chris in the thigh and scrambles back up to the bench. "Didn't catch your name," he says to Lorelei as Angela resituates herself, draping her legs over his.

"Lorelei."

"Lorelei. Cool. Jackson. And this is Angela."

"Angela," Angela affirms. Then she nips at Jackson's earlobe.

"So how do you two know each other?"

"Lorelei came to the show on Saturday," Chris says. "We started chatting. Turns out she goes to Venice too. Obviously."

"Oh, right," Jackson says. "You said. I remember now. You coming to watch us practice?"

Lorelei shakes her head. Her brothers are probably already waiting for her in the parking lot. She should go now before they start to wonder, or, worse, look for her.

"I should go, actually," she says. "Gotta find my ride."

"I can get you a ride home after," Chris offers. "If that's the issue."

"Oh."

All of yesterday's weird, ominous warnings swirl up in her head: the story of Oma singing and being silenced, and the emptiness of her father's glassy, exhausted eyes. But then she looks at Chris, sunny, smiling, normal and happy, and it seems impossible that anything about this could be dangerous. He's just trying to pull her into his world of band practice and hanging out, catching rides, maybe even eventually making out on a bench somewhere too.

Screw it, Lorelei thinks.

"If it's not gonna be a problem?" she says. Chris shakes his head emphatically. "Let me just go tell my— I'll be right back."

She finds Jens and Nik waiting impatiently and tells them that she's going over to Zoe's. Someone will drop her off at home later. She's never lied to them like this before, but it's easy to make her voice come out steady and even. Of course they believe her. Where else would she be going?

"Tell Oma," she says. "And Mom and Dad, I guess."

"Sure," Jens says. He's sitting in the driver's seat, already turning the keys in the ignition. "Hey, Nik, this means we can—"

The rest of his suggestion is lost as the engine roars to life and the twins start to roll their windows up. Lorelei sees, though, the suspicious look that Nik gives her as they pull out of the lot, the frown that formed at the corners of his mouth when he listened to her lie.

She shoots Zoe a text while she's walking back to Chris and company. *Chris asked me to come to band practice to hang out (!!!) told J & N I was going over to yours hope that's okay.* She thinks Zoe will understand and forgive her for trying on a lie all by herself. Lorelei keeps hoping to bump into her on the walk, to squeeze her hand and maybe steal another swipe of lip gloss. But the sea of faces she passes through on the way seems blanker and more unfamiliar than ever.

Chris's smile, when she gets back, is warm and welcome. She reaches out a hand and he grabs it and pulls himself up. He doesn't let go while they walk. He keeps her close so they can talk a little bit, low and private. Jackson and Angela go on ahead and he lets them. Lorelei loves how open and easy he is with her, like he's known her all along.

6

THE TROUBLE PRACTICES IN a studio space Bean's parents rent for them. "He's a great drummer," Chris explains, "and an even better rich kid." It sounds fancy. Lorelei doesn't know what to expect, but when they get there, the building is just a bunch of big rooms on either side of an echoing concrete hallway. The walls are thick with insulation, and everything smells dry and empty and industrial.

They've personalized the studio by making it a mess: the floor is littered with tangled strands of Christmas lights that someone got tired of tacking to the walls, plus pages torn out of magazines, and plastic pieces from novelty toys. There's a bag of kazoos stashed in one corner. The air is sweet with a skunky smell Lorelei recognizes from the boardwalk as weed smoke. The walls are plastered with posters showing half-naked women lounging and half-naked men playing guitars.

Angela split off when they got to the parking lot, so it's just the three of them at the space. Bean drifts in a little while after. Lorelei sets herself up on one of the ancient armchairs, clearly a Goodwill salvage, and listens politely while the boys banter back and forth.

Her phone buzzes in her pocket and she pulls it out, grateful for the distraction. There are two texts: one from Zoe that just says, *DETAILS AT LUNCH TMRW PLEASE AND THANK U*, and one from Nik that reads, *Oma making schnitzel for dinner tonight, be home by 6.* She ignores Nik and sends Zoe *I'm sitting in a chair they haven't started playing yet I feel awkward help?*

The response is almost instantaneous: *You're a bad bitch, girl. Just act like you're in charge.*

Lorelei feels nothing like a bad bitch. She feels like a little girl hanging out with the big kids for the first time, painfully uncertain about what to do with her hands, arms, legs, and face. She imagines Carina here in her place but that's not so helpful, because Carina would be outside smoking a cigarette, or else joining in the banter about some band— whoever they're talking about, Lorelei doesn't recognize the name—but neither of those things is really an option. Instead, she feigns boredom, drapes her legs over the chair, and fiddles around uselessly on her phone.

It's a relief when they actually start practicing. This means playing through a whole song once, usually, and then breaking it down to its component parts, working out a bass line, a guitar riff, the precise staccato rhythm of a drum fill. It's a little like how Oma taught her to sew, Lorelei thinks— turning shirts inside out, checking the seams. She's starting to see the way The Trouble constructs sound.

They spend the last half hour working on a new song, something slow and driving. Chris presses up against a mic for a full-on croon. One unruly curl falls into his eyes, and he tosses it back, impatient. His mouth is warm and moving. Lorelei sits up straight in her chair. The energy of the sound comes in at the crown of her head and shakes her down to the soles of her feet.

"Shit," Jackson says, eventually. "I gotta go in a minute. I didn't realize how late it was."

Lorelei checks her phone: it's five-thirty, which means she's about to be in trouble.

"I wanna go through it once all together," Chris says. They've been playing in fragments, going over the chorus, the bridge, a sketched-out second verse. He's still positioned in front of the microphone, unmoving. "I just want to hear it—the whole thing. Anyway, my ride won't be here for a minute. We've got time."

"Just once," Jackson agrees, tapping his fingers against the fretboard of his bass.

The song starts off slow and deliberate, the beat strong and undulating. Chris moves his hips in time with the music. He catches Lorelei's eye and gives her a long, slow smile. She feels a thrill deep in the pit of her stomach, but it's nothing like what happens when the first chorus kicks in. The guitar, bass, drums, and Chris's howling wail all come together to fill her up, and tumble over. It's too much, and not enough, and Lorelei's skin is so fever-hot she can't stand it a minute longer.

"I'm sorry," she gasps. Chris stops playing. "I'm— It's just—too much—"

She bolts before she can think about it, out through the doors and down a long, dusty hallway, running the wrong way, not caring. She bursts through another set of doors and out onto an abandoned loading dock. She sits down on the concrete ledge and puts her face in her hands, trying to catch her breath.

The sun has just finished setting, and the marine layer is rolling in again. The day's last light has a surreal quality, an almost-green tint that makes her feel like she's much farther away from home than she's ever been, like she's deep underwater, and only just now noticing how hard it is to breathe.

She stays out there for five minutes, maybe, just long enough to get really, really embarrassed by what she's done, before Chris pushes through the doors and drops to a squat beside her.

"Are you okay?" he asks, putting a warm hand on her back. She leans into it.

"Fine," she says. "Fine, sorry, I don't—I don't know what happened back there."

"It's okay," he says. He shifts to his knees, and, when she doesn't protest, swings himself around so that he's sitting at her side. "It's— Is it weird if it's a little cool?"

"Huh?"

"I just— No one's ever been moved by our music like that before." He shrugs and smiles a dopey, lopsided grin.

"I thought you would think it was weird," she admits. "Like, really weird."

"Nah," he says. He cocks his head to one side, angles his face toward hers and pauses, considering. "I have a feeling about you," he says. "You're sensitive. Deep. I knew it when I saw you at the show. You look— You can tell on your face that the whole world affects you. That you're open to it in this really cool way."

Lorelei considers the idea. Maybe it's true, and maybe that's what it is about her and the women in her family. Maybe they're all deep and sensitive, and delicate. Maybe it's the purity and clarity of her voice that's too much for anyone to hear. She touches the curve of her cheek and tries to let her expression be open, to look at Chris like he's looking at her: enthralled, entranced.

"I want you to sing with us," he says. "It seems like you love music, and I want you to help us make it. I think it could be, like, really amazing."

For the first time Lorelei understands instinctively exactly what Oma was trying to keep her from: wanting something so powerfully that saying no to it feels impossible. His face tilts toward hers and comes in close, closer, like they're magnetized, closer and closer, so close now, so close that—

He leans in and seals his mouth over hers.

Lorelei has never been kissed before. Chris's fingertips come, gentle, to the corner of her jaw, guiding her forward. He kisses her long and slow and sweet, easing her into it. She loves how it feels, his smile warm and moving against her lips.

He jerks back when the door bangs open behind them. *"Chris,"* Jackson says. "Your mom's here."

"She's—shit—what?" Chris leaps to his feet. "She isn't supposed to be here. Greg said he'd give me a ride."

"I don't know what happened to Greg," Jackson says. "But she's here, and she's waiting, and she wants to know where the hell you are."

"She's not inside, right?" Chris grabs Lorelei's shoulder and urges her up, pulling her back into the building with him almost as an afterthought.

"Bean's stalling her out front."

"Oh, thank god, I— Lorelei—can you—I'm so sorry, but can you find another ride?" He's so sweet and desperate that she finds herself nodding slowly, watching him rush as he ducks back into the studio and throws his guitar into its case, a few stray papers into his backpack. He pauses next to her, just inside the doorway, and brushes an apologetic kiss across her forehead before scrambling out, down the hallway, and disappearing around a corner. Then it's just her and Jackson in the room.

He sighs and then smiles politely. "You'll be asking about that ride now, I expect," he says.

⌖

Jackson doesn't even try to make conversation while he drives. The silence in the car wouldn't be so awful if Lorelei's brain wasn't chanting *Late, late, you are so late* at her as the tires turn. Guilt courses through her, keeping pace with her heartbeat. Her phone buzzes a few times from her backpack but she ignores it. It's just going to be Nik or Jens giving her crap, and it's not like she doesn't know.

Jackson keeps the radio on low, as if to make the quiet between them more pronounced. *I get it,* Lorelei wants to say. *You don't like me, you don't approve of me, you wish I—* But she doesn't know what he wants, and maybe that's the problem. She gets Chris not wanting to introduce her to his mom yet, but Jackson's coldness seems almost theatrical.

"Sorry about this," she says eventually, just to fill up space. "I really didn't—"

Jackson keeps his eyes fixed on the road in front of them. "I know it's not your fault," he says. "This is what being friends with Chris is like. You're not the first girl I've covered for him with his mom, and, like, no offense, but you probably won't be the last."

Lorelei knows enough to say, "None taken."

"Because this is gonna be the deal for you," Jackson goes on. "If you think he's gonna, like, fall in love and get serious about you, you have another thing coming. He's never going to break her heart like that."

"His . . . mom?"

Jackson's laugh is hollow. "You gonna answer that phone?"

"It's probably just Nik," she says.

"Nick Fitzwell?"

"Nik Felson," Lorelei says. "My brother." She might be imagining the startled sharpness of Jackson's blink, the way his hands grip suddenly white on the wheel. A half second later, whatever it was is gone and his expression is vacant again.

"I know Nik," he says casually. "There are two of them, right? The twins?"

"Yeah."

"Does he know you're hanging around Chris?"

"Not exactly."

It occurs to her that she hasn't given directions in a little while, but Jackson keeps making the right turns anyway, like he knows where he's going. Maybe he knows Nik better than he's letting on.

She changes the subject. "Do you think I'm making a mistake?"

"Chris is probably worth it," Jackson tells her. "Or he's worth a lot, anyway. He's one of the best dudes I know. But you shouldn't get hung up on him. He's not— He never lets anything last."

"I might be different, though," Lorelei says. She feels bold with the memory of his mouth still warm against her lips.

"You might be. You never know," Jackson says. "But I'm not trying to be mean when I say: I doubt it."

They pull up in front of her house. Nik opens the front door and steps onto the porch, like he's been waiting for her to arrive. Lorelei is too far away to tell, really, but she thinks he looks a little off, unsteady on his feet.

"Where have you been?" he asks, calling out into the darkness.

Jackson rolls down her window and leans across her body. "Don't be so hard on her," he calls back.

Lorelei definitely sees something, this time. A change comes over Nik when he hears Jackson's voice, a tightening. The porch light is stark overhead, so the planes of his face are sharp.

He says, "Lorelei, you need to get in here." There's a pause. "And don't tell me what to do, Jackson." A funny undertone laps at the edge of Nik's words. Jackson leans a little farther and opens Lorelei's door for her.

She tumbles out into the night, through their front gate and onto the lawn. Nik waits for her on the front porch, silent and stern. Jackson's car is still idling at the curb.

"Don't lie to me," Nik says when she reaches him. "Don't—don't do that shit, Lorelei. You don't even— Where the *fuck* have you been?"

"Band practice. Jesus. I went to see them play for a minute." Nik takes this in and doesn't say anything. "Would you have let me go?" she asks.

He doesn't respond.

"Are you going to rat me out?" she asks, then, instead. He shakes his head slowly. "I won't do it again," she promises.

"Okay."

"So come inside with me. Is there any schnitzel left?"

"Some. But listen, there's— Something happened. With Oma."

"What kind of something?"

"We don't really know yet. But Mom and Dad are at the hospital. Jens and I were waiting for you before we left."

The world drains itself of noise, of color. Panic sets a fire in Lorelei's stomach. Her knees buckle and she reaches out blindly, clutching at Nik's sleeve, his shoulder. He curls an arm around her and draws her all the way in, holding her against him. Lorelei doesn't mean to start crying; the tears don't gather or threaten, they're just *there*, streaming down her face, hot and miserable.

"It's okay," Nik murmurs. "It's okay, she might be okay."

But I was gone, Lorelei thinks. *I was off thinking about singing, kissing boys, I was gone, I was gone.* Jens appears over

Nik's shoulder and they hand her off one to the other, working in their usual silent tandem.

"I'm just gonna go say thank you to Jackson," Nik says. "We'll go in ten?"

"Sure thing," Jens says, pulling Lorelei over the threshold, into the house. "Hey there, little L," he says. "Let's get some dinner in you before we leave?"

7

OMA IS NOT OKAY. She's alive, but barely, and sunk deep into a coma by the time they arrive. It was a massive stroke, the doctors explain. It's unlikely that she'll wake up on her own, and even if she does, she'll be damaged. Lorelei swims through the words the doctors keep saying: *significant loss of gross motor function, linguistic impairment, looking into long-term-care facilities.* What they mean is: one way or another, your grandmother is not coming home again.

"Let her go," Petra says when the doctors try to discuss treatment options. "Just let her go already."

"You sure, Mom?" Jens asks. He's stationed himself by her side, along with Henry, who clings to her, useless, undone. Lorelei and Nik are set up on some chairs nearby, where they have a pile of vending machine snacks they aren't eating and an *Us Weekly* crossword they can't concentrate on enough to do. "We can sleep on it. She's not going anywhere. We don't need to decide right away."

"I've made my decision," Petra says coolly. "And you know her. She certainly wouldn't want this."

Papers are shuffled and passed around. The doctors confer. They try to talk to Henry, but he can't stop crying. He's clutching desperately at his wife's thin wrist, like she's the one who's dying. He hugged them all too tightly when they arrived, and Lorelei was disgusted with herself for being relieved: at least for a minute he'd forgotten to be scared of her.

Jens isn't eighteen, but he looks it, so he takes over.

We're a mess without her, Lorelei thinks. Oma has always been in charge of the whole family. Always.

It takes hours for nothing to happen. Lorelei goes in to sit at Oma's bedside while everyone else argues in the hall. Oma is one of three patients in the room, and Lorelei catches glimpses of the rest of them through fluttering curtains: other still, silent bodies, and crying relatives. The curtains pretend to keep their grief private but there's nothing they can do about the sounds, the gasp of respirators and the beep of heart monitors, the stifled sobs that issue softly from the living.

Oma seems peaceful, at least until you look too closely. Her face is serene, but there are IVs in each of her forearms, and bruises spreading purple under her papery skin. Her long braid is coming loose, and tangling.

If Lorelei looks long enough, Oma's slack face takes on a kind of violence. There's no one home, certainly not Oma, who was always vital, always moving. Her body without her spirit is empty, and the emptiness is awful, and wrong. Lorelei thinks she knows what her mother means when she says, *Let her go already.* Oma wouldn't allow herself to lie in bed with messy hair and a machine pushing air into her lungs. Oma—the real Oma—is already gone.

It's one o'clock in the morning when Jens finally comes in. "Oh, L," he says. "I didn't know you were here."

She stands up automatically. Like there's something to do now that he's here. He doesn't say anything, though. Jens just gathers her against him in a hug.

It's nice to be sheltered in the cove of her brother's arms. It's not like hugging Oma again would be—Jens is bone and sinew, still teenage lanky, but he's warm, and he's hers.

"I've convinced Mom to give her another day, at least," he says. "C'mon. There's nothing more we can do here."

Lorelei pulls away to say goodbye to Oma, and it hits her that this parting might be for good. *I said goodbye to her this morning,* she thinks. *I say goodbye to her every morning.*

She wants to leave Oma looking comfortable, at least. A little bit like herself. She reaches out to straighten the bed-clothes, but her grandmother's body is heavy against them and they won't be stirred. Silver hair is escaping wildly from its pins, curling softly around her face, and she looks young in a way Lorelei doesn't recognize, which seems unfair; Oma should look like she always does, if this is going to be the last time, if this is—

She decides that she has to redo it: the whole long plait. Lorelei pulls out the bobby pins she can reach and the thin elastic at the braid's end. She runs her fingers through Oma's hair and then realizes she'll have to move her head, just a little. She might get in trouble, but—

"Hey," Jens says. His hand comes to her shoulder again,

but this time his grip is firm. He isn't forceful with her, but there's no escaping him without a fight. "We've gotta go, Lorelei. You can do this in the morning."

Lorelei looks back as the door swings closed behind them: Oma's hair is messier than ever, streaming silver over the pillows, waves and waves of it looser than it ever was in life.

☙ ❧

That night Lorelei can't sleep. She comes downstairs for water and finds Nik bent over a textbook at the dining room table. She flinches against the harsh overhead light he's got on, just more evidence of how frazzled everyone is: it's three a.m., and no one has bothered to remind him to go to bed.

"What are you doing up?" he asks.

"I wanted water," Lorelei says. "My throat hurts."

"It's late."

"Yeah."

Lorelei goes into the kitchen and doesn't bother flipping on the light. Nik closes his book and comes in behind her. He goes to the refrigerator and opens the door while Lorelei pulls two glasses from the cupboard. Her brother is illuminated by the fridge's white glow on one side and the spill of yellow light from the dining room on the other, his body turned abstract and incoherent between them, just shape and shadow. Maybe that's why she's bold enough to ask the question that's been niggling at her, quiet, since she got home.

"So you and Jackson know each other," she says. Nik

pulls out the Brita, closes the fridge, and blinks as his eyes adjust to the deeper darkness.

"Uh-huh."

"I didn't know that."

"I guess not. But I didn't know you guys were friends, either."

"We aren't, really."

"Good."

Lorelei doesn't like his tone. "Why good?"

"I don't know." He pours them each a glass and puts the Brita back in the fridge. "So how did he end up giving you a ride home from band practice?"

"Chris Paulson invited me," she says.

"Oh."

"This is so not fair!" For a split second the day falls away from her, and she's just arguing with Nik in the kitchen, playing her little-sister role, hunting for information. "You totally know them, and you totally have an opinion on them, and you should tell me what it is."

"I don't know, Lorelei." Nik moves as if to leave. "It's late."

"You really aren't going to warn your baby sister?" she asks. She does remember, then, about Oma, and the things that he can't protect her from.

"It's not anything, really," Nik says. "I knew Chris a little bit when he was dating this girl Lisa, I guess. We used to play pickup soccer after school sometimes, before he joined that dumb band, winter of junior year. Jens was doing the play then, so I had a lot of time to myself."

Nik pauses, and seems to decide something. When he

speaks again, the words come more easily, like the story wants to be told. "His dad wasn't sick yet."

This part of the legend Lorelei has heard: that his dad passed away last year, and left Chris the old silvery Mercedes he drives when it's running. She knew the car in the parking lot long before she knew who it belonged to.

"Or I guess he was, but we didn't know it, and we'd spend—Jesus, hours, just running around, playing. Getting high sometimes, watching the sunset, whatever. He's—I mean, you've talked to him. He's a nice guy, right? Like, he'd always been popular—since seventh grade, basically—so I assumed he was a dickhead athlete like the rest of them, but he was funny. He surprised me. He and Lisa were always fighting over shit, but they were happy about it. They both kind of liked it, I think, the fighting.

"Until his dad— His dad got really sick, really suddenly, you know? Like, one minute he was fine and then he went to the hospital for something and they were, like, *You have three months, tops,* and that messed Chris up. Obviously, I guess."

Lorelei deliberately doesn't think about Oma's pale face and silver braid in that stark white unfamiliar bed.

"So you guys stopped hanging out?"

"It wasn't that simple," Nik says. "Because at first he just slipped away. He was at the hospital, like, all the time. Which I thought was funny because they weren't that close before, him and his dad. But I still saw him at school and stuff. And then all of a sudden he was *gone.*"

"I'm sure Lisa loved that." Lorelei only knows Lisa a tiny bit, from seeing her around on campus. She's tall and very pretty, with black hair and big green eyes, and she's

60

almost always got someone hanging around her, boys trying to touch her and girls trying to talk to her. She doesn't seem like a person who you could keep waiting.

"She was okay," Nik says. "She was actually great about it. They'd been together on and off for a while, at that point, so she had met his family. I think she went to be with them sometimes, at first."

"But then?"

"They broke up after he died," he says. "That's really what happened, his dad died and his mom just got, like, crazy possessive and jealous. She told Chris he had to be home right after school, and he was like, okay, you know, it's been a rough couple of months, I can do that, and then she told him he had to stop bringing Lisa around and he didn't love that but he did, and then—" Here he pauses to find the exact right words.

"She caught them," Nik says. It's sweet that he's being careful with her, Lorelei thinks. Like she won't know what it means, or can't imagine. "In his car, up on one of the bluffs, I guess. He said he had to be somewhere after school and his mom followed him, saw them. Naked. In the backseat of his Mercedes." His dad's car. "Chris missed, like, a week of school, after. I never found out exactly why. That's when they broke up."

He leans back in his chair and meets her gaze. "Chris is a good guy," he says. "He's been through a lot, and that's— what it is. But I know something about his family, Lorelei, and I don't want you getting mixed up in any of it. He's not worth it."

He's worth a lot, Jackson said in the car. Lorelei is sick of other people telling her what she deserves, when she's only just starting to figure out what she wants. "Don't you think he needs someone?" she asks. "To help him, to care about him? To get him *away* from her?"

"He could get himself away if he wanted to," Nik says. "It's— Love is like one of those Chinese finger traps, L. Remember those? How the harder you pull, the tighter it snares you? And it's hard to know that until it happens to you, until it's way too late. I don't want you to get caught up with him. Or anyone else."

"You sound pretty sure about that," she says.

"Trust me," Nik says. "Please just—trust me on this one."

"Love is like a trap," she repeats.

"Love is like a spider's web," Nik says. "It doesn't look all that dangerous when you're on the outside, but once you're in it—good luck ever trying to get yourself unstuck."

8

"YOU'RE GOING TO NEED a dress for the funeral," Petra
says.

Lorelei looks at her mother. Her hand tightens compul-
sively around the banister. Her response is instinctive and
absurd: *I want breakfast first.*

She slept later than she meant to after the long, strange
night, and woke up to the sun at an unfamiliar angle. She
got three, maybe four minutes of peaceful confusion in before she remembered, and her stomach and her throat iced
over with sharp-edged dread.

Her mother's words shatter through that.

"Oh, she's still alive," Petra corrects. "But she won't be
for long, and you don't have anything to wear."

"I don't want anything to wear," Lorelei says.

"You need something whether you want it or not."

Lorelei's eyes are open enough now to see that her mother
is freshly showered. She's dressed in a soft blue shift instead
of her usual dark, severe work clothes. The color catches a
feverish brightness in her eyes.

It's a practical thing to think of, and Oma has always been nothing if not practical. Lorelei can't imagine it, though: spending Oma's last hours or days looking for something appropriately somber. Nothing she feels is appropriate.

"I have to go to school," she says, though she's seen the clock and they probably aren't expecting her by now. It's already hours too late. She must have forgotten to set her alarm last night. Nik stayed up after she went to bed; he's probably still sleeping too. Maybe he could come with them. "What about the twins?" she asks.

"What about them?"

Petra has looked past Lorelei almost every day of her life, her gaze focused on horizons seen and unseen, sliding around her daughter's body like it isn't even there. Now she confronts her head on, and Lorelei is surprised by her mother's intensity.

"You're a very pretty girl," she says when Lorelei doesn't answer. "You should have a dress to wear. Something new. Something nice."

∾♾∾

They go to the Third Street Promenade, which is choked with tourists even though it's midday on a Tuesday. It's surreal to walk through the crowds together, the two of them side by side like nothing's going on. It's a mother-daughter shopping trip. On another day, in another family, this would have been offered as a treat.

Lorelei has always hated shopping with her mother, though, and when they enter a store, she remembers why.

Petra's work is all about how much nice things are worth. She goes through racks methodically and hands Lorelei things to try on. She touches everything, assessing each piece evenly, but the fever Lorelei saw in her eyes earlier is still burning, glowing steadily under her skin.

"Pity you'll look so sallow in black," she observes at one point.

Lorelei doesn't recognize her own reflection when it passes in mirrors and plate glass windows: she's just some anonymous teenage daughter, trying to pick out a dress for an occasion. Shopgirls ignore her surly indifference as a symptom of her age. She feels blank, and numb.

The dress she ends up in fits beautifully. There's a loose thread in the skirt's hem. Lorelei picks at it while Petra watches.

"Don't sulk," her mother instructs.

Something rude and ugly flares up in Lorelei. "Don't tell me what to do," she says.

Her mother pays for the dress without looking to see how much it costs. Is this mania? Lorelei wonders. Is this her mother's way of losing her mind? But it doesn't seem like that, not exactly. Petra has always been distant and quiet, like bare, dry earth. Now she's swelling up and filling out, like she had to wait for Oma to wither and fade before she could blossom.

The sadness that's been sitting heavily over everything else Lorelei feels heats up with the flare of her anger until it's boiled away, and she's left with nothing more than slow-simmering rage. She saves it until they've left the store. She's still her grandmother's girl. She isn't going to make a scene.

"Don't you care?" Lorelei asks. "This is sick, Mom, to be *shopping,* at a time like this."

"I shouldn't have let her raise you," Petra says, instead of answering. "You're so serious all the time, Lorelei."

"I'm not being serious! You're being crazy!"

"What, because she was my mother?" Petra flips up her sunglasses and steps close enough that Lorelei can see the way that the light makes her thin skin translucent, illuminating the tiny cracks and folds around her eyes. The feverish intensity pinking her cheeks has turned her mouth red and chapped. "No one is obligated to love her own mother," she says. "You know that."

Lorelei is stunned into tears. No one has ever come at her like this, nakedly furious, needling sharp. The suddenness is like a kick to the stomach. "I love you," she says. "Of course I love you, you're the one who—"

"People are looking," Petra says. Lorelei's outburst has calmed her. The hectic light in her eyes dies down, and she seems sober and human again. "Oma and I had a complicated relationship. Thinking about losing her reminds me that you won't have me forever, either. I thought this would be a nice thing for us to do together." She drops Lorelei's gaze just as suddenly as she held it. "There's a Starbucks over there," she says. She sounds stiff and uncomfortable again, like the mother Lorelei recognizes. "We could get a coffee before we go."

"Okay," Lorelei says. The rest of her sentence, left unsaid, keeps ringing in her ears: *You're the one who never loved me. You're the one who never wanted me in the first place.*

66

Petra chooses a table in a corner, where sunlight is streaming in through the floor-to-ceiling windows, so that she
can keep her sunglasses on. She gets a decaf for herself and
a chai for Lorelei. The steam keeps fogging up her lenses
and making her face strange, like an alien with enormous,
opaque dark eyes. Lorelei doesn't know whether to feel like
she's being seen or just examined.

"How's school going?" Petra asks.

Lorelei tries not to laugh. This is what her mother wants
to have a heart-to-heart about. "Fine," she says.

"Nik had a hard time at the beginning of his sophomore
year," Petra says. "I was wondering if—"

"I'm not Nik."

"I know."

Does she, though? Lorelei has never been sure how
much attention Petra really pays to her. She was an accident,
after all, or that's what she's been assuming since she learned
what that kind of accident was. The twins were a different
kind. It's not the type of thing she can ask her mother—how
she ended up with three kids when she's never seemed to
want one of them—but she wishes she could.

"How's . . . um. Work?"

Petra shrugs and looks away. "I'm sorry," she says. "We
don't have to do this."

"It was your idea!"

There's a silence. Petra picks up her bag, and then puts it

back down again. Lorelei wonders how many missed calls she has, how many emails have piled up on her phone. This is the first time she's ever seen her mother take a voluntary day off. She wishes she felt flattered instead of tricked and trapped.

"Will you miss her?" Petra asks.

Lorelei is so stunned she can't answer.

"Of course you will," Petra says, almost to herself.

Lorelei can't bring herself to say, *And you won't.*

Petra says, "I didn't make her stay, you know."

"I don't know what you mean."

"In the house," she clarifies. "As soon as we were settled, I told her she could get a place of her own, or go back, if she wanted to. She helped arrange the move for us, but she didn't have to come too."

"You didn't want her to stay?"

Petra's shoulders twitch into a reluctant shrug. She considers her answer and sips her coffee. "I knew I would be a bad mother," she says. "That I would make a mess of it. But it wasn't her responsibility to clean up my messes."

There it is, the admission: not just an accident but a mess.

"She was trying to take care of things," Lorelei says. Defending Oma feels useless, but she can't not do it.

"That was what she did," Petra says. "Taking care of everyone and everything. It would have been— I would have been bad at it—like I said. But it would have been all right. Not having a perfect mother doesn't ruin a person. Necessarily." She looks out the window. Her phone vibrates steadily in her bag.

"Do you need to get that?" Lorelei asks.

"Sure," Petra says. "We should probably go, anyway."

They're quiet in the car on the way back, and the space of their silence gives Lorelei time to think. Oma is—was—always a presence when she entered the room. She was used to being in charge, and she didn't take suggestions or criticism. Lorelei was always grateful for her grandmother's harsh edges; Petra is unpredictable, but Oma, even when she was difficult, was sure and certain.

Her mother was young when she had the twins. She's young now, still. She's never lived in a house without her mother before.

Lorelei feels something inside her soften toward Petra, and it scares her almost as badly as anything else that's happened in the space of the last day. Petra is unpredictable, and loving someone who changes like that is dangerous. That's something she's known since she was a much littler girl.

That night her mother and father leave after dinner to go to the hospital. Lorelei is still unsettled by the conversation she and Petra had: she feels like she's adrift in open water, like a boat that's tugged free from its moorings.

They don't tell her why they're going, but when they come back, Oma is dead.

Her mother comes in while she's getting ready for bed. The morning's fever is burning hot now, scalding, and her eyes are molten with fury. "She told you, right, Lorelei?" she says, without preamble. "She must have told you too what you could and couldn't do."

Lorelei assumes she means the singing. She had planned to ask more from Oma, to find out the whole story, but she can't do that anymore. The distance between her last conversation with Oma and the present seems impossible, a blur of static, all snow on the screen. "Sure," she says. "Yeah, she told me."

"She told me too," Petra says. She grabs Lorelei by the wrists. "She was always telling me how to live my life. She put a spell on me. She cursed me, you know. She probably cursed you too."

Lorelei tries to twist away from her mother and can't. Her grip is too strong. She looks possessed. Not the way her father did when he heard her singing, which was a distant thing, like he'd become a vacant body, a zombie. Petra looks like there's a spirit inside her, making her mouth move too quickly and giving it strange shapes.

Lorelei says, "She just told me—"

"Not to sing, never to sing. She told me the same thing, baby, but now I think we might be free."

"You can't possibly think Oma was, like, . . . a witch."

If anything, it's her mother who's the witch, always shut away from the rest of the world, bound up by a tight smile and this angry suspicion. She looks like she could do magic right now if she could channel the energy sparking behind her eyes into her fingers and her mouth.

"I know what I know," Petra says, but she loosens her grip a little. "Trust me. What she did to me—I hope she didn't do it to you. I hope it all goes away now that she's dead and gone. Maybe now it will all be over."

At this point, Lorelei is sick to death of crying, but she feels tears gathering behind her eyes, anyway. Her body stopped obeying her the minute Nik said, "Something's happened. With Oma," the minute she looked close enough to see the resignation written across his face, and the dark soft sadness welled up in his eyes.

Because she's starting to understand, and wishes she wasn't. From a certain angle—at seventeen, say, and terrified—bad luck can look a lot like something worse. What her mother must mean is: Oma cursed her, and she ended up pregnant. Petra sang for Henry, and slept with him, and somehow her babies are Oma's fault. The morning's conversation, and the air it seemed to breathe into her mother's life, crumbles in on itself. Petra doesn't want to take responsibility for anything. She wants to blame Oma for everything that's gone wrong so far, and start over again like Oma never existed.

She believes their family is her curse.

"How can you say that?" Lorelei asks.

"You don't know her like I did," Petra says. "And you weren't there when—"

But Lorelei can't bear to hear any more. "You said this morning that you loved us," she starts. "That you wanted to take care of us, that you were scared, and now you're saying—that having Nik, and Jens, that was a *curse*? Thank god you didn't raise us, if that's how you feel."

This, finally, stills Petra. Her face goes blank and white. "That's not what I meant," she says, but it comes out mechanical. She must not have realized what she was really saying. What she was confessing to her daughter, who's part curse too, or cursed, or who knows.

"Sure." Lorelei is a minute, maybe less, from crying. She thinks that if her mother doesn't get out of the room before it starts, she's going to scream, or die, or just explode. "Okay. You told me. Please leave now."

"I'm sorry," Petra says. She slips out the door with her shoulders hunched.

Lorelei refuses to feel sorry for her.

She falls asleep on top of the covers in her clothes, and wakes up to a face that's stiff with tear tracks. She stares up at the ceiling and licks delicately at the salt crusted against the upper corner of her lip. There's an ocean's worth of sadness inside her that's just started spilling out. It's briny and sharp against her tongue.

9

EVERYTHING IS COMPLICATED IN the days that follow Oma's death. Grief is not straightforward, and Lorelei's is full of twists and turns: sadness followed by anger, and then whole minutes where she forgets, and then has to remember again.

Oma died on Tuesday night. Wednesday is lost in a blur of sleeping, or trying to, or staring at walls. She calls Zoe when she knows she'll be in class so that she can just leave a voice mail explaining where she's been. Jens tells her when to come down for meals and reminds her to eat while she sits at the table, lost. Everything tastes like sand and feels just as heavy in her stomach.

On Thursday, she's vaguely aware of the planning going on downstairs. Henry's taken the week off from his teaching, so between grading papers he calls crematoriums and funeral homes and relatives on the other side of the ocean. She hears German coming up through the floorboards and it sounds completely foreign and somehow familiar, a language she's learned to recognize but has no idea how to speak.

Petra avoids her. After that feverish confession, she seems to have run out of words. She keeps watching Lorelei, though, her eyes hawk-bright and sharp. Lorelei watches her back. She almost wants to look at her mother's wrists to see if the blood that flows there is actually black, sludgy and mean, instead of bright red and human with pain. They're all devastated by Oma's death, of course, but to basically call her a witch, and act like asking them not to sing was some kind of curse—

Lorelei's fury with her mother hones itself into something so sharp and shining that it resembles a knife's blade inside her, always testing its edges on her fingertips and toes. It needles her with questions: How dare Petra? What in the world could she have been thinking?

What tore her mother and grandmother apart, all those years ago?

Lorelei doesn't mean to go looking, exactly. She just doesn't know how to stop herself.

Oma's room is still the way she left it: the bed is neatly made, and the blanket she was knitting is half finished on her bedside table. There are clothes in the hamper and lipstick-kissed tissues in the trash can. Lorelei closes her eyes against the feeling of seeing it, and takes her first few steps that way, arms outstretched, fingertips seeking blindly.

Don't be silly, she tells herself. *Pretend it's a mission. Pretend it's a game.* All she's doing is playing detective and looking for evidence—of what, she doesn't really know. Something awful that one of them did or said twenty years ago. The roots of a tree that's grown up twisted, and snared her in its branches. She's just like a cop on television, coming in to untangle what happened before she showed up. She can investigate Oma's room if she pretends it was someone else's, moving through beats she learned on the screen.

So Lorelei opens her eyes and walks a short circuit around the room. She taps her knuckles against the walls, but they all sound the same. The floorboards don't yield any secret compartments or unusual cracks. *Where would Oma hide something?* she asks herself. *How would Oma hide something?* She hates the idea that Oma hid anything. It isn't like her. Wasn't like her.

The only off-limits piece of furniture (aside from the closet in the weeks before Christmas) was Oma's writing desk, a heavy, solid old-fashioned thing, with dozens of cubbyholes and small, specific drawers. Her laptop is sitting at the center of it, an incongruous modern detail in the room.

Oma wasn't opposed to the digital age. She didn't Skype, but she emailed regularly, sitting here or at the dining room table downstairs, tapping out missives to everyone she'd left behind in Germany. Lorelei watched her open it enough times to know that it's password-protected—and she has no guesses as to what the password might be.

There are a few physical letters on the desk too: a bill half out of its envelope, waiting to be paid, a notice about health insurance, an offer from the Humane Society she hadn't gotten around to throwing out yet. On the right-hand side, carefully stacked and squared, are two envelopes addressed and stamped, ready to go.

Lorelei takes the pair of them and puts them on the bed. One is another bill. The other is personal, addressed to an apartment in Hamburg. It's for Hannah, a name Lorelei doesn't recognize. The envelope is standard-sized and it feels light, almost weightless.

The bill should get sent, obviously. Probably they both should. Lorelei tries to imagine what her grandmother would have needed to commit to paper, and pay all that postage on. Something important, maybe, something someone is waiting on thousands of miles away. Or maybe they've heard the news already, and have stopped expecting the letter. Maybe if she puts it in the mail, a few weeks from now Hannah will see an envelope with that curved, familiar handwriting on it and catch her breath, go white and then blue with shock.

Lorelei turns back to the desk, like it will help her make her decision, and sees what she missed before: the little pull that was hidden underneath those envelopes. When she tugs on it, it lifts up a panel of the desk's wood to reveal the space below it, which is filled with stacks of more letters, each one labeled with a year. 1998 through 2016: one for every year of Oma's self-imposed exile. Some stacks are much thicker than others, like there were years when the talk ran dry for a while before it swelled up again. When she rifles through them, each one is signed by the same Hannah.

Each one is also written in German. Lorelei can't read a word.

Language has always been a tricky thing in her life: her father teaches English as a second language classes at the local community college, and he spent most of the twins' freshman year of high school trying to convince them to take

Latin instead of Spanish, so that they would understand *the roots of their words,* he said. But all the adults in the house already have a second language—a first one, actually—and they've kept it carefully from their children. Zoe's parents make her go to Farsi classes on Sunday mornings. Lorelei looks at what's in her hand and recognizes the alphabet, and nothing else.

It's a treasure trove or a trash heap, and no way of knowing which. There are probably dozens of secrets hidden here, plenty that Lorelei wants to know and more she really doesn't.

Before she can stop herself, she lets one hand dart out to grab the earliest, thickest stack. Oma left too soon, and she left a million mysteries in her wake. Lorelei touches the paper reverently and imagines it's full of answers, things that will make her miss Oma less somehow, and make her absence bearable. Things that will make her family work like a family should.

She imagines that she is one of those TV detectives again, tough and untouchable, and she'll have all the answers by the hour's end. She just looks down at the paper as she walks out of the room, instead of around at all of the evidence of the life Oma lived, and then left, disappearing too fast to be pinned down and held in place.

⚬⚬⚬

Friday is the funeral. Only the family comes.

Later that day, Lorelei mails the last letter. It drops into a mailbox and disappears. Just like that: gone.

10

SATURDAY IS THE LAST gasp of hot September. A lick of oven-warm wind rolls and gusts across the city. It makes the house seem unbearably small, so as soon as she's done with her homework, Lorelei goes for a walk. She heads down to the beach and then up toward the Santa Monica Pier, where she can get lost in the crowd. She eats cotton candy, which sticks to the corners of her mouth and unspools from its paper cone in the breeze. The Ferris wheel is huge and hot, gleaming brightly under the relentless sun. Lorelei watches couples get on and go up, up, up, before they come back down again.

The air is so clear and empty that she can see for miles, straight out to the humped backs of the mountains that cup the city from the south, the east, and the north. Los Angeles sits in a basin, at the bottom of a bowl, and the ocean stretches out sparkling in its belly.

A song itches itself in the back of her throat, something high and sweet in counterpoint to the rustling breezes and the low ocean roar, but she doesn't dare sing it. In the clear light of day it's even harder to believe that there's anything to Oma's warning or Petra's curse, but she doesn't want to take her mother's permission, or break her grandmother's rule. Lorelei knows who really raised her, and who she's loyal to.

❧

When she gets back to the house after her walk, the twins are wrapped up in last week's homework, Jens quizzing Nik for a history test in the living room. Her mother is in the kitchen, and her father is sorting through work sheets at the dining room table.

Lorelei hovers in the front hall for a moment, not wanting to disturb the house's peaceful equilibrium with her presence. The usual silence is softened by small human noises, the twins' voices and her father's papers rustling, her mother opening and closing cabinets, looking for something she can't find.

There's a stack of mail on the hall table, and Lorelei notices a letter from school poking out of it. It's probably nothing to worry about—some minor administrative update—but she wants to open it first just in case.

When she tugs the envelope free, the rest of them come with it. Lorelei moves to grab them out of the air and knocks over the metal tray they've been sitting on. It hits the ground with a crash. So much for peace. She kneels and sweeps the mail back into a pile.

"Lorelei?" her dad calls from the dining room.

"Yeah, Dad," she calls back. "Sorry, I just knocked something over."

The top letter in the rearranged stack catches her eye as she lifts it back up. She recognizes the writing. *Hannah*, the return address says. She tears it open without thinking—it has to mean something, it has to—but of course it's written in German, just like the rest of them.

"Oh, you're okay." Her father hovers over her shoulder. Lorelei didn't hear him coming. "What have you got there?"

"A letter. To Oma."

Henry frowns and tugs the sheaf of paper out of her hands. Lorelei doesn't know how to say *No, stop, I need that.* When he scans it over, something in the contents makes him smile sadly.

"From family, at home," he says. Oma never called it *home*. She said *back there*, mostly, like her life in Germany was far behind her. "I don't think you knew—Hannah is your grandmother's sister."

"I didn't." Lorelei knew Oma had sisters. She never learned their names.

"I guess we don't talk about that much," Henry says. "Maybe we'll visit someday. Your grandmother never wanted to, but—" He cuts off his sentence as soon as he realizes what the rest of it will be: *now that she's dead, we can.*

Lorelei can't help loving the idea of meeting great-aunts and cousins, and discovering the scattered constellation of her own family: more girls and women with her grandmother's stern, beautiful face. Maybe they were raised in quiet houses too. Maybe they're people who would understand.

But her father's silence guilts her: Who is she to be happy now that Oma's gone? How can it feel like freedom to lose someone you love?

"Are you talking about Mama?"

Lorelei's head snaps up, but it's too late: Petra snuck up on them both. She tugs the letter out of Henry's hands and doesn't look at it.

"A letter came from Hannah," Henry says.

"Oh." Petra's hand tightens and the paper crumples in it.

"Can I have it?" Lorelei doesn't mean to ask. The words just come.

"For what?" Petra asks. Her eyes narrow. Lorelei doesn't know how to explain. "You can't read it, anyway," she reminds her. She turns and heads back to the kitchen with the letter still wilting in her hand.

Henry follows her. Lorelei watches him go and realizes that's the most she and Petra have said to each other since Oma died. Since long before that, probably, too, not counting the coffee shop the other day. Which she would rather not.

Just like that, her good mood evaporates. She can't bear to stay in the house with her silent, greedy mother or her pliant, self-involved father, or her brothers, who are always conveniently keeping out of the way. The tightness she felt in the air this morning closes in on her again. "I'm going back out," she yells, and slams the door behind her before anyone can tell her not to.

❧

By the time she makes it back to the Pier, the afternoon is tumbling into evening. She walks fast to the far end, where it's marginally less busy and she can stare out past everything at the day's last brightness. Behind her a crush of late-season tourists crowds the neon-lit amusement park. The air is heavy with their scent: human bodies and stale fry grease and sugar and salt and sweat. Before her is open water, endless, unsettled.

She leans against a railing and her fury boils over into air. The song just flies out of her, as high and clear as she's been imagining. It feels soothing in her throat, to her skin and eyes and mouth. It's physical, the way singing empties her out: like everything she's been clutching too close can finally, finally be set down.

She's so distracted by relief that at first she doesn't notice the way people have drawn closer to her, clustered in a loose group of fifteen or twenty. Every one of them is listening intently, rapt in the sound.

When she does notice, what she sees is that every face is slack with wonder and wracked by grief, tears falling silently out of bright, unfocused eyes. It seems natural, for just a moment, that everyone is as stricken as she is, bone-weary, like sadness is the thing that threads the world together.

Around them the Pier bustles on about its business, but Lorelei is enclosed in a circle of her own making, the quiet center of the lonely, left-behind universe. A woman reaches out to touch her: the hem of her T-shirt, the ragged threads of her cutoff shorts. The bodies around her stir and shuffle in closer. Too close.

As Lorelei shakes herself out of the song, she starts to see the wrongness: these people are enchanted, fevery like her father was the last time she sang. Like her father, they're sick with something she gave them. The light behind their eyes doesn't belong to them at all.

"No," she whispers, but no one moves. "Stop," she says, louder. They're not doing anything aside from crying, a steady stream of tears dripping from chins and cheeks. She half expects when she turns to run that someone will stop her, but they let her leave, parting gently around her body and staying still, stunned silent in her wake.

The idea that there might be something to Petra's curse after all is too exhausting to take seriously. That night Lorelei looks at herself in the bathroom mirror. She wishes Zoe was here to make her over with the mask she wore at the Roxy: the face of someone older and prettier, just someone *else*. She hums tunelessly while she brushes her teeth.

"I'm cursed," she whispers at her reflection, but the lights in the fixture overhead burn on merrily, unblinking, and her mouth tastes of mint and she feels nothing more than tired and sad, achy, like usual. "I'm cursed," she insists to herself, tracing the lines of her face on the mirror's cold glass.

She looks just like she always does. She shouldn't be surprised. She's always had Oma's curse in her, or whatever it is, just like she's always had her mother's fury and her father's absence. If Petra was cursed before Lorelei was born, she's never lived without it.

I'm the same as I always was, Lorelei thinks, and flicks off the light on her way out.

11

IN THE MORNING, before she's awake enough to think better of it, Lorelei picks up the oldest letter. She types the words into a Google translate box, one sentence at a time. She has to find keyboard shortcuts for unfamliar characters. It seems to take forever. *Ich würde gerne fragen, wie es dir geht, aber ich bin mir nicht sicher, ob das eine Frage ist, die du jetzt beantworten wolltest.* I would like to ask how you're doing, but I'm not sure if that is a question that you wanted to answer now. *Ich weiss, dass die letzte Zeit schwierig war.* I know that the last time was difficult. *Jetzt, da du da bist, muss ich einfach daran glauben, dass alles wieder gut wird.* Now that you're there, I just have to believe that everything will be fine again. *Ich bin wenigstens froh darüber, dass du gehen konntest, weil du es wolltest.* I'm at least glad that you could go, since you wanted to.

It was Henry's side of the family who arranged the actual emigration; they were government people and diplomats going back generations. He grew up traveling, learning languages in first one city, and then another, and then another. He was the one who chose Los Angeles for them; at least, that's the way Lorelei has always heard the story. *Your*

mom knew she was going to have two babies, and she wanted to
raise them somewhere warm and sunny, where they could play
outside all day. I told her: I know just the place.

That story left a thousand details unspoken. Some of
them Lorelei has filled in over time: that Henry had always
loved Los Angeles, but also that they were running from
something they were too ashamed to discuss in their native
language when they came here. Then there are the things
she's only learning now: that the pregnancy might not have
been the only source of worry, or shame. That her grandmother might have done something she was ashamed of too.

The letter is not a revelation. It's chatty and full of news
of people whose names she doesn't recognize, domestic details from homes she's never seen. Halfway through she gets
bored with the laborious process of typing and reading, and
trying to piece together what the computer can't translate or
conjugate. It all feels broken and impossible, like a nest of
words so tangled that she can't find the first thread to pull.

She takes sentences at random from the letter, and then
from the next and the next one. Today, we found some of your old
school papers. Should we forward them to you, or throw away? When it
rained the other day, I wanted to make the chicken soup from your recipe,
but we didn't have any garlic and it seemed impossible for me to go out
in the rain. Of course I miss you all. I miss Petra's singing in the house.

Lorelei has to read it again. I miss Petra's singing in the house.

Of course she must have sung, to know there was a
curse on her, or—whatever it is. Lorelei just can't imagine
Petra singing, is all. She tries to picture her mother young
and happy and carefree, sitting in her mother's home,
surrounded by their family, humming while they talked and

washed dishes or made tea. What she comes up with is like a holiday commercial; it has nothing to do with the mother she knows.

She can't imagine her mother happy, or the days when her parents were just starting to fall in love.

Lorelei types in the next sentence, and the next. I know you won't want me to say it, Silke, but I think there has to be another way for her, and for you.

Her hands are shaking now.

You treat it like a curse, and so she will too.

You've probably stopped reading this letter already, or if you haven't, I will get some blistering reply. It will come all the way across the ocean and still it will burn me when I open it. There's so much space between us, now, and you probably still don't think it's enough.

I'm sorry to make you angry, and remind you of the things you don't like to think about. But if I don't, who will?

Love always,
Your sister

Lorelei smooths the paper in front of her. She was hoping that Hannah's letter would explain it all away, and give this thing a name that was normal rather than magical. But instead it's the final click of a lock coming closed. *You treat it like a curse.* Whatever *it* is, Hannah knew about it. They both did. The blank faces of all those people on the Pier flash in front of Lorelei, and she shivers.

On the other hand, if Oma only *treats* it like a curse, that means it isn't one. *There has to be another way,* Hannah says in the letter. Yesterday Lorelei sang from the bottom of her own grief, but maybe if she was feeling different—if she *was* different—she could give people happiness instead, or wonder, or love. Maybe she could use the obscure power she holds in her throat for something beautiful.

She shivers again, and this time it feels heady and lovely, like something she wants to feel again.

12

ZOE COMES TO VISIT that afternoon, and brings all the normalcy of the real world rushing back in with her. She also brings a satchel of missed homework from the teachers and a card signed by their friends. "Chris asked about you on Friday," she says, huddling up with Lorelei on her bed.

"Oh!" Lorelei is thrilled, and then upset with herself for being thrilled.

"I told him," Zoe says. "I hope that's okay."

Lorelei nods. She's glad to have been spared the awkwardness. It's a big thing to say, and she's already learned that no one really knows how to respond.

Zoe doesn't say anything for a while. She strokes Lorelei's hair at her temples, soothing and sweet.

There's a particular quality to the quiet between them, something different from the oppressive silence that usually fills the rest of the house. They could be talking. Zoe could be trying to fill up space with words and Lorelei would let her. Instead, they both allow the absence. They choose it together.

When Lorelei starts to cry, it happens in her chest, like something ripping open, sobs tearing through her over and over. Zoe holds on to her, an anchor so steady Lorelei can finally let herself drift. She cries until she's ready to be quiet again.

"I don't know what I'm going to do," she says at last. What she means is: *I don't know what my family is going to do.* She's been so busy thinking about singing, and the letters, and the idea of big, powerful mysteries, that she hasn't let herself look too closely at the truth: every day from now on, she'll wake up and Oma will still be gone. Who will run the house in her absence?

"Oma took good care of you," Zoe says. "She always— She kind of raised you, right?"

"Yeah."

"When my mom's mother died, she totally lost it," Zoe says.

Lorelei can't imagine it. Zoe's mother seems so assured and controlled.

"She didn't get out of bed for a week. And at the gravesite—I mean, she *screamed*. She and her mother had such a complicated relationship, though. I think she didn't know how to mourn her, really. Because they fought so much when she was alive."

"It's not like that with Oma."

Or is it? Lorelei doesn't even know how to feel about her grandmother right now.

"Of course it isn't. I just— If it was like that for her, when it had been so complicated, I can't imagine what it's like for you, if, you know, it wasn't. I remember Dad telling

Carina that it's okay if grief is ugly. That you just have to get through it, however you need to."

Oma's absence is like a huge, aching hollow: it's not ugly, it's gutting. Lorelei has a new dress in her closet and she messed up Oma's braid and she made all of those people cry. She took the letters and no one stopped her. There's no fixing it now. There is no going back.

What's ugly is how she feels about the living: Petra's bright eyes, and her mistrust, and the way she's made Lorelei start to ask questions that Oma can never answer.

It shouldn't be this hard, Lorelei tells herself. To Zoe, she says: "I feel like an orphan. Which is crazy, because—"

"Oma raised you," Zoe says again. "And anyway, I'm pretty sure that you're allowed to feel whatever the fuck you want."

❧

It's dark out by the time they go downstairs to say goodbye.

"See you at school tomorrow?" Zoe asks.

"Yeah," Lorelei says. She unlocks the door and pushes it open. Chris is standing on the front porch.

His hands are stuffed in his pockets and his shaggy head is hung low in the dim yellow light. He's half turned away, as if he lost his nerve at the last minute, or thought better of coming in the first place.

He looks up at them and says, "Oh."

Should she let him leave? Lorelei gives him a tiny wave. "Hey."

Zoe says, "Hey," and she and Chris nod at each other. "I was just going, but I'm glad you came."

It feels good to know she has Zoe's blessing: that Zoe trusts her, and thinks she's doing okay at this, with him. Lorelei watches her friend skip down the steps to where her mother's car is idling quietly at the curb. Then it's just her and Chris on the porch, hemmed in by the darkness all around them.

"I wanted—" he says, and stops. The smile he gives her is happy but puzzled, strained at the corners. "I really wanted to see you. I wasn't sure if you wanted me to come."

"It seemed weird to ask," Lorelei says. "We don't really, um, we don't know each other that well."

Chris doesn't say anything. His hands are still in his pockets. His body inclines toward hers but he doesn't touch her. It's like he's deliberately holding himself back, but she can't imagine why. Isn't he older? Shouldn't he be sure?

She steps in a little closer and marvels when he does the same.

"I didn't want to see people, sometimes," Chris says. "After my dad."

"You're not bothering me," Lorelei says. "I'm glad you're here."

At this his smile breaks out, wide and white and dazzling, and he reaches at last to loop an arm around her and tug her in close at his side. She noses at the folds of his sweatshirt, inhaling the strange, musky boyscent of him, clean laundry and his sweat, his skin.

"It's actually been kind of boring, being shut up in the house all week," Lorelei says.

"You want to get out of here?" he asks. "I mean, can you? We could go for a drive or something. If you want."

Lorelei looks behind her to where the front door is still just slightly ajar. Jens is in the kitchen, starting to get dinner ready. Nik and her parents are still upstairs. She's wearing leggings and a sweater, and there are probably flats kicked off under the dining room table. Her keys are hung over a hook in the front hall. "Yeah," she says. "Hang on."

Jens has three different pots on the stove. It doesn't smell half bad, actually, but he looks pretty frazzled when he hears her come in and turns around.

"I might go out for a minute," she says.

"Yeah, okay." He stirs a wooden spoon through something thick, and frowns. "You'll be back to eat, though, right?"

"Sure."

"Tell Zoe I say hey," Jens says.

Lorelei doesn't correct him. The lie needles at her, small and sharp. She chooses to ignore it.

She slips out the front door again and closes it behind her, feeling the snick of the lock sliding into place all the way down to her bones. Now she's alone with Chris and the whole huge, dark night.

In the car, the city flashes around them, dim, narrow residential streets quickly giving way to Venice Boulevard's wide lanes. Well-lit window displays and the occasional neon sign mark their progress, though Lorelei doesn't think Chris knows where they're headed, exactly.

"Zoe said you and your grandmother were pretty close," he says eventually.

"Yeah," Lorelei says. "She lived with us."

"That must have been nice."

"I guess."

"I don't really know my grandparents." He slips the car three lanes to the left, hanging a turn at the next intersection. The streets get smaller again, quieter. "My mom's parents are both dead, and my dad's are pretty far away."

"I guess that's tough for you guys," Lorelei ventures. "Being just, you know. The two of you."

"It's hard on her," Chris agrees.

"Is that why she comes to your shows?"

Chris heaves a long sigh instead of answering. He navigates a few more turns, purposefully, now, like he has some sense of where he's going.

"Sorry," Lorelei says. "You don't have to tell me."

Chris pulls over to the curb and turns off the car. He runs his hands through his hair and fiddles the keys out of the ignition. Lorelei tries to be patient. Inside the car it's quiet and warm, and—intimate, she thinks. That's the word. She's surrounded by the stuff of Chris's life: crumpled essays, fragments of gum wrappers, loose change and empty Starbucks cups and stray guitar picks. Her own life seems distant and abstract in comparison.

"It's weird, right?" Chris says. "That she comes."

"I don't know. I guess everyone's family seems weird to people who aren't in it."

"She and my dad used to come together," Chris says. "When I was playing in orchestra, in middle school. When he was good. I mean, they had to drive me, so obviously they came, but—my dad was a musician, have I told you that?"

Lorelei shakes her head. Chris keeps talking. "She was never much for it, but he was so excited that I played. So when she comes now—I don't know, everyone hates it, everyone in the band thinks it's so lame, and I do too, but—" He turns to her and splays his hands, helpless. "She's my *mom*," he says. "What am I supposed to do?"

It's a question without an answer. There are no rules, Lorelei knows now, about how love works, or how family makes you feel. Everyone knows what they're supposed to feel, of course, but what if you don't? There isn't a law against it. There's only the black fact of your own heart.

"At least you love her," she says finally. "I don't think that's a bad thing. Right?"

Chris's hand hovers for a moment before it slips across the gearshift, landing lightly against the outside of her thigh, the bony ridge of her kneecap. "I'm crazy about you," he says. "That's— Is that a bad thing?"

"Why would I think it was?"

"I don't know." Chris gets bolder. He keeps the hand on her thigh and slides his other one up to her shoulder, brushing against her throat. The network of veins there pulses keenly at his touch. "I barely know you." His fingertips find the hollow where skull meets neck and slide up, into the tangle of her hair. "You might want me to play hard to get."

"I don't want anything to be difficult," Lorelei says. "More difficult than it has to be, anyway."

Chris surges forward and kisses her breathless, his hands on her tightening like he's desperate to keep her. Lorelei has no intention of going anywhere. She wriggles her way toward him, one blind hand coming up to clutch at his ribs through his sweatshirt.

"This is crazy," Chris says again, mumbling against her mouth. "You—you—"

"I what?" Lorelei does pull away just a little bit, uncertain. Her mouth is buzzing, humming, swollen.

"I couldn't stop thinking about you," Chris says. He unwinds himself from her and leans his forehead against the curve of her seat. "When you were gone. I wanted to see you, and I kept thinking that I shouldn't. I'm the last thing you need to be thinking about right now. But it was like—like you were calling to me. Like I could hear something echoing. I don't know." He sounds lonely, and lost, like he's somehow far away from her even though they are so close. "Sorry. I can stop being weird."

Lorelei thinks she knows what he means, though. That was how she felt after she saw him in the hall that first time: like he was echoing in her, bouncing off her hollows, resounding again and again.

Chris shifts back so that he's facing forward again, not looking at her at all. "There's a coffee shop down the block. That's where we were going before I got distracted. If you want to."

"Yeah, I could—yeah."

The place is small and cozy. Chris is apparently a regular: the women working the counter greet him by name and get to work on his order. Lorelei asks for chamomile tea. When it comes, slopping at the edges of an enormous orange mug, it smells like Oma, like home.

Lorelei takes a deep breath of the sweet steam before she asks her question. "How did you handle it? Going to school with all of that happening with your dad, and everything?"

"I didn't have a choice." Chris is unsentimental. "I just kind of muscled through it."

"Oh."

"You don't have to, though. I mean, whatever, I don't know, it's just . . . It's really hard. I don't think I understood how hard it was going to be."

"Zoe said I was allowed to feel however the fuck I wanted," Lorelei says. "When she was over, before."

"Yeah." Chris nods thoughtfully. "You can," he says. "You should."

He reaches for her again, but this time his touch is reassuring, just solid and warm. Lorelei leans into him and thinks, *So this is what having a boyfriend is like.* Here is someone who looked at her and saw what she needed. He'll help her put her life together again.

Chris presses his face into her hair. "It's so hard. But I'll take care of you," he murmurs. "If, I mean. If you want me to."

13

THERE'S ANOTHER THE TROUBLE show. "You should come," Chris says. They're spending the last minutes of their lunch period together, lying in the grass. It's been three weeks, and it never stops seeming magical to Lorelei that she can hang out with him whenever she wants. He smiles when he sees her. He makes room and time for her in his day. "It might be a little weird because of my mom and whatever, but I'd like it if you came."

He laid out the rules for her over tea that Sunday night. He isn't allowed to date, so he can't make too much time for her, and can't bring her home, and doesn't want to meet her parents, either. Lorelei almost doesn't care—she can't imagine ever wanting anyone to meet her mother—but she minds it in moments like this, when the specter of Mrs. Paulson hovers over the little bits of time they're supposed to have for themselves.

The truth is that she'd be dying to go even if Chris wasn't playing. She's made her way through the first stack of Oma's letters and gotten midway through the second without finding another word about music; apparently Oma's reply was blistering enough to put Hannah off the subject. Lorelei's questions are still mostly unanswered, but she wants to get back into a room filled up by sound now that she knows what to expect from it. Maybe she'll find a way to sing something of her own—humming, even. A tiny test. An experiment. To see.

Hannah said you didn't have to treat it like a curse.

So Lorelei weighs her options and asks Nik for a ride to the show while they're supposed to be setting the table for dinner that night. He surprises her by not putting up a fight.

"I've never actually heard them play," he says. "I'll come as long as Jens doesn't need the car."

Lorelei didn't mean to ask him to accompany her, exactly, but she can't tell him that now. "What would Jens need the car for?"

"It's his car too," Nik says, instead of answering. "Or he might want to come with."

Great. Lorelei feels, not for the first time, that two is an excessive number of brothers.

Jens and Henry walk into the dining room, carrying plates of food.

Jens says, "Come where?"

"To see The Trouble on Saturday."

"I have an enormous history test Monday," Jens says. "I'm not going anywhere this weekend."

"Does that mean you have a test on Monday too?" Henry asks Nik.

"I'm not in AP," Nik says. "Mine's next week."

Lorelei does have a test on Monday, but she and Henry haven't spoken directly to each other since the thing with the letter, so he doesn't know that. He doesn't ask her if she ought to be studying. A tiny piece of her is disappointed. Lorelei is still learning the contours of an Oma-less life. The freedom is a little bit dizzying. She doesn't want her brothers to watch over her, exactly, but she misses knowing someone else was keeping track.

❧

The show falls near Halloween, which means costumes. The band gets skeleton sweatshirts. On Friday, Lorelei goes with Chris after school to pick up palettes of face paint, and sits with him in the bathroom at the practice space while he coats his face in white and sweeps streaks of black along his bones: his nose and cheeks, and then across the swell of his mouth.

She expects it to be harder for one or both of them, but he doesn't look like death at all: it's just Chris as a cartoon. He pulls some funny faces at his reflection, and then at her in the mirror. He forgets himself and kisses her, smudging them both with gray.

She and Zoe spend Saturday scrounging up thrift store punk outfits: tight jeans with holes in the knees and safety-pinned tank tops. They rat their hair up into faux hawks.

Lorelei narrows her eyes and practices making tough faces. "You're such a marshmallow," Zoe says. "You look like one of Carina's angry troll dolls."

Lorelei frowns down at her outfit. "Is it dumb?" she asks. "Should I change?"

"The point of Halloween is to be whoever you're not," Zoe replies philosophically. "I mean, you are definitely not a street punk."

Lorelei is nervous, but the drive there soothes her. Nik and Zoe are both good at distracting her. They might even be flirting with each other a little bit. She watches her reflection in the window flash by under each passing streetlight, and it looks—okay, she thinks. Not so crazy, now that she's away from her little-girl bathroom at home.

They park somewhere up in the steep, sloped hills above Sunset. Nik is wearing a tight black T-shirt and a pair of bunny ears taken from Lorelei's old dress-up box. She's surprised to find that he's handsome enough to get away with something like that. He's just her brother. But when Zoe looks at him, Lorelei can kind of imagine how other girls see him too.

Carina drives over from UCLA to join them. She knows Bean even though he's a year younger than she is, and she's curious to hear the band play too. She meets them at the bottom of the hill. When they stumble down to her, she's halfway through a clove, wreathed in its pale smoke. She isn't dressed up, so she looks like she always does: tough, casual, careless.

"Carina," Lorelei says, "this is my brother Nik."

Nik and Carina have met once or twice before, but only

ever in passing. It's strange to see the two of them together. It feels like they *should* know each other already, just by osmosis.

"Nice to meet you," Carina says. She gives Nik a split-second once-over and then turns her attention to Lorelei. "I hear one of these dudes is your boyfriend now. Nice going."

"Uh," Lorelei says. "Thanks?"

Nik cocks his head at Lorelei. "Chris? I didn't know he was your *boyfriend*."

"He's—"

"The show's gonna start," Zoe says before Nik can ask any more questions. "Let's go inside, yeah?"

Carina takes one last, long drag on her cigarette. The smell of her exhale is so thick and sweet that it makes Lorelei a little light-headed. "Sure," she says. "Whatever."

Carina's smoky scent envelops all four of them as they walk into the Whiskey, giving them an air of unquestionable, indifferent cool. Chris is already onstage. He's tuning his guitar, haloed in white light, exactly where he belongs.

"*That's* my boyfriend," Lorelei says, allowing herself one satisfied smile when Carina draws her breath in through her teeth. Someone else must have done his makeup tonight: the lines are slim and precise, stitches radiating out from around his lips, his dark eyes surrounded by a sea of black.

"He certainly looks like trouble," she says.

Nik says, "You have no idea."

The two of them share a look over Lorelei's head that has her instantly feeling five again, maybe twelve, definitely young and left out. So she leaves them behind and bounds up to the stage, leaning against its lip to look up at Chris. "Hey, baby," she says. Chris smiles back and then freezes.

"Hey," he says. "Shit, we, uh— Remember, we talked about this? My mom?"

Mrs. Paulson is once again stationed at the back of the room. She's as silent and watchful as ever.

They did talk about this, about how she would be there, how Lorelei shouldn't do exactly what she's doing. "Sorry," she says.

"Nah," he replies. Chris flicks his hair out of his eyes, his little habitual gesture. It's familiar, endearing, and it soothes the hot lick of shame Lorelei feels. "I'm glad you want to. But. Later, maybe?"

"Find me," she says. "I'll be around." She tries to walk back to the rest of the group with some measure of confidence and cool.

"Not in front of the Mrs.," Nik says. He looks at Chris's mother. His gaze lingers on the group of kids around her and then flicks up to the stage where the boys are finishing their sound check. He used to hang out with some of them, Lorelei remembers. Jackson, soccer, all of that. She wonders if he's embarrassed to be seen with his little sister.

Nik says, "Carina's at the bar trying to round up a beer or two. I won't tell if you want to have some sips."

❧

There are a couple of guys at the bar who Carina knows. They're Chris and Nik's age, seniors at a different Valley private school than the one Bean goes to. They're badly groomed and neatly dressed, the stubble covering their chins marking them definitively as older than Lorelei's smooth-skinned classmates. Carina introduces them all around—the dark-haired one is Daniel, and his friend, a blond, is Paul. Daniel has a fake ID with someone else's face on it. He flashes it at the bartender and buys them all their drinks.

Lorelei can see the boys doing the math in their heads: three girls, three guys. Nik is charming Carina as easily as he charmed Zoe in the car; Zoe tilts her face up toward Daniel's when she talks. He motions that he can't hear her. She rises onto the balls of her feet and props a hand against his shoulder to steady herself.

Paul and Lorelei catch each other's eyes, and smile, and look away. For the first time Lorelei understands the appeal of a wedding ring: some silent symbol she could flash that would say *off-limits*. Not unfriendly, just unavailable.

"Have you heard these guys play before?" Paul asks.

"Yeah," Lorelei says. "A couple of times."

Should she be flirting with him, and trying to get a rise out of Chris, who's tuning his guitar onstage? It seems pointless to pretend. Instead, she sips at her icy beer, so cold it doesn't really taste like anything, and lets the chill and the alcohol numb her from the inside out. Chris not kissing her stings less and less and less.

"So they're good?"

"I think so," she says. "Pretty good." Lorelei nods at Chris on the stage. "He's my boyfriend, so. You know."

"Oh," Paul says. He smiles at her. "Got it."

By the time the band comes on, Lorelei is buzzing. She feels like a firecracker about to go off: tightly wrapped, full of sparks. She knows all the songs by now, from the last show, and the practices, and Chris humming them unconsciously under his breath.

It's different, though, when the band comes together, when the sound rolls up and spreads through the air in the room. Instead of concentrating her inside herself like the first show did, this one connects her to everyone around her. It's nice to look at a crowd and see every face in it: to think, *You and you and you and you.* At the first show she wasn't sure she belonged, or whether she could move in a mass governed by a beat. Now it seems easy. Natural, almost. She understands how to let her body tell her what to do.

If she was the one onstage, her voice might snare all of these people the way it did on the Pier. When it first happened, Lorelei was horrified by herself. She doesn't want anyone under her thrall. But the power Chris wields, up front, holding the microphone—that's something she recognizes. It's something she wants to have, and if she can't have it, she wants to touch someone who does. Chris finds her in the crowd and Lorelei lifts her hands up to him, mouthing along with his words.

Zoe nudges something cold against her thigh, and she looks down to see another bottle of beer being quietly handed her way. Lorelei shakes her head to clear it, and purses her lips to take a sip.

∽◠◡◠

Zoe and Lorelei retreat to the bathroom after The Trouble's set ends, taking turns in the single relatively clean stall.

"Ugh, I feel like I've had to pee *all night*," Zoe says. She has to yell to be heard over the din coming in from outside and Lorelei running the sink.

"I know," Lorelei yells back. "Wait, how many have you had?"

"One and a half?" Zoe emerges, a little unsteady on her feet. "Two, actually, I guess. I had one, and then I split that one with you, and one with Daniel."

"Yeah. So. Daniel."

"Daniel," Zoe agrees. She smiles at Lorelei in the mirror. She looks pleased and pretty, pleasantly distracted. Lorelei wonders if that's how *she* looks when Chris is around. "He's, like, cute, right?"

"Cute," Lorelei agrees. "Maybe don't let him buy you any more beers."

She doesn't want to sound like a downer, but she's never seen Zoe's eyes shine like this before, and she doesn't know anything about how much beer a person can drink. In the wake of the music, she's feeling steadier, but still slightly off-kilter, like there's a thin layer of static between her and the world.

"Oh, come on," Zoe says. She turns to lean her back against the sink's damp ledge. "Have I given you shit about Chris? I have not. Your dumb brother might, but I have been—" She covers a hiccup. "I have been very supportive. And I'm not gonna, like, marry this dude, or even go home with him. Carina would never let me. I'm just seeing what I can do."

That makes sense to Lorelei: she thinks of the moments on the Pier before she realized that anyone was watching her, when singing almost felt like stretching her wings. Her voice lies coiled up inside of her most of the time, unacknowledged and unused. Most people don't even know she *has* it. The power of it scares and seduces her in equal measure.

"Just be careful with yourself, then," Lorelei says. "You might not plan on going home with him, but you're— He would be an idiot if he didn't try."

Zoe laughs and ducks her head against the intimacy of the moment. It's hard to talk about, Lorelei knows: the feeling you have for your very best friend, the kind of love that isn't romantic and isn't family. It's just love, the kind that hooks into your heart and *pulls*.

She does love Zoe, and doesn't understand how anyone could not want to spend time with her, how anyone could not think she's the coolest, the greatest, the funniest and smartest. Of course some dude in a bar is buying her drinks, trying to buy himself a slice of her time.

"You know I can take care of myself," Zoe says again, looking over her shoulder as she pushes the bathroom door open. "Coming?"

Lorelei follows her back to the bar. Chris is over with his friends, but she isn't allowed to talk to him, so she talks Carina into sharing more sips of her beer instead. She figures that if Zoe's still standing after two, a little more won't undo her. This one is Rolling Rock, slippery with condensation in its green glass bottle.

Zoe picks up her practiced flirtation with Daniel, and Lorelei leaves her to it. Paul has long since disappeared, and the assurance she felt earlier in the evening has mostly evaporated.

When she sees Chris slip backstage, she goes to follow him.

It's not even really a backstage: just a narrow hallway from the back half of the stage to the alleyway where they load equipment. Hidden from the crowd, she grabs Chris's arm and rocks forward into him. She's a little unsteady on her feet. He's mostly washed the paint off his face, so he's pink-cheeked again, looking like himself.

"Hey," he says, laughing, leaning down to kiss her.

"Hi," she says, and goes back to the kissing. It feels different when she's tipsy, honey-warm and loose. She just wants to be *closer*.

"Did we sound okay?"

"Sounded great."

"Better or worse than the first time?"

"Better?" Lorelei doesn't really want to talk about music right now, for once.

"We didn't play the new song," he says. "The one that freaked you out."

"I wondered about that."

"Wanted to get it really right," he says. He's pulled away a little bit, but he leans in and brushes the tip of his nose against hers. "I wanted to see if you'd sing it with me, actually. We could do a little duet."

"You've never heard me sing," she says.

"Have so," he counters. "I hear you humming, sometimes,

when you don't think anyone's listening." She blushes. "It's cute," he insists. "And I'm sure— I know you're talented, okay, I just know it."

"That's a big bet," she says.

"We'll practice," he says, kissing her again.

Lorelei thinks about telling him: *It's a little complicated, because there's—a thing, with my voice, and my family. My grandmother wouldn't talk about it. My mother thinks it's a curse. And I want so badly to believe that they're both wrong, and it's safe. That I'm safe.*

Her train of thought drifts off the track as he kisses her again. And he keeps kissing her until Bean bangs into the hallway. Chris says Bean is basically married to his drums. He has no time for women, and even less patience for his bandmates' needy girlfriends.

"You seen Jackson?" he asks. "We need him to pull the car around."

Chris sighs and peels himself away from Lorelei. "Probably making out with Angela in a corner," he says. "I'll take a look."

"Thanks, man," Bean says. He's already jumping up the steps to start pulling the last of their equipment down.

Lorelei drifts out the back door and breathes in the cold, clean air of the night. She leans against the building's exterior wall, stucco prickling the backs of her bare arms. She looks up to the cloud-covered sky and tries to shake the excess energy out of herself. She almost misses the tentative sounds of scuffle at the narrow end of the alley.

There are two bodies there, one shoved up against a wall, the other curving over it. As her eyes adjust, she can see that there's no threat to the way they're touching, even if it looks like a struggle.

It dawns on her slowly, unwillingly: One shape resolves into the outline of Nik's familiar silhouette, his rabbit ears knocked askew above him. The other one is so unlikely that it takes a minute before she can put a name to it. Jackson isn't inside. He's here, leaning against the wall and tilting his throat up to be kissed. That's Jackson in her brother's arms.

Lorelei is frozen to the spot. Jackson turns his head and sees her. His open mouth turns into a snarl. Nik doesn't seem to notice. Lorelei shakes her head frantically, silently. She whirls and darts inside without looking to see if he's following.

Carina is still by the bar, flirting with someone new. Daniel has one of Zoe's hands in his; she's got a third beer in the other. Chris is all the way in the back, talking to his mother, whispering in her ear. Lorelei pulls out her phone and texts with shaking fingers.

Where are you? she sends to Nik. *Let's get out of here. I'm tired. I want to go home.*

14

LORELEI DECIDES NOT TO tell Nik she knows. She worries that Jackson might do it for her, but days go by without him mentioning it, so Jackson must want to keep it quiet too.

She'd like to support Nik, but she can't figure out how, when he hasn't asked for any support. She thinks about asking Jens but can't bear the idea that he doesn't know, either: that Nik doesn't trust anyone but *Jackson*, of all people. She understands why it isn't public, pretty much—it's easier not to talk about that kind of thing if you don't have to, and Nik was raised by Oma just like she was. It's not in any of them to make a fuss.

It should have been his to decide what to do with, is the thing.

Lorelei wishes she could give them both the moment back.

Because it's one thing to know that everyone has interior layers and private worlds. It's another thing to find herself with unasked-for access to some of them. Who knows what other secrets Nik is keeping? It gives her a queasy sense of

vertigo to think about it, the hollow-belly sensation of falling without quite knowing when or if she'll hit the ground.

Lorelei is consumed by restlessness. She tries to pretend that
other people are the reason for it: Chris asks her to sing with
him again, and Jackson keeps kissing Angela like nothing
has changed, and she can't ever seem to find Zoe, or catch
up to her for more than five minutes at a time.

But it gets worse when she's alone. Eventually there's no
escaping the knowledge that there's a song that's haunting
her, melody like a ghost making its home under her skin.
Desire sears her veins and turns her insides to dust. Her eyes
itch. Her throat burns.

She gets distantly curious about how long she can stand
it. Oma taught her discipline, and she learned her lesson
well. Her mother hasn't sung for years now, and Lorelei is
certainly as tough as Petra.

She bears it until she can't.

It's an ordinary kind of Thursday when she puts down
her homework and slips out the front door. The sky is settled
low and heavy, mist drifting through the air as she heads
toward the beach. The surf is quiet, and the shore is almost
deserted.

Lorelei walks down to the water—as far from people as
she can get—before she gives in. The sound that emerges
from her mouth is so huge that even she is stunned by it.
Her wail arcs up into the soft, still air. That night, for the
first time since Oma died, she sleeps deeply and well.

In the morning she starts going through the letters again with a renewed sense of purpose.

The first time Lorelei sang, she felt awful, after, and haunted by the people she'd taken with her. This time she feels so good she can't imagine what could be wrong with doing it again. Its effect on other people is chilling, but singing by herself, to herself—that's fine. Whatever Oma's curse/not-curse was, or is, it's worth investigating until she understands what she can do, and what she can't. She won't let herself be silenced forever.

Lorelei starts looking for letters from the year she was born. Hannah is thrilled about the pregnancy—she sends short notes that clearly accompanied packages, funny little gifts for the new baby, as soon as Oma tells her that Petra is pregnant again.

Lorelei wishes keenly that she had Oma's side of the correspondence in hand too. Was she excited? Or was she already exhausted by the twins, tired of living in a foreign country, resentful of the way her daughter just kept making inexplicable decisions and then forcing everyone else to live with them?

The only real clue comes from a letter Hannah wrote in March, a few months before Lorelei was born.

I know pregnancy was hard on Petra the first time. And this one you've been so quiet about, which means either it's much better or much worse. Of course I hope she's feeling better, but if she isn't, you know I'm happy to come visit if you just tell me when. I think it would be good for both of you to have some community again—and don't tell me you have your little circle of friends there, Silke, because you know it's not the same. Friends are not the same thing as family—and our family, in particular.

Hannah has a habit of doing this, Lorelei has discovered: feinting at something that she and Oma clearly understood, and disagreed on, before darting away again like she never meant to touch the topic. It reminds her a little bit of the way the twins handle their parents, one of them planting seeds while the other makes sure they never notice what's being encouraged to take root. It swells something in her to think that her brothers' mischievousness is inherited: that there is a family legacy other than silence and anger, fear and guilt.

On the other hand, it means that Silke and Hannah had their own kind of silence between them, something they could interpret and decode. Now Lorelei is left with the letters she can only barely translate—often literally. She's gotten better, but her notes are full of scratches and question marks and keyboard shortcuts for foreign symbols she can't name.

She's learned enough vocabulary that sometimes she thinks she's catching the drift of a sentence, only to plug it in and find out that she had wisps of the content but no idea of the context. German grammar is a nightmare, loosely organized and barely structured. Lorelei wants to find an index, a Rosetta stone, but every day that she sifts through the piles of correspondence, that seems less and less likely.

And maybe there isn't an explanation, really. Maybe there's just something in her voice, and her mother's voice, and her grandmother's voice, and no one knows what it is.

Helen of Troy had a face that launched a thousand ships and started a war. Some women are just that beautiful. Would the story be so different if she had sung them out into the ocean, to battle?

Beauty in any form can bend the world to its will, and its shining surface can work dark magic. Lorelei thinks of the way the ocean glints and calls, and of poisonous snakes and frogs in the rain forest, painted with neon caution signs on their backs. Their beauty is an invitation and a warning. Her voice might serve the same kind of purpose.

Lorelei carefully puts down the letter that she's holding and lets herself stare into space. She's sitting cross-legged on her bed, wearing the sweats and T-shirt she changed into after school ended. Her phone is at her side, waiting for a text from Zoe—she sent something a couple of hours ago, just a *hey what's up*, and has been waiting for a response ever since. She made a deal with herself that she could read letters until it comes, but that's starting to seem foolish the longer Zoe stays quiet.

Hoping to hurry the process, she skips through the letters from the intervening months and finds the one that must have come just after her birth announcement reached Hannah in Hamburg. A girl! her letter says. The writing is round and sloppy with excitement that warms Lorelei. Someone, at least, was uncomplicatedly thrilled when she was born. And such a lovely name. Did Petra let you choose, or have things really unthawed so completely? Lorelei doesn't know what to make of that.

Her phone throbs against her knee, lighting up with a

text. It's not from Zoe, but Chris is just as good. It says, *You coming to practice tomorrow?*

Lorelei wants to—she always wants to. She turns back to her laptop and clicks away from the translation site she's on to her calendar, to skim through and see if there's any reason to say no. But the week is mostly free of tests and essays, and Nik will still cover for her. Jackson will be there, and maybe she can get him alone long enough to clear things up with him too.

Yeah, she texts back. Between the phone and the computer she can't keep from noticing what time it is: past the hour for putting this down and picking something practical up. Lorelei folds the letter onto her pile of already-read, stacks the to-read on her bedside table, and opens her backpack.

She'll return to all of it again, tomorrow, and the next day, until somehow it actually gets done.

15

CHRIS DETOURS ON THE way to practice to pick up McDonald's drive-thru for everyone. It's been three hours since lunch, so of course all of the boys are going to be starving. Lorelei gets French fries and extra barbecue sauce, mostly just to be companionable.

She's glad they have the food, because as soon as they walk in and Jackson sees her face, he shuts down like a light being flicked off.

"We brought burgers," Chris says.

Jackson takes the paper bag he's offering without saying anything back.

A month ago Lorelei would have felt awful. She would have curled in on herself and gotten small and silent, hoping that the awkwardness would somehow resolve itself around her, or just wash itself away. Now she looks at Jackson's bad mood and thinks, *If you would just talk to me, you'd know there's nothing to worry about.* She folds down onto the floor next to Chris and holds out her own bag in Jackson's direction. She tries to sound neutral when she asks, "Want fries?"

Jackson shrugs, and takes one. It shouldn't break the tension, and it doesn't, entirely, but it fractures enough of it that Lorelei's shoulders loosen. She's done her part without making a big deal out of it. Bean comes to join them and starts joking with Chris; after a while, Jackson chimes in. Lorelei lets them have their boy-banter. *See?* she thinks at Jackson. *I'm not trying to take anything from you. I promise.*

The food disappears so quickly it looks like a magic trick, or stop-motion animation: Lorelei sees it happen in flashes, and all of a sudden it's just her and the boys and a sea of greasy wax paper. No one seems to be in a hurry, though. Bean folds his napkin into a floppy origami mouth, and Jackson is lingering over the last of her French fries. The talk turns toward music like it always does when they're together.

"I want to play another show before the end of the year," Jackson says. "We do better when we're practicing for something, instead of just, like, dicking around."

Bean wads up his napkin and tosses it vaguely in the direction of Jackson's head. "Like now, you mean?"

"We'll get to it," Chris says. "In a minute. You think I brought Lorelei out here just to make her smell your farts all afternoon?"

"Wouldn't want Lorelei to be bored," Jackson says.

"I've got homework," Lorelei says. Maybe she shouldn't try to placate Jackson—there's no reason for him to be a dick—but she's not really in the mood for the afternoon to turn sour, either.

"Forget that. You should practice with us," Chris says.

Lorelei makes a face. Of course she'd love to sing with

him—for him, even—but that's not something she's ready to try out in front of a group yet. She's just as worried about her family's mysterious legacy as she is gripped by plain old stage fright. "Nah."

Chris tips sideways so he can lie down and rest his head on her thigh. "Someday you're going to say yes," he tells her. "And you're going to blow us all away."

"You'll have to say I'm good, after you've spent all this time trying to convince me."

"You will be," Chris insists.

"We'd tell you if you sucked," Bean cuts in. "Just so we'd never have to hear this argument ever again."

"Oh, please." Jackson's voice is cold and furious. "Lorelei will never do it. She just wants to make sure Chris has to keep asking her."

Lorelei's face goes white and then red.

"That's not—" she starts.

"Oh, shut *up*," Jackson says. "I know he's gagging for it, but some of us are tired of the sound of your voice."

Lorelei reacts without thinking: she pushes Chris's head off her leg and stands up shakily, grabbing her backpack as she goes. Distantly, she can hear Chris saying something, but it doesn't matter: whatever it is, she doesn't want to hear it. He doesn't try to stop her when she slips out of the studio. He doesn't follow her down the hall, or come running out the front door of the building.

Lorelei pulls out her phone—and stops. Shit. If she asks Nik to come get her, he'll have questions, and if she can't answer them, he might stop covering for her when she needs him. Jens will have fewer opinions but even more questions, and she doesn't want to draw his attention if she doesn't have to. She weighs her options and hates each of them. In the end she texts Jens, mostly because she's sure he'll come no matter what. *I went to a thing with Zoe and Carina but now I'm not feeling great—can you pick me up?* she sends.

A minute later he says he will, and asks for the address. Lorelei hopes she can pretend she's too sick to talk. She almost wasn't lying about that: now that the initial shock has worn off, all she feels is the nauseating pulse of her anger.

She leans against the building's front railing and trembles, little starbursts of rage exploding under her skin. How dare Jackson talk to her like that. How dare he act like she's just some awful girl, when she's done everything she can to be good for Chris, to be good for everyone. He has no idea what she's protecting him from. Something dark spills loose in her, and she thinks: *I could show him, and then he'd really be sorry.*

When the building's door opens again, it's not Chris coming to see her. It's Jackson. He doesn't look like he's going to apologize.

He comes down the steps and stands next to her. "Jesus, seriously," he says. "Did you put that dude under a spell or something?"

Lorelei starts, guilty, but—no, she didn't, that's the whole stupid *point*.

"He wouldn't let us get on with it until I came out to say sorry."

There's a deliberate silence in which Jackson does not do that.

"I haven't told anyone," Lorelei says, finally. She owes

him this much, and no more. "I haven't talked to Nik about it or anything. About what I saw."

"Okay," Jackson says. "That's not even the point."

"I know it's none of my business—"

"It really isn't."

"I just—"

"It really isn't," he says again.

He's my brother, Lorelei wants to say. *I love him and I want him to be happy. I wouldn't do anything—anything—to mess with that.*

"It's not serious," Jackson says eventually. "It's just a thing we do, sometimes."

"So, Angela?"

"I love Angela," Jackson says. "I like girls, okay, I love her, she's—it's just— Nik and I started messing around a while ago. You know, before. Chris was gone a lot, dealing with his dad, and we had time to kill, I guess. And then there was Angela, and we stopped," he says. "And if you hadn't started hanging around Chris, Nik would have stayed out of my way."

"That's ridiculous," Lorelei says. "This isn't my fault!"

"Oh, right, okay. How silly of me. Of course nothing is *your* fault. Because what have you ever done wrong? Nothing. Nothing. You're golden. You have no idea what this is like. You have everything. Enough to just—" He makes a little gesture: dismissive, royal, unconcerned.

That's what he thinks of her life, and why wouldn't he, from what he's seen of it? He thinks that just because she has Chris, she's never wanted anything she couldn't let herself have. Lorelei chokes back a laugh.

Jackson corrects himself. "No one has everything they want," he says. "Duh. Yes. Okay. But you seem like you're coming pretty freaking close."

Lorelei slumps against the railing, the sun-warmed metal biting hard against her back. She doesn't want to defend herself. She shouldn't have to. Just because she knows one of Jackson's secrets doesn't mean he can begin to guess at hers.

"Look," Jackson says at last. "You can probably sing. I don't know why the hell you're pretending you can't, but I know that Chris deserves better from you. He loves music. He loves it so much. It reminds him of his *dad*. And if you're lucky enough to be in love, and to have someone want to share something they love with you—then don't waste it. Sing it for me now. The first verse. Don't think. Just do it."

The darkness that spilled loose in Lorelei earlier is all through her, now, threaded across the network of her veins and into her lungs, her marrow, the thick muscle of her heart. She takes in a breath to tell Jackson to be quiet, and the air finds new space in her, in the hollows created by that blackness. When she breathes out again, she knows she's going to do it. It's not a thought; it's a physical fact. She opens her mouth and closes her eyes.

She doesn't really remember it, after. All she knows is that while she sang, she was seized in the grip of the sound, channeling something bigger than herself: conducting electricity. The music was white-hot and bright, sparking in her wrists and behind her eyes. It was like she could reach out and touch him: just Jackson, the hidden parts of him, his sadness, his loneliness, his quiet. She could pull at his inner life with her bare hands.

It came to her instinctually, like kissing, like breathing. She didn't have a name for what she was doing. Her whole self was absorbed by the space the sound made between them. It was the first time she had directed a song at someone, making it for him as much as for herself.

Lorelei gave away feeling without meaning to, with her father and that day on the Pier. She thought it might work like a mirror, turning her listeners into reflections of her own emotional interior. Singing to Jackson, though, and coming back after, she's distantly aware of something more complicated going on.

There he was, laid bare for her, his mind open to her mind's touch. It wasn't that she gave him what she was feeling. She convinced him to feel something specific. The words came to her as unbidden as the song, but she recognizes them. They're the ones she's been biting down on for days and days.

They echo in her mind after Lorelei has fallen silent. *Listen to me*, she told him. *Believe me, you asshole. From now on, you listen for me. And you believe me when I tell you what I feel.*

The first real thing she sees after is Jackson like she always sees him, standing in front of her. Now, though, he's wide-eyed and shaken, and very white. He reaches out and touches her face with his fingertips, as if to check and see that she's real.

"What—" he asks. "What are you?"

"I'm—" Lorelei says, and doesn't know how to answer.

"You're so—" he says, and stops again, fumbling for the words. "You—I could *feel*—"

Jens's car pulls around the corner, and he leans over to open the door and yell out at her. "Come on, Lorelei, I'm supposed to meet Nik in, like, half an hour." She pulls the door the rest of the way open, and slides into her seat.

For the first time since this whole mess started, she sang to someone on purpose. She let her voice loose, and let it tell someone what to do. Lorelei doesn't know what it means that she did it, or whether she'll be able to undo it, or whether she cares.

All she knows is that she loves it. She loves what she can do.

16

SECRETS HAVE THEIR OWN specific weight in the human body, some unidentifiable but precise number of ounces, of pounds. Lorelei starts to feel all of the things she's not telling dragging on her like weights on her shoulders, or barnacles on the bottom of a boat. Letting go of that one phrase—*listen for me, believe me*—made her conscious of how much other stuff she's been carrying.

Jackson texts her a few times that afternoon: *can I see you* and *I need to talk to you.* She deletes the texts as fast as she can and tries to pretend she never read them. She calls Zoe, gets her for once, and arranges to meet up with her on the boardwalk, just to get herself out of the house for the rest of the day. At the last minute she leaves her phone inside when she goes. She doesn't want the distraction, or the reminder.

It's an especially chilly afternoon, with a storm threatening over the ocean. Zoe is wearing jeans and boots and an oversized windbreaker, her long hair pulled back into a neat bun. Lorelei has never been so grateful to see anyone in her life. Zoe's tall, slender form against the darkening sky seems like a beacon along a rocky shoreline, guiding her somewhere familiar and safe.

"I'm glad you called," Zoe says when Lorelei reaches her. "I totally have news."

"Good news?"

"I think so, anyway." They start walking along the paved path that runs parallel to the shore. "I gave Daniel my phone number when we were leaving the Whiskey the other night," Zoe admits. "Just to see. I didn't think he would call but he, um . . . he did. So we've been hanging out. Kind of a lot." She is shining with pleasure.

Lorelei is happy for her, but also nervous in a way she can't quite parse. Chris has always been a known quantity but Daniel is alien, in addition to being older. He'll pull Zoe further away from her and their friendship. She was probably with him the other day, Lorelei realizes, while she waited for Zoe's text like an idiot.

"That's cool," she says.

"You sound even less enthusiastic than Carina did."

"She doesn't like him?"

Zoe waves a dismissive hand. "She doesn't know him."

"I thought she introduced you guys?"

"I mean she, like, knows him, like, she knows his name and stuff. But she's just pulling older-sister bullshit: *be more careful, I know what's best for you,* whatever, whatever."

"And you don't think she does?"

"Whose side are you on, exactly?"

"I mean, *I* just don't know him," Lorelei clarifies. "And he's. You know. A senior."

"Speaking of which, how are things with your older boyfriend?"

"Fine," Lorelei says.

"Just fine?"

"Not *just* fine." Lorelei looks out over the ocean. The sky and sea are tinted by the same gray darkness. "I don't know, I've never— I don't have anything to compare it to. But I'm happy, so."

"You still going to band practices and stuff?"

There goes not thinking about Jackson. "Yeah."

Lorelei doesn't realize that she's stopped walking until Zoe nudges her and asks, "What?"

She shakes Jackson out of her head. Nothing comes to take his place. "I don't know," she says. "Chris wants me to sing with them, I guess."

"That's kind of random? Because you don't really sing, do you?"

"Not really." Lorelei searches for the right thing to say. She settles on "I think it's just his way of trying to let me be closer."

"You guys seem like you're pretty close."

Lorelei feels this for the dig it is: she disappeared into Chris's world before Zoe even met Daniel. No wonder Zoe's excited that someone is paying attention to her, and taking up her time.

"It's weird with his mom and everything," she explains. "That's why we have to, like, sneak around, and hang out at school and stuff. I'm sorry about that, by the way. That I've been a little MIA."

"It's whatever."

"I guess if you and Daniel get serious, you'll be busier too."

Zoe shrugs. "You'll have band practice," she says without malice.

"No I won't." If it comes out a little too fierce, Zoe doesn't seem to mind. "I mean, just, we can find other things to do together. And you and I can make time for each other. If you want."

Zoe doesn't say anything in response, but she knocks a shoulder against Lorelei's again while they walk. Her arms are wrapped tightly around herself. She's folded in against the wind, but she straightens long enough to drift into Lorelei's space and then back into her own. "I've missed you," she says quietly. "I don't want to be selfish or anything, but it sucks when you're not around."

"I've missed you too," Lorelei says. "I'm sorry. I know it's my fault."

"It happens." Zoe disentangles herself and shoves her hands in her pockets. She looks out philosophically at the bleak boardwalk in front of them. "But, you know. It would be nice if it didn't happen to us."

17

LORELEI SPENDS THE WEEKEND buried in the letters and finds piles and piles of nothing.

Chris called to apologize that night, but he does it again first thing at school on Monday. "I thought maybe Jackson would be able to work it out with you on his own," he says. "Clearly not the case. He came back in all glassy-eyed and quiet, and I was like, *Oh shit!* I don't know why I thought he could behave himself. He was probably stoned or something."

Lorelei shrugs. She doesn't want to talk about it any more than she has to. If Chris asks her about Jackson's strange behavior, she has no idea what she'll say.

"But it also made me realize," Chris goes on, "that it's kind of crazy of me to ask you to sing with the whole band as, like, the first time you do it. Of course you're shy about that. And my mom's working late tonight. So I was thinking if you wanted to come over, maybe I'd play a little bit, or whatever. That it might be nice. And it would be just the two of us."

The words *just the two of us* swallow the rest of the sentence. *Yes,* Lorelei thinks. She says, "Yeah."

"Cool."

Chris considers her for a moment. Then he touches her cheek with his fingertips and pulls her face toward his, cupping her jaw with his palm. He kisses her, and his other hand comes to rest at the back of her waist, low. He curls against her, pressing her tightly to him. The kiss sings with its own slow intention. Suddenly Lorelei understands all of what, exactly, she's just said yes to.

She texts Zoe, *SOS gonna need an emergency conference at lunch Chris wants me to COME OVER after school??* Followed by a bunch of X-mouthed, blushing emojis. She's just slipping her phone into her backpack, rooting through the main pocket to make sure she's got her workbook for first period, when Jackson appears at her side. He seems casual at first glance, but when she looks again, he's white-knuckled and thin-lipped, in the grip of something intense.

"You didn't answer my texts," he says. "What's up with that?"

"Sorry," Lorelei says. "Busy weekend."

"That's *bullshit.*" He stops and she stops with him, too startled to realize that she should shake him off and keep going. "I saw Nik," he says. "He said you were home, and that you saw Zoe but—"

"You asked him about me?"

"I had to," he says, and then again: "You weren't answering my texts."

"Where was Angela during all this?"

"Don't worry about Angela."

The first bell rings and everyone seems pulled as if by gravity into their classrooms. It's just the two of them alone in the halls.

"I can't stop thinking about it," Jackson says. One hand reaches out to grab Lorelei around the wrist. His fingers dig into the bones there, burning against her skin. "Sing for me again. Do it. Please. Do it now."

"Here?" Lorelei looks around them frantically but the hallway is empty, echoing.

"We can go somewhere if you want," he says. He tugs again, insistent. She pulls back against him and he rounds on her, furious light blazing in his eyes. His pupils have narrowed down to pinpricks. "Don't make this difficult," he says. His voice is rough and awful, scraped and ugly. "Please, Lorelei, please. I have to hear it again. I just have to know what you're thinking, what you—"

"Okay," she says. "Okay, fine, I will. I promise. I will." She was hoping to distract him, but his grip only tightens.

Lorelei doesn't know what she's frightened of, exactly, or what she thinks he'll do to her. She only knows that she doesn't want to be pulled against her will, forced to sing, or told what to do. She knows that Jackson isn't himself right now, not hardly, and that whatever she gives him will only fuel the fire that seems to be consuming him from inside. He's already ashen with need.

She can only see one way out of it, and her throat tightens at the thought.

She waits until they're pulling level with the classroom she's supposed to be in, first-period Spanish with Ms. Brady. He stops when she does. "I'll do it here," she says. Jackson draws in too close for comfort. She starts to hum a melody, something sweet and broken. It's a song she sang to the waves.

He slackens into it, body loosening, his hand finally falling away from her wrist. His pupils swell in pleasure. His mouth dilates into a soft rounded O.

"Listen to you," he murmurs. Lorelei hears the echo of her own words: *listen to me, listen to me.* The sharp humiliation that follows comes out in the sound, and Jackson jerks back like he's been burned. Lorelei takes the opportunity to wrench the door open and trip into her classroom, slamming it shut behind her.

Maybe it worked, and he'll believe that all she wants is for this to stop happening.

Every head in the room turns her way. She barely notices. She's still buzzing with the aftermath of the song and the pull of Jackson's attention, and the weight of the thing she could feel between them: her mind at the edges of his.

She finds her seat and spends the rest of the period in a dull-eyed daze.

Jackson isn't waiting for her when class ends.

Lorelei usually eats lunch with Chris. Today she's glad to have somewhere else to be, since she doesn't want to deal with him and Jackson and the complicated mess she's been making out of her life. She texts him, *eating w Zoe, see you after school?*

The morning's twitchy, nervous energy recedes as soon

as she sits down at Zoe's side. She feels like the shore being bared as the tide pulls away from it: only so many miles of soft, flat sand. The other girls sitting with them keep up their usual chatter. Lorelei drifts further toward calm on the familiar sounds.

It's only near the end of the period, when Zoe elbows her and gives her a knowing grin, that she really remembers why she's there in the first place. They slide down to the end of the bench for some privacy. "Are you freaking out?" Zoe asks. "Honestly, I would be freaking out."

"It's sort of about the singing thing, actually," Lorelei says. "He wants to play for me. And have us try it out alone."

"Right. Instead of playing for you in the nice practice space they also have available."

"It's a big deal that he invited me over at all," Lorelei reminds her. "You know. With his mom and everything."

Zoe regards her gravely, and tucks an errant strand of hair behind Lorelei's ear. Lorelei has been meaning to get it cut, but she's been so busy lately that she keeps forgetting. It's gotten a little wild, actually. When she wears it loose, she comes home at night to find it hopelessly tangled, no matter how carefully she brushes it smooth each morning. Chris says he likes the way it frames her face: *like ocean spume*, he said, and then laughed at himself. *You know, the white part, the spray.*

It's very different, the abstract idea that she's pretty and the way it feels when he traces the curve of her cheek and tells her so.

"You know what you're doing, though, right?" Zoe says. "You want to be with him, really."

"I do."

"Because you know you don't owe him anything. Not just because he's making an effort. Not ever."

"Yeah." Lorelei looks down the long bench to the rest of their friends, mostly pretty, serious girls. They're gossiping and laughing, a few bent over late homework. Things felt safer in so many ways when she sat here every day, and ate in quiet while they talked.

With Chris everything is terrifying because it's new. And it's that fear that's made sharp corners between her and Jackson and Nik and Angela, between her and everyone else in her life. She's never loved someone and had to expect to lose them before. She's realistic about where Chris will be headed next fall: to college, probably, which even if it's in-state will be a different world. She can't expect he'll try to take her with him.

She's never been alone in a house with a boy who wanted to kiss her before. She's never sung with anyone, either, and she's not sure she'll be able to, even though she wants to so badly it burns. But she can't say that to Zoe.

"I don't think I'm afraid because I don't want to," she says instead. "I think I just . . . don't know what to expect."

"I'm looking forward to your report back," Zoe says. The same hand that smoothed Lorelei's hair comes up to hover in the air between them for a moment, and then falls back down. "Your first reports from the, ah, unexplored territories."

There's no excuse for them to touch but Lorelei leans against Zoe's shoulder anyway. Touching Chris always feels complicated, explosive. Zoe's warmth at her side feels like animal comfort, like home.

"Do you think you will? With Daniel?"

"Who knows?" Zoe says. "I wouldn't rule it out, I guess."

"It's up to you," Lorelei says. "I mean, obviously, it's fine with me, if you do. Whatever you do with him. I trust you."

"I'm glad." Zoe really does sound relieved. Lorelei wonders exactly how much crap Carina's been giving her, and resolves to be better about the whole thing. Zoe deserves it.

The bell rings. The sound is so shrill and sudden that Lorelei flinches. All of the morning's fears rush over her again. She wants to cover her ears to keep everything out. Instead, she forces her breath to slow before standing and swinging her backpack up onto her shoulder. Zoe, still seated, looks up at her. "Be safe, Lorelei," she says.

"You too," Lorelei says. "Okay, Zo? You too."

❧

She spends the rest of the day walking close to the lockers and checking behind her every few steps to make sure she isn't being followed. Jackson's imaginary presence haunts the hallways; she wonders if she's haunting him too, the ghost of her voice ringing in his ears. She's so jumpy that Mrs. Whitlock pulls her aside at the end of class to make sure everything's all right.

I can't go to Chris's like this, she thinks desperately, making her way through the hall. *I can't—what can I—* Jackson will be waiting with him on their usual bench out in front of the school. He'll see her, he'll say something, he'll—

"Watch it," someone says as Lorelei brushes too hard

against traffic moving in the opposite direction. She looks up to apologize and it's Nik, only playacting at being gruff. He's seemed a little more relaxed lately, something smoothing the corners of his eyes.

He turns around and falls into step with her. "You seem distracted," he says.

"Mmm."

"You catching a ride home with us again or are you, uh, studying at Zoe's?" He raises his eyebrows once, twice, three times.

"Zoe's," Lorelei says.

"You have the patience of a saint," Nik tells her. "After that show, man. I don't think I could listen to those songs over and over every week." He thinks she's just going to band practice. Lorelei doesn't see the point in correcting him.

"They're pretty good," she says instead. "I don't mind."

"You don't mind for other reasons."

"It's nice to be around," Lorelei says. "Sometimes. Just. All of that sound."

"Yeah," Nik says. "Our house is pretty quiet, huh."

"It kind of blew my mind, the first time I went to one of their shows. It was just—*loud*."

"They are definitely loud."

"Shut up!" Lorelei elbows her brother.

"I'm glad you're getting out of the house, though," he says. "I used to worry about you a little bit. Jens and I have been screaming since we were kids, but you seemed to fit into that quiet in a way I never understood. You were always trailing Oma like this little blond shadow, and you never wanted to play or get dirty or loud. It seemed like you were happy to just—I don't know. I think it's good for you, getting out."

"Even with Chris?"

"Even with Chris."

They're nearing the bench. Chris is idly strumming his guitar. Jackson is rigid at his side. He turns his head as they approach and his eyes skip right over Nik, landing hard on Lorelei. She swallows around a lump in her throat.

"Hey," she says. Her mind races desperately and hooks into the first terrible thought it finds. "Do you think you could talk to Jackson?"

"Why would I want to talk to Jackson?"

The camaraderie of their walk dissolves. Nik looks at her with flinty eyes.

"Um. He mentioned that you guys hung out sometimes? The two of you?"

"Not really."

"Well, he said— I'm supposed to go over to Chris's," she admits in a rush. "And he doesn't think it's a good idea, but, you know, you just said, he's good for me, and we're not gonna do anything, really, so, it would, uh, it would be nice if you could just distract him. Jackson. For a minute. For me."

"What do you know?" Nik asks. "What did he say?"

Lorelei is torn between wanting to protect herself and knowing she owes Nik the truth: That Jackson never said anything. That he never would and never will. (*For better or worse*, she thinks.)

"He didn't say anything. I might have seen something. Once. Just for a minute."

Nik's face flashes hurt, the expression so raw that Lorelei gets caught and cut by its sharp-toothed edge. He says, "You didn't tell me."

"I wanted to let you keep it," she says. "I didn't want to— I didn't think it mattered. If I didn't tell."

"You can't ask me to do this." Nik looks at the bench, where Jackson has turned away from them to talk to Chris. The longing he allows himself is a brief, bare moment. Lorelei only catches a glimpse before it disappears completely. Then he's composed again.

"I'm sorry," she says in her smallest voice. "God, Nik, I'm sorry." She had assumed it was just like Jackson said it was: they messed around, and then they stopped. She had never considered that Nik might not have wanted it to.

"You didn't know."

"I didn't. I thought you were okay with it."

He laughs humorlessly. "I'm fine with it," he says. "C'mon, we'll talk about this later."

Then, like it's nothing at all, he does it. Nik puts on a face Lorelei hasn't ever seen before, something too loose and sunny to be real. The tightness that stays around his eyes gives him away. Jackson doesn't seem to notice.

Chris sees Lorelei and gets up to greet her. He wraps an arm around her and starts walking them both toward the car. As they leave, she turns back to watch Nik and Jackson sitting and talking in public. So this is what Nik will allow himself: the part where he sits in the sunlight, and pretends he isn't feeling anything out of the ordinary.

18

CHRIS AND HIS MOTHER live at the border between Santa Monica and Venice in a nice house in a pretty, well-groomed neighborhood. Whatever else has been going on in Mrs. Paulson's life, she's kept the property up beautifully: there's fresh paint on the eaves, and flowers are blooming in the garden. Inside it's all dark wood and big windows. The whole place shines with glossy, lacquered stillness.

The house is quiet in its own way, not like Lorelei's, in which quiet is just another quality of the air. Here there's a thick, stale sadness she can almost smell, something musty and pervasive that refuses to be swept out or wiped up. For a moment Lorelei imagines Chris's mother on her knees, scrubbing and scrubbing, going out of her mind trying to make the house right again. Then she shakes herself out of the fantasy. Mrs. Paulson probably doesn't even do the cleaning. Maybe they have a maid.

Chris's hand is warm in hers. He tugs her past the living room, and the den, toward the stairs.

"Hang on," she says. She might be stalling, just a little bit. "I don't get the full tour?"

"It's a pretty boring tour," he says. "The downstairs is really Mom's domain. Unless you have an interest in interior decorating I didn't know about?"

Lorelei shakes her head. She doesn't know if it's her place to ask, but he brought her here. Maybe she has the right to be bold. "I thought— You said your dad had instruments," she says. "I was wondering if they were still around."

"Some of them are in storage," Chris says. "People packed them up before Mom could stop them. But the rest are still—"

He pulls her with him, toward a set of sliding doors Lorelei assumed led out to the porch.

Instead, they open onto a small sunroom. It's a little gem of a space: French doors look out over the backyard, and light is streaming in through the windows, winter-bright. It catches on three guitars, a couple of basses, and the black back of an enormous piano that sits in one corner. Lorelei pulls away from Chris to trail her finger-tips over it. The sunlight is so white that it turns her skin translucent.

He brushes a hand over her shoulder, and rests it gently at the nape of her neck. "Can you play?"

"Nah," she says. "I never learned."

"You should." He drops a kiss on the top of her head, and circles around her to sit on the piano's bench. The hinges are silent when he lifts the lid. "Mom keeps it tuned," he says. His hands are soft on the keys. "He barely played it, and I'm not—I hardly know how, but—she keeps things going," he says, almost to himself. "She does." He shakes his head and smiles up at her. "Anyway. Lorelei. Lorelei. Do you know that song?"

"What song?"

Chris hums a few notes before he starts to sing. *"You told me tales of love and glory / same old sad songs, same old story / the sirens sing no lullaby / and no one knows but Lorelei."* He tries to pick it out on the piano and can't quite get it right. "Seriously," he says. "No one's ever sung you that song before?"

"Nope."

But that's what Hannah must have meant about her name—that it was a reference to this, or something like it. She wonders whether her mother or her grandmother picked it out for her, and what she meant by it, exactly. Just now it seems like a cruel kind of joke. Same old sad songs, same old story.

"My dad loved the Pogues. I can't believe I haven't sung it for you before. Maybe that's your song."

"Maybe." Lorelei circles around the piano and sits down next to him on the bench. "Seems kind of narcissistic, though, to sing about myself."

"You're a siren on the rocks all right," Chris agrees. "My Lorelei."

She knows what he's talking about, but for a second she hears it wrong, and thinks of a siren like a bell sounding or a klaxon warning danger. A wail piercing the peaceful air.

Chris sings the next line softly, just to her. *"River, river have mercy / take me down to the sea / for if I perish on these rocks / my love no more I'll see.*" It's the sweetest thing Lorelei has ever heard.

"I'm ready to go upstairs now," she says.

Chris closes the lid on the piano keys carefully, and then takes her hand in his to lead the way.

⸎

Lorelei has never kissed a boy on a bed before. It makes more sense, basically: The rucked-up mess of Chris's sheets and quilt is soft under her back. They can fit together, here, and find space to get comfortable. He hovers over her and doesn't kiss her. "We don't have to," he says. "I didn't just bring you here for—whatever. I mean. We don't have to do anything."

Lorelei thinks of Zoe saying the same thing earlier, how abstract it all seemed, sitting next to her in the cafeteria. Then it was just concepts: mouth, hands, and, or— Now it's her and Chris, and the way their bodies want to touch each other.

"What if I want to?" she says, and leans up to kiss him instead.

Still, he's careful with her. His hands smooth gently over her T-shirt and down to the sharp corners of her hip bones. He touches her like she's unfamiliar territory, which, she supposes, she is.

"You've done this before," she says at some point.

"Not with you."

The light in the sky falls low. Lorelei knows what sunset

141

looks like from the coast, at the earth's raw edge. Now she knows what it looks like sprawled across Chris's bed, from behind her eyelids. She takes her shirt off and takes his shirt off. He's a little surprised.

"I didn't think I would be in charge of this operation," she says when he hesitates.

"I didn't know what you'd want," he says. He takes his hands off her and gestures to the space that's opened up between their bodies.

"I'm not sure I know, really," Lorelei says. "I'm just making it up as I go along."

"Improvising."

"Sure." A thought occurs to her. "If you don't want to—" she says. "We don't, um, I don't expect anything. Obviously."

Chris laughs and butts his forehead against her shoulder, pushing her back onto the pillows. They smell like him, like his soft, sleeping body.

"I want to do everything with you," he says. "I just— You're younger than I am, you know? And you've never— before?"

"Not really," Lorelei admits. She feels unaccountably safe, even now, as bare as she's ever been. Chris leans over her and looks down at the plain black bra Zoe helped her pick out at Victoria's Secret just before this whole thing got so, so real.

"So maybe we take our time," he says. He's delicate when he leans down farther and kisses the side of her neck and the branch of her collarbone.

"Okay."

He comes up again and kisses her mouth. His hands

find purchase at the sides of her waist and then slip lower, one delicate finger pausing at the button on her jeans.

"We can start here," he says, and presses a palm against her.

Lorelei nods yes. Her voice is lost somewhere in the back of her throat.

He undoes the button. He pulls down her zipper.

19

IT'S DARK BY THE time they stumble downstairs. Lorelei's clothes feel like they've been put on wrong; they don't quite sit right on her body now. Or maybe it's her skin that feels different: lit up and glowing, too warm, too soft, too tender. She wants to strip down and run straight into the ocean, and feel the water cold and stark against her skin. She wants to lie down in the sand and trace every place Chris touched on her body, the paths he made from her head to the soles of her feet.

She finds her backpack in the sunroom, dropped beside the piano.

"C'mon," Chris says. "We've gotta get out of here. Mom texted a minute ago. She's on her way back already."

"Yeah," Lorelei says. She's distracted by fishing out her own phone. She has three missed texts. One, from Nik, just says, *You owe me, L.* The next two are from Zoe. *Having dinner w Daniel he says he's having a birthday party in like 2 wks maybe The Trouble could PLAY IT.* And then *he thinks you singing sounds super cute. I say go for it :)*

The song Chris was singing echoes in her head again: *same old sad songs, same old story.* Her father, enchanted; those people on the Pier, crying; Jackson desperate for the sound of her voice.

Isn't it time for a new story? Lorelei wonders. If Hannah said it wasn't a curse, maybe it's time to prove her right. And singing with Chris couldn't possibly be sad, or awful. They would stand together in the spotlight's hot circle, and he would put his arm around her, and their voices would move together. It would be beautiful. She wouldn't be dark or tempting or angry or sad: she would make everyone in that room feel like she feels about Chris right now.

"Hey, hold on," she says, pulling him back into the room. "You might have convinced me after all."

"What does that mean?"

"Zoe wants you to play at her boyfriend's birthday party," Lorelei says. "She wants us to sing."

"Would you do that for her?"

Lorelei expects the question to have a little heat behind it. He's asked her so many times. She's always said no. "I would," she says. She holds his gaze when she says, "The thing is, I want to."

She expects Chris to kiss her, but instead he moves past her to pull one of the guitars from its stand. He sits on the couch with it, and she joins him. She loves him in this moment: she loves that he loves to share his music with her just as much as he loves to kiss her.

Chris strums the opening notes to the song that made her cry on that first afternoon at band practice. With the whole band behind it, it sounded dark and driving, but when it's just him, it opens up into something earnest and almost pretty. The coaxing turns to longing. Lorelei gets ready to join him on the chorus.

She's so relaxed, so deeply in her own skin, that she forgets to be careful: the highest, purest part of her voice is gathering itself up when she opens her mouth. There are clouds of sound in the air in her lungs. Lightning crackles behind her eyes.

She catches Chris's gaze and gets overwhelmed by how well she knows him, now, and how much she feels for him. *You should tell him,* her heart says, beating hard against her rib cage, hammering at the pulse points in her wrists and neck. *Sing him how you feel.*

I will, she thinks, and she opens her mouth to do it.

She only gets the first two words out before the front door swings open and they both go silent.

"Chris?" Mrs. Paulson calls. "Chris, who's singing?"

Mrs. Paulson insists on driving her home.

Lorelei sits in the front seat of the car rigid with misery and fear. She wants to text Chris but she's afraid Mrs. Paulson will see, that she'll yell, or that she'll do anything, really.

The woman is mostly a character from stories, as far as Lorelei is concerned. She's the gargoyle hovering over her boyfriend's shoulder and keeping them apart. She thinks about the story that Nik told her, and thanks god she wasn't naked in the back of Chris's car, or naked anywhere at all. It was bad enough to be caught out with her guard down, when she was happy and relaxed, and thinking nothing in the world could touch her. She thought she was too safe to be found out.

Lorelei gives halting directions to her house. Mrs. Paulson doesn't respond, but she follows them. Outside, the sky is strangely pale, a thick cloud cover reflecting the city's neon lights. Lorelei wonders if she's imagining the feeling of something wild massing in the air, the ocean blowing inland, making waves. Mrs. Paulson doesn't say anything until they've pulled up in front of Lorelei's house and she's parked and turned off the engine.

It's only then that Lorelei turns to look at her, Chris's demon mother up close at last. It's dim in the car, illuminated mostly by a nearby streetlamp, so that Mrs. Paulson's features are rendered in shadow and sodium yellow. She looks like she might have been pretty once. Lorelei wonders how long she would have to look at that face before she saw Chris's in it.

Mrs. Paulson surprises her when she speaks. "I'm not a monster," she says. "I don't want him to be alone."

Lorelei doesn't know how to respond to this. She was expecting a lecture or a threat. Instead, what she sees is a woman at the edge of herself. Mrs. Paulson's breathing gets ragged, like she might— But she can't be about to cry. Lorelei wonders where she keeps her rage.

"I just miss him," Mrs. Paulson goes on. The raggedness is still there but not breaking, not yet. "I miss him so much."

Lorelei wants to reach out and touch her, to offer some grounding human contact, but she doesn't dare. "Chris?"

"*Jacob*," Mrs. Paulson says, her voice cracking at last. *His father*, Lorelei thinks. She never knew loss, not really, before Oma, but she knows it now. It's breathtaking, still, sometimes, the moments in which Oma's absence brings her up short.

"I miss him so much," Mrs. Paulson says for the third time. "And I hate that Chris knows it. I don't want to ruin him. I don't want to ruin anything. I didn't mean it, that time. It was so soon after. I was so sad."

Lorelei thinks of Lisa, and shivers in spite of herself. "Why are you telling me this?" she asks.

Mrs. Paulson turns in her seat and regards Lorelei for the first time head-on. She looks at her strangely, as if searching out something she can't quite remember. "Something—" she says, a little faint. "You were singing. When I came in."

Fear rises cold and metallic in the back of Lorelei's throat. If Mrs. Paulson caught anything, it should have been love and affection, desire, want. Or maybe Lorelei colored the song with something else and didn't realize it? It hits her all at once how incredibly stupid it is, to keep playing with a force she doesn't understand just because she wants to. Just because she wants to believe she can.

Mrs. Paulson isn't blank or insistent, though. She's not like Jackson was. Lorelei doesn't know what to make of her. "I don't know," Mrs. Paulson says. "I don't know. God, I never want to see you again. Get out of my car. Go home. Just—go home."

Lorelei bolts out the door and stumbles over her feet. She drops her keys in her hurry to get them into the front door's lock. It doesn't matter. Mrs. Paulson's car peels away from the curb. For a few long, silent moments it's just Lorelei on the porch in the darkness, trembling and small against the hugeness of the night.

20

THE FAMILY IS GATHERING for dinner when Lorelei walks in. Her mother has taken Oma's old spot, so she's seated silently at the head of the table while Henry and the twins carry out plates of food. Lorelei drops her backpack and leans against the door for a long moment, catching her breath. *I'm safe,* she tells herself. *It's okay, I'm here, I'm safe.*

She digs her phone out of her pocket and tries to text Chris, but what? What is there to say? Mrs. Paulson will make it home soon enough. She's seen Lorelei now, and knows her face. She knows who's been taking up so much of Chris's time. Lorelei hates to think about that awful woman tightening the reins and pulling Chris in.

She can't bear the thought that he'll let her.

All the high energy from earlier, the willingness to sing, is still gathered up in her chest. The contained electricity crackles against her bones before settling slowly into something bigger and darker and angrier, thunderheads booming misery through and through her.

"Stop being lazy, Lorelei, and come help," Nik calls to

her from the kitchen. "We all heard you come in. You can't hide out and wait for dinner to be served."

"Sorry," she says. She drops the phone on top of her backpack. *Just get through dinner,* she tells herself, trying to quell the storm rising in her veins. *Just get through dinner, and you'll figure the rest of it out.*

Henry and Jens are sitting down in the dining room, so when she walks into the kitchen, it's just her and Nik. They're supposed to set the table together. Usually they do, but tonight it's already done.

"I would have helped," she says.

"Didn't know when you'd be home. If you'd be home."

He tries to turn to leave the room, but Lorelei is faster. She grabs his elbow. "I'm really sorry," she says. "We can talk about it, or—"

"We're not talking about it," Nik says.

The dinner table is always quiet, but somehow tonight Lorelei can tell that she's being given a deliberate silent treatment. Nik doesn't even ask her to pass things; he just points.

It gets so uncomfortable that Henry takes it on himself to make conversation, which he almost never does.

"Did you have fun at Zoe's?" he asks Lorelei.

At least Nik wasn't so mad that he wouldn't lie for her.

"Yep," she says. "Lots of fun."

"You've been over there a lot recently," Henry says. "You sure her parents don't mind?"

"We just do homework," Lorelei says. Her stomach gets tight. She swirls her fork through the soggy lettuce on her plate, dragging the tines in a slow, tight spiral. "It's not a big deal."

"Still." Henry turns his head and then turns it back: it's an old, instinctive gesture, of looking to Oma for support. "I was thinking that it would be nice to have you around the house more," he says. "You have been gone a lot."

Lorelei feels a flash of burning guilt. It's unfamiliar: she didn't think she felt like she owed her parents anything. But then, she didn't think they cared—she especially didn't think her dad cared. She's never tried to pull away from them before. She's run out all of the slack in the line, and now she feels them tugging her back from the other end.

She's stubborn, though, and exhausted. She's been pulled in enough directions in the last few hours and over the course of the last few days. The words come out of her mouth before she can think better of them. "Tell it to the twins," she says. "They're home way less often than I am, and they never get shit about it."

Before anyone can respond, Petra speaks. "Oh, leave her alone," she says from the head of the table.

Every face turns to look at her. Lorelei grips her fork so tightly that her fingers start to cramp. Since Oma's death, Petra has transformed herself in a dozen tiny ways: tonight she's wearing a pale pink sweater, a spring blush color that makes her look lovely and young. She's still removed but seems less isolated, somehow. Like she won't come to them, but if they wanted to, they could find a way to come to her.

"Petra," Henry says. The frustration drops out of his voice. Her mother is her father's soft spot, always.

"She's young," Petra says. "Let her explore the world a bit."

The corners of Henry's eyes wrinkle with confusion. "If that's what you—"

"It is," Petra says.

He's too surprised by her expressing an opinion about the kids' lives to argue.

"I'm sorry about the cursing," Lorelei says. She almost wants them to be mad at her, to keep disagreeing the way normal parents would. "It just—"

"If that's what they're teaching you at Zoe's," Jens says, "then you might want to take a look at your choices, young lady."

"The company you keep reflects back on you," Nik says, picking up Jens's thread. They continue the joke for a while, until Henry asks about their after-school activities, their classes. The conversation moves away from her, and Lorelei focuses on her food. She just wants to go up to her room to sleep, to get away from everyone and everything for a little while.

"Your hair is getting long," Petra says quietly. She reaches out and touches the frizzed edge of one of Lorelei's curls. The air outside is damp, and over the course of the day, it's started to lift and kink wildly. This morning's neat ponytail is tangled in knots. "Come up after dinner and I'll give you a trim."

Lorelei has never had her hair cut anywhere but at home. There are pictures of her sitting in the kitchen sink as a baby, Petra smiling guardedly over her, and a few similar images from her early toddler years. In the last one she's three, standing on a step stool with her hair streaming like dark honey over her shoulders, already wet. Petra is staring at the camera with a blank, fathomless look. Soon after that, Oma took over.

As a baby, Lorelei hadn't required quite so much raising. Petra took care of her before she really learned how to talk. But Oma did all the heavy lifting in the years that came after, when there was heaviness that needed to be carried. She told Lorelei not to sing, and for a long time made sure she didn't. She was the one who combed through the tangles and cut away the split ends.

Lorelei is a little anxious about putting herself in her mother's hands again. Part of it is vanity, pure and simple, but it's also more complicated than that. She knows her mother too well to trust her with sharp scissors, and her bared throat. Lorelei doesn't think that Petra wants to hurt her; it just seems like Petra doesn't know how to avoid it.

On the other hand it's a chance to talk to her mother, which she hasn't done, really, since that strange, heated confession. Lorelei knows more, now. She has questions Petra might be able to answer.

Petra has Lorelei sit on a low stool next to the edge of their old-fashioned bathtub. She cushions the back of her neck with a towel and brings her head to lean over the rim, tilting it back. The faucet is slightly too far away to duck under, so she fills a bowl with warm water and pours it over Lorelei's hair. She hasn't forgotten how. She just didn't want to do it. Her hands are gentle and sure.

"Mom used to do this for me too, you know," Petra says as she scrubs through the tangles. "When I was growing up. She always cut my hair."

This is the second time since Oma died that she's tried to talk like this—to have a conversation. Lorelei doesn't even know how to respond to the idea that her mother seems lonely. Instead, she nods and closes her eyes, and tries to let the tension that's been simmering under her skin drift out the ends of her hair. She imagines it washing down the drain as Petra fills the bowl and rinses her, fills it and rinses again.

When she's been rinsed a final time, Petra wraps Lorelei's hair in a threadbare white towel and sits her up in front of a mirror. "Just a trim, yes?" she asks.

Lorelei has worn her hair long since she was old enough to choose how she wanted it cut. She likes the loose weight, and that she can pin it up or pull it down. She uses it to hide her face or the burning tips of her ears when she's blushing. It's strange to see her face unframed, decontextualized. She looks rounder and less pretty, she thinks. Too pale.

"Just a trim," Lorelei agrees.

Petra unwraps the towel turban and her hair falls down in a heap. The water has turned it from pale gold to a dim, wheaty shade, underscoring the purple-black smudges dark under her eyes.

Petra readies her scissors and makes the first cuts. She works in silence for a while, turning Lorelei's head with her fingertips, considering her from every angle. Lorelei wonders at the instinctive, physical thing she feels for her mother. It has nothing to do with reason, or even really with feeling. It overrides her wariness from earlier easily, like it's just an animal thing, bred in the bone.

"Thank you for doing this for me," she says eventually. "I'm glad that you want to."

Petra smiles at her in the mirror. Lorelei can see it, then: how beautiful her mother must have been when she was happy, when she was young. The sight makes her bold.

"Mama," she says. "Can you tell me more about what happened with you and Oma? With the singing?"

Her mother's face shuts down again, whip-fast. "Why do you want to hear about ugliness?" she asks. "Why does it even matter?"

"Because she was my grandmother," Lorelei says. "Because I don't think it was a curse, and because she—I—I have it. I am it. Whatever you are. I am too."

"Who did you sing to?" Petra puts the scissors down and pulls Lorelei to her violently, fingertips digging painfully into her upper arms. "Jesus, Lorelei, what did you *do*?"

"I didn't say I sang to anyone!"

"You did, though," Petra says. "You wouldn't know unless you had." She lets go of Lorelei to pause and consider it. "But then, if you really knew, you wouldn't ask. You wouldn't want to talk about it at all."

"I did," Lorelei admits. "I sang just, like, a tiny bit. To one person. Once." She's only counting the time with Jackson. Tonight was just a few words, and Mrs. Paulson and Chris both seemed fine after. "So don't worry or anything. I'm not in trouble. It's under control."

"You think it's under control." Petra picks up the scissors again. Lorelei tries to shy away but her mother holds her firmly in place and begins to cut again, focused, almost vicious. "I thought so too, and I was fooling myself just like you are. There is no under control with this. Either you do it or you don't, and you *can't*."

"Okay!" Lorelei reaches up and brushes fine bits of hair from her nose and cheeks. "But I'm just saying, it would be a lot easier to not do it if I understood what I was not doing, and why."

Petra puts the shears back in their drawer and pulls the towel from around Lorelei's shoulders. "Go downstairs and make us some tea," she instructs. "Come to my room. I'll tell you. I'll tell you all about what happened to me."

21

IN THE KITCHEN, Lorelei makes mint tea in mismatched mugs. Her father and brothers are clearing up the last traces of dinner, clattering plates into cabinets and silverware into drawers. As she goes up the stairs again, quiet closes itself in around her.

Petra didn't specify, but Lorelei knows that "my room" means her little office rather than the bedroom her parents share. Her mother is always there when she's awake; sometimes she even sleeps in the workroom, on the futon. The door is half open, light spilling out into the dark hallway. Lorelei thinks she remembers doing this when she was younger: standing outside her mother's door, wondering if she was allowed to come in.

Petra is sitting in front of her laptop, which is open to her email, glowing white. Lorelei puts the tea down and settles herself on the futon. Petra doesn't turn around when she starts speaking. Her voice is low and rough.

"You never knew your grandfather," she says. "But he was a good man. He loved Oma beyond all measure—the way I remember it, anyway. And the way people talked about him." He died when Petra was a teenager. Oma was a widow for so much of her life. "When he—after—I was wild," Petra says. "Reckless. I skipped school, you know, ran around town with boys. The way girls do." She shuts the laptop but doesn't turn around.

"I met your father just after I turned seventeen," Petra goes on. "I was too wild to keep, he said, like an animal, all eyes and teeth. He wanted someone steady and stable. But I was in love with him." She turns, finally, and looks at Lorelei with a gimlet gaze. "You know how it is, I'm sure."

Lorelei thinks of Chris's hands on her all afternoon long: the way he touched her chin, and her breasts, and the insides of her thighs. The way he picked up his guitar and offered her his song. She nods in agreement.

"And I wanted him to love me back." Petra bites down hard on her lip. Her mouth takes on the familiar sour shape it's held for so much of Lorelei's life. "So I sang to him over and over again.

"Oma had told me not to, of course. The same way she told you, I imagine. I had forgotten it by the time I started wanting to. And anyway, your father was slipping away from me. I didn't care what I had to do to keep him."

Lorelei wants to stop her to ask more about this—whether Oma explained why, or if Petra ever asked. But her mother is far away, lost in the story.

"Oma was so wrapped up in her own grief that she never noticed," she says. "Never noticed how often he was around, or that he would stop by the house when I wasn't there and just wait for me, for hours, sometimes. And I thought— I don't know what I thought." She smiles a dark, secret smile. "All I thought was that it was working."

Lorelei can't help herself. "When did you decide it was a curse?"

"When she found out," Petra says heavily. There's a long pause. "She just kept saying *Petra, Petra, what have you done?* But when she found out I was pregnant, she would just say instead: *What have I done?*"

"With the twins?"

"With the twins."

"And you think just because she said—"

"She's the one who warned me," Petra says. "No one else knew about it. No one else would have cared! Whether I sometimes sang a song or not. But she was always twisted about music, after the way her mother destroyed her career onstage. She couldn't bear it if I had something she didn't have. Or if I left her behind. If she had to be alone again, in her own miserable quiet house."

"You don't think her mother asked her not to because her voice was just like yours? Because it could— It was, you know, powerful?"

"I always thought that she must have brought it on herself," Petra says. She sounds almost shy, admitting it. "She asked for too much, and we all ended up cursed."

Lorelei wants to argue with her mother's version of events, her carefully constructed personal mythology, but it's not like she has any evidence to support her own theory. The difference is that she doesn't want to believe that this is Oma's fault, and her mother does.

And anyway, something else is dawning on Lorelei, so slowly that she doesn't realize how massive it is until it's too late. "But. I mean. So let's say she did it on purpose, or by accident, either way, that she did it. Since you got Dad—since you got what you wanted—why is it a *curse*?"

But she already knows the answer to this question. She just needs someone else to say it, so she doesn't have to.

"All love spells are curses," Petra says. "To make someone feel what they don't, and do things they wouldn't. To take a person's body, his mind. What else could you call it? Of course it was a curse."

"So Dad is the one who the curse is really on," Lorelei says. "I mean. It's on you, still, but you don't have to sing anymore. He can't stop being in love with you."

"I tried to get him to leave when I figured it out. I told him what I'd done, and it didn't make any difference. Eventually, it seemed like it might be kinder to bring him with us. To give him what he thought he wanted."

Lorelei feels seasick. The world keeps shifting itself underneath her. Their family is her father's blessing and his curse: it's the only thing he's ever wanted, and having it is the reason he can't want anything else.

"So you see why I had to let your grandmother raise you, when she offered. I had tried to love someone once, and I ruined his life," Petra says. "Oma was difficult, but I thought: at least she'll teach them control." She shrugs her shoulders up by her ears and wraps her long, thin arms tightly around herself. "Everyone in our family is hungry for something. The women, as long as I've known them, they've been starving. There's only one way to survive that kind of hunger. You have to learn discipline. You have to learn it from the very first day."

Lorelei gets up to leave.

"I'm sorry," Petra says. "You were the most selfish thing I ever did, you know. Having a daughter—giving Henry another baby—and Oma another one to take care of— It's not your fault you were born into all this mess, Lorelei. I would take it back if I could."

"You wish I'd never been born."

"No!" Petra stands and grabs Lorelei's wrist. For once her grip isn't menacing; it's tight with desperation that tugs on Lorelei like the tide. "I wish you had been born into a better family. None of this is your fault."

"It wasn't until I started singing," Lorelei says. The family legacy is hers, now, and it doesn't matter where it comes from or what anyone calls it. It's been tainting her blood since the day she was born, but she chose to open her mouth.

Petra's hand on hers slackens.

Lorelei leaves before either of them can say anything else.

22

LORELEI WAKES WITH THE echo of a song in her head: the one Chris sang yesterday. The one with her name in it. Usually she translates a letter first thing, while she's still fresh, but today she's too anxious to focus. Instead, she pulls up the Pogues playing "Lorelei" on YouTube. *Sirens.* She takes her copy of *The Odyssey* off the shelf. They read it in English last year; she's pretty sure it has sirens in it.

It does, but barely. Odysseus is warned against them, and then he figures out a way to hear them without succumbing to their song. So he sails right on by without actually seeing them. And that's it. Lorelei does remember, now, because she asked a question about it in class: Why did he risk it? What was the point?

Her teacher had an answer ready, something about how narratives need detours, and heroes need challenges to prove that they're heroes. She didn't press the point, then, and wishes now that she had. Though Mr. Colombo probably wouldn't have had answers to the kinds of questions she has now, either.

Like, did Odysseus spend the rest of his life dreaming about that song?

Her father's abstraction from their lives makes so much more sense now that she understands what he's been listening for all these years.

And then, beyond that—what was it like for the women on that island, who reached out with their voices, and watched the hero and his story leave them behind? Because *The Odyssey* is about a man coming home to his human wife. The temptations that other women—even magical women—offer are just detours. The sirens are a chorus of faceless voices on an island. They live forever, but they do it in history's margins.

Even in ancient myth, their lives escape off the page.

No wonder Lorelei doesn't understand what the hell she is.

The internet doesn't have much to add to this. Lots of cultures have siren stories, but they're all pretty similar. Sometimes the women have bird's heads or bodies, in addition to their bewitching voices. They all promise wrack and ruin: a seduction that invites you to betrayal.

Lorelei's own name is a reminder of all that. It's taken from a tall rock in a narrow river, a place where men die so often it seems like there must be something unnatural at work. Lorelei thinks of her mother's desperation last night, and looks down at her ribs, and the hollow between her legs. She wonders how many men will shipwreck against her before she learns how to keep them—and herself—safe from the dark pull at work in her and her voice.

23

AT SCHOOL THAT DAY, Lorelei is listless. She and Zoe take their lunches out and eat on the bleachers overlooking the basketball courts.

"I don't understand why you're not more excited about singing with him," Zoe says through a mouthful of grilled cheese. She wants to talk about The Trouble playing Daniel's party, and Lorelei keeps trying to avoid the subject. "This is a good opportunity for all of you, actually. Some of Daniel's friends know, like, producers and stuff. It could be their big break or something."

It's so impossible: sitting in back of her normal high school with her normal best friend, talking about boys and dates and bands, and thinking about the mess she was born into, and how to keep herself from getting any further into it.

Zoe gets tired of saying things Lorelei won't respond to. She lets it get quiet, picks at a loose thread at the hem of her sweater, nibbles cheese from the edge of her sandwich.

Her strategy works. Lorelei says, "I don't really know what's going on with me and Chris after yesterday."

"Whatever, he's totally obsessed with you," Zoe says. "And if he lets his *mom* boss him around— I mean, do you really want to be with a guy who's so whipped?"

"It's more complicated than that." Lorelei tilts her head back and looks up at the powdery sky, thin clouds scattering light so that it's even and flat and surprisingly bright. "He doesn't want to hurt her. I get that, you know? Like, it's actually kind of—"

"If you say sweet, so *help* me, Lorelei, seriously? That's creepy. It's super not okay."

"Ugh. I mean. I know. But it's also— They've both been through a lot. I think maybe they don't really know how to be good to each other anymore. In a less codependent way."

"Have you talked to him about it?"

Lorelei shakes her head. "He didn't call after I left, and I haven't seen him yet today."

"Oh my god, you are *ridiculous*. You're actually pining over someone who hasn't even dumped you yet?"

"Yeah, exactly: yet." Lorelei told Zoe the story about Lisa and the backseat of the Mercedes at some point. She doesn't need to repeat it. "Anyway, I'm just being realistic."

"You're just being defeatist." Zoe finishes her sandwich in one enormous bite. She takes her time chewing and swallowing, watching Lorelei contemplatively while she does. "Do you care about him?"

"Yeah," Lorelei says. "Yeah, of course."

"And he cares about you."

"It's different. It's his *family*."

"You could be his family," Zoe says. "And, look, the point is: what's so wrong with getting what you want?"

That's exactly what's wrong, Lorelei thinks. What she wants is too much of everything. Her father is her mother's curse. She is too.

She doesn't say that. Instead, she says, "I don't know. I'll think about it, I guess."

"That's almost the spirit," Zoe says.

Lorelei smiles at her. It's so nice having Zoe on her side. Zoe can believe in her enough for both of them. "I'm working on it," she says.

"Good."

She finds Chris after school, mostly just out of habit. He's managed to shake Jackson and Angela, so it's only the two of them. He says, "I'm sorry about all of that yesterday. With my mom and everything."

"It's my fault," Lorelei says. "You said we should leave, and I—"

"You didn't do anything wrong."

Lorelei stifles a snort. People keep telling her that. "Anyway."

"You know how she is about me," Chris says. "And I—"

"Don't want to hurt her. I know."

"I don't want to hurt you, either." He turns to her and takes her hands into his. It's a simple gesture, almost casual. Lorelei remembers the first time he found her deliberately at school, how he walked her to class and his knuckles brushed the backs of her hands and wrists, and she felt that little touch light her up all over. His body was unfamiliar then, so much strange territory. He himself was a stranger.

He's restless too. He asks, "Can we— I don't know, you want to get out of here?"

"Sure."

They drive aimlessly for a while. Lorelei suggests stopping for coffee, for sandwiches, and Chris says, *Yeah, maybe,* and doesn't slow down. She decides to leave it alone. They end up on the Pacific Coast Highway, crawling up the California coastline in a snarl of slow-moving traffic. Chris keeps one hand on the steering wheel and the other threaded tightly through one of Lorelei's. He hums along to the radio and doesn't say much of anything. When he glances over at her, his face is soft.

They make their way toward Malibu, where bougainvillea vines spill purple over the white walls of houses. The hills are wild with fall rain, and the ground is loose and heavy and wet. There are mudslides to the north of them, and blinking orange signs warning of road closures ahead.

When Chris pulls over into a parking lot, it isn't anywhere Lorelei recognizes. They're at the top of a high, rocky cliff, with wooden stairs winding to the shore below. He pulls a dusty blanket from his trunk and throws a spare jacket at Lorelei. The wind is bitterly cold, so biting that she almost wants to ask if they can just stay in the car. Instead, they sit on the hood together, wrap the blanket around their legs, and stare out toward the setting sun.

"What did she say to you?" Chris asks. "My mom."

"She just said she didn't want us hanging out anymore." That was part of it, anyway. "She talked about your dad a little, I guess. She said she missed him."

"She talked about him with me too," Chris says. "After she came home. She never does that. It was like you had knocked something loose in her. I thought maybe you'd be different." He sighs, blows out a breath that gets lost in the wind.

You were singing, Mrs. Paulson said. *When I came in.*

All love spells are curses, Petra told her last night. But it isn't just a love spell: it's something stranger and more powerful than that. Either way Chris seems fine, still, mostly.

But if she tries too hard to keep him, he won't be.

Chris's hand finds Lorelei's under the blanket. "I thought maybe I could find a way to make it different, with you."

She means something different than he does when she says, "That's what I was hoping too."

"Did anyone, you know, warn you?"

"Everyone. Or Nik, anyway, and then Jackson."

"And you still stuck around."

"Where else was I going to go?"

Chris shakes his head, his gaze still turned outward. "*I* should have warned you," he says. And then: "She met my dad when she was in high school. That's one of the things she was talking about last night."

"Huh."

"They were together for almost thirty years before he died."

"She doesn't— I mean, that's not what she's worried

about, right? That I'm going to, like, steal you away and marry you? I was planning on at least getting my driver's license first."

Chris laughs. For a moment it all seems possible again, but then his face darkens and closes, and his shoulders draw toward one another in a protective hunch. "She wants me to be happy," he says. "She really does. I think she just knows that I have no idea how to take care of two people. How to have that much time, I guess. How to love you, and to love her, and not hurt either of you."

Lorelei lets the weight of his words settle. "Do you love me?" she says, then, because she can't form the other sentence just yet.

"Yeah," he says, looking at her, finally. Finally. His voice is thick, but he looks at her steady and certain: sure. "Yeah, I think I do."

"I think I—" Lorelei says. "Okay. Yeah. Me too."

"Me too?" He leans his forehead against hers. "That's all you've got?"

"I love you," she says before she can psych herself out of it. The words bubble up and spill over. For just a minute, she suspends herself in a world without consequence.

Chris kisses her with his eyes closed so tightly that it looks like he's in pain, but his mouth on hers is slow and sweet. Soon the kiss gets faster, frantic. He loosens his hand from hers and puts it around her waist. Their cheeks are burning with cold but they're warm under their clothes. Chris keeps trying to haul her in closer. Lorelei thinks: *This is where I belong.*

When he pulls away, he's gasping. Lorelei doesn't understand. What could he be thinking of in this moment? What else could there possibly be? He digs a hand into one pocket and comes up with his buzzing cell phone.

She doesn't have to look to know that it's his mother calling to reel him back home. The urge to do something—to toss his phone into the ocean, to open her dangerous mouth all the way—rises so wildly and sharply that she can barely swallow it in time. Immediately after, she's disgusted with herself, and terrified. How could she even think about singing again, after what Petra said last night?

He silences the call and says, "Oh, Lorelei." He reaches for her again but she resists, and starts to unwind the blanket from around her legs. "I mean, we could—"

But they can't. She knows they can't. He'll keep trying to split the difference between her and his mother, and she'll let him until she can't bear it anymore. And then she'll curse him, and they'll end up just like her parents. She can't protect herself from heartbreak, but she can protect him from her love.

"I can't keep doing this," she says. "I love you—I love you—but I can't be your secret. I can't have any more secrets, Chris."

He holds his hands out, empty and open. She always knew who he was, and what he could offer. That hasn't changed.

"I want to keep you," he says.

Lorelei doesn't let herself think about what she wants, or what she'd do to get it if she gave herself the chance. "Take me home. I just want to go home now, please."

Home, where everything will be quiet and still. She hops off the hood and lands too hard on the parking lot asphalt.

The ocean calls to her but she doesn't turn and run down the rickety stairs. She doesn't think about throwing herself into the cold, stark water, or even just putting her toes in. She gets in the car and slams the door. The silence, after so much wind and so many words, is deafening, and comforting.

24

THE DAYS PASS QUIETLY for a while. Lorelei sets her sights on Thanksgiving: a break from seeing Chris in the halls and avoiding him. Jackson tries to talk to her once or twice, but even he gives up eventually. Angela, of all people, is nice to her about the breakup. Their lockers are near each other; sometimes the two of them walk to class together, making small talk about nothing in particular.

And it's not all that bad, even. She comforts herself with the thought that she did what Oma would have wanted her to do: she behaved. She saved Chris instead of herself. And now she has more time for homework and studying, and her own little family research project, which seems even sillier now that she knows more. How could she have thought she'd find the answer to her mother's loneliness and her grandmother's magic in a few bundles of old letters?

Instead, she learns dozens of useless facts from Oma's domestic life: the names of old friends in the old country and the recipes she missed and wanted to re-create in her new kitchen. The more Lorelei reads, the more she thinks she didn't know her grandmother very well at all.

It makes her conscious of her own family, and how little she knows about the lives going on all around her. She stops using the drive to school to catch up on English reading so that she can talk to Jens while Nik naps; instead of asking Nik for rides from the studio space after school, she sits on the sidelines and watches his soccer practice. Lorelei even starts taking her math homework to her mother, whose work as an accountant has made her exceptionally good at word problems. They don't talk about anything else during these sessions. Lorelei still can't figure out how to talk to her father at all.

From the outside, at least, she looks as normal as she ever has. Her family looks normal too. It's just that she feels like there's a limb that's gone to sleep somewhere, except it's not an arm or a leg that's fuzzy, it's something much deeper down.

Lorelei describes it to Nik and he laughs and says it's just normal breakup stuff. She believes it, mostly, but she also can't help noticing the way her reflection in the mirror each morning keeps dimming. Her hair is always tangled. Her skin gets patchy and dry. She wears her mother's makeup, but it just makes her look worse: big, empty eyes over hollow, too-pink cheeks.

After a while she has to wonder if it isn't just heartbreak. The thing within her starts to feel genuinely corrosive, like it's eating her up from the inside out. She looks more like her mother every day, and it's not just the makeup. Petra's skin is thin too, pulled tight by the rictus of her smile. It's like Oma's skin was, translucent and papery.

Mostly what she feels is heavy, and tired. Her body moves through the world like there's something pushing back on her with every step.

～⊙～

When the break from school for Thanksgiving finally comes, Lorelei switches her focus and spends days buried in family photo albums, looking for more of these family resemblances, hoping they'll tell her some secret that the letters can't. They're just as cryptic in their own way, though, mute images instead of untranslatable words.

She brings them to Petra and asks her to identify the photos' subjects. Maybe her mother will want to talk again. She doesn't, though. Instead, she squints at the pages like they hurt her eyes, and points listlessly to one or two faces. "I think that's Pietr," she says. "He was my—second cousin? One of Oma's cousins' kids, I think."

Her fingers slide over the page, leaping up as they pass over a few of the faces.

"What about them?" Lorelei prompts. Oma's in this one, in the center, with her arms around two women about her age. They're all smiling the static smiles of people in old photographs; it's impossible to tell if they're happy or not.

"Hannah," Petra says. "That's Hannah, and your Oma, and Eva."

"Her sisters," Lorelei says.

Petra looks at her daughter, startled. "Yes," she says. "Her sisters."

Petra stands to leave, then, and Lorelei lets her. She's too busy staring down at Hannah, who she's only known in letters up until now. She's not as pretty as Oma was: her face is broader, and she's got a way of looking at the camera that's so frank it's almost off-putting. But the longer Lorelei looks, the more Hannah's face seems to come alive.

"Here," Petra says. Lorelei didn't hear her coming. Petra shoves another photo album into her lap and turns like she's going to leave.

"What is this, Mom?"

"It's mine," Petra says. She's holding herself perfectly straight and stiff. "I thought you might like it."

"Okay," Lorelei says. "Thanks."

"You can look at it downstairs. I have to concentrate up here."

It's the Saturday after Thanksgiving—what work could she possibly have to do? But Lorelei doesn't want to argue, so she takes the album downstairs to the living room.

Petra must have made the album when she was still a teenager: it's full of crappy shots from disposable cameras, all of the background cut away so that she could cram as many versions of her friends' smiling faces onto the page as possible. There are a few captions written out in her familiar scrawl, and Lorelei knows enough German now that she can read some of them: *me and Anna at the beach last weekend*, *Steph and Frank at "our" table at the café*. Everyone looks impossibly happy, and young, and terribly dressed.

Lorelei doesn't recognize anyone other than her mother

until she gets to the last page Petra used, about halfway through the album. Then, suddenly, her father's face is grinning at her, unfamiliar and unmistakable at the same time.

He's sitting on a park bench in the middle of winter, bundled in an enormous down coat. He has the hood drawn over his head but he's tilting his face toward the sunlight, smiling up at the camera. Lorelei doesn't know what he looked like before her mother cast her spell on him, but surely she'd done it by the time this was taken: his gaze is so open and kind that she has trouble tearing her eyes away from it.

The caption says, *Henry, the day we met.*

Lorelei traces her father's face with her fingertips. She looks like him too: she has his high forehead, and the curl in her hair is just like his, rough and wavy.

She knows all about her mother's legacy to her, but what is her father's? What does it mean to have been born to a man who could love so thoroughly and openly, and who could let himself be taken in by magic, and who, even when he knew what had been done to him, refused to leave the person who had done it behind?

Lorelei closes the album and stares down at the cover, like it will have answers written for her there.

"Lorelei?" She turns to find her father hovering over her shoulder. Even though she's known him this way her whole life, it's shocking to see his adult face so soon after the younger one on the page.

"Mom just gave me this," she says. "I was looking at the old ones."

"Wow," Henry says. "Can I?"

He takes a ginger seat next to her on the couch. Lorelei almost wishes he would stop being so careful around her—it just reminds her of that awful afternoon, Oma trying to warn her, and all the things she didn't know, and thought couldn't possibly matter.

Henry smiles while he leafs through the pages. "Steph introduced us," he says, pausing on the picture of her. "Me and your mother."

"I didn't know that." There are so many questions that just never occurred to her, before. Her family seemed like a fact—or maybe a force—of nature. Not something people had stories about.

"Sure. Steph and I had grown up together. She met your mother at school. She thought we might get along."

"So it was a setup?"

"Yeah." Henry flips another few pages and finds his own face staring up at him. Gently, he closes the book on it. "But even if it hadn't been—god, she was beautiful."

"Love at first sight, huh?" Lorelei asks.

"I don't believe in that," Henry says. "Not really. It's more complicated." He squints a little at Lorelei, like he's trying to size up what she knows. She can't bring herself to tell him. It's nice, for a minute, to pretend she's still his small thing, his uncomplicated, unruined daughter.

"But I wanted to love her," he says. "From the moment I met her."

"Do you love her now?"

"What a question! I love all of you." For just a minute, she wants to believe him more than she wants the real an-

178

swer. Henry reaches out an arm to her: an offering. Lorelei lets herself fall sideways into a hug. It wasn't a yes, but it wasn't a no, either.

It isn't a curse.

It's so much more complicated than that.

25

HENRY'S REASSURANCE DOESN'T LAST, and when it wears off, Lorelei feels worse than ever. Does anyone love her? Has anyone, ever? Pushing Chris away starts to seem crazy, and she can't let herself think that way.

Lorelei doesn't have Oma's patience for letter writing. She and Hannah seem to have used longhand to enforce cooling-off periods, but Lorelei's had plenty of time to think this over. And anyway, enough already with old-fashioned letters, and half answers, and family myths and legends. She just wants something simple, and solid, and certain. For once.

She finds her great-aunt on Facebook. She has to pull Hannah's married name from the return address on her letters; there are fifteen results when she searches. Five of them live in Hamburg. Only one looks to be the right age. She's old enough that her profile isn't locked up tightly. Lorelei copies and pastes her email address into a blank window and stares at it, the plain black letters of it, for a long time.

If her translations make sense, Lorelei's letter says:

Dear Hannah,

I am your grandniece. I've been reading the letters between you and my grandmother, Silke. I think there's something you could tell me that I need to know. What am I? What does it mean that she told me never to sing?

Thank you.
Lorelei

26

LORELEI DOESN'T RECOGNIZE EITHER of the boys at first. She and Zoe are sitting at Coffee Bean after school, plodding through homework, and when someone taps on Zoe's shoulder, Lorelei thinks he's going to ask them for the wi-fi password or something. Then Zoe gets up and throws her arms around him.

Right, Daniel. She said he might stop by.

She didn't say he was bringing a friend too.

"You remember Paul, right?" Daniel says. Lorelei doesn't. She tries to make her shrug look neutral. "From that show—The Trouble?"

"Oh," Lorelei says. The blond one who wasn't Daniel. "Right, sure. Good to see you."

"We're getting drinks," Paul says. "You want anything?"

Lorelei says, "Tea, please. Chamomile." She's already drained her chai, and she's buzzing with caffeine and sugar. She was counting on it to keep her awake through the long afternoon of doing boring work, but with Paul and Daniel here she's starting to feel a little twitchy.

She tries to hand Paul a couple of dollars, but he waves them away. "I've got it," he says. Lorelei looks to Zoe to see if she should argue, but Zoe's face is turned against Daniel's shoulder. It makes her miss Chris so much she can barely stand it.

She nods at Paul. "Thanks."

Lorelei opens her book again, but she keeps getting distracted by Zoe and Daniel talking, and the song playing over the speakers, and her pulse thumping in her ears. Of course this is Zoe's idea of how to fix things.

Paul is cute. He's got wide-set blue eyes and thick, sandy hair, broad shoulders, long arms. He's probably a nice boy, or nice enough.

Lorelei goes over to stand with him and wait. "I thought I could help you carry, at least," she says.

"Oh yeah." Paul nods. "Thanks."

He doesn't say anything else.

"So you and Daniel go to school together?" Lorelei tries.

"Yeah," he says. "And you and Zoe?"

"Yeah."

What did she and Chris talk about, that first night? Nothing special. Lorelei remembers, distantly, that it seemed awkward, then, but it's hard to believe it was ever this awkward.

"Cool."

Another agonizing minute of silence passes. Lorelei looks at the Polaroids of the store's regulars pinned to a bulletin board, at the floor, the girl making their drinks, the backs of her hands.

"What are you, uh, what were you working on?" Paul asks.

"English," Lorelei says. "Doing some reading."

"Chamomile tea and an iced coffee, for Paul," the countergirl says.

Zoe comes up behind them. Daniel's next to her now, one arm still slung around her shoulders. "You want to get out of here?" she asks. "We were thinking about taking a walk."

At least it will give Lorelei and Paul something to do while they try to talk. "Sure," she says.

In the shuffle of leaving, the boys pull ahead and Zoe drops back while the two of them shove books into their backpacks. "You don't have to fall in love with him, or anything," she says. "I just wanted you to remember that there are other guys out there. I probably should have warned you."

"It's whatever," Lorelei says. "He's nice."

"He's one of Daniel's best friends." Zoe worries at the zipper on her backpack. "I don't know. You've been so sad, lately, and distracted. I wanted— I'm sorry if this wasn't right."

"I just feel like such a weirdo," Lorelei says. "Like, I have no idea what I'm doing. I don't want to make you look bad, or make things awkward. That's all."

"Don't worry about me, man. And seriously, you don't have to fall in love with Paul. We're just going to go up to Wolves in Winter," she says. "Daniel wants to buy something to wear to his birthday party."

Lorelei knows the store; it's teensy and fancy and expensive, with bare wooden floors and five identical white shirts hung from antlers on the walls.

"You can stay if you'd rather. I can say you're getting work done."

"Nah," Lorelei says. "It's cool. I'm cool."

"Cool." Zoe grins and throws her backpack over her shoulder. She practically skips out the door to Daniel's side, and Lorelei goes up to meet Paul.

The walk is a little better, a little easier. He's trying, and she's trying. They discuss her English reading, and then whether they like to read. Paul plays water polo; he gets carsick on the buses to and from meets, and then he gets home exhausted, and his grades are shitty but polo is going to get him into college, probably, so whatever. He's just as nice as he looks. Lorelei can't help liking him a little bit.

He doesn't compare to Chris, though.

After a couple of blocks their conversation hits a lull. Paul takes advantage of it, and changes the subject.

"I don't know if this is weird to say. Daniel mentioned that you'd just broken up with someone."

"Oh," Lorelei says. "Yeah."

"Me too. I think they thought they were doing both of us a favor."

"Yeah."

"I just wanted to say— I don't know. I just wanted to get it out there. That that's, like, the situation."

Lorelei has been glancing at shops as they pass by: fancy thrift stores, little boutiques, a juice place, another coffee place, a café. She sees an awning up the block that she recognizes but can't place. It looks familiar, and inviting, fabric glowing crimson in the afternoon sun.

"I appreciate that," Lorelei says. "I feel like—maybe it makes things less awkward?"

Paul nods. The sunlight gilds the edges of his features, turning them sharp and bright.

"Can you read that sign up there?" Lorelei asks. "The one on the red awning?"

"House of . . . Spirits?"

Of course. This was one of the first places Carina took them when she got her driver's license: on a field trip to buy a pack of tarot cards. She did readings for Zoe and Lorelei under a bedsheet tent in her room. Somehow their futures were always full of dark, mysteriously handsome strangers.

"I kind of want to go in there," Lorelei says. They're close enough, now, that she can read the sign on her own. It's funny how distinctly she remembers coming here, how her world was transformed just by knowing an older girl with a car.

"Are you a Wiccan? Daniel definitely didn't mention that."

"Ha. No. I might get a birthday present for . . . my mom," Lorelei says. What a lie. "She likes that kind of thing."

"Want me to flag those guys down?"

"Nah," Lorelei says. "You should go ahead. I have to get back to school to meet my brother soon, anyway. When he's done with soccer practice. He's giving me a ride."

"Oh. Cool."

"Yeah."

Paul's hands are shoved in his jeans pockets. He moves like he's going to pull them out, to hug her or shake her hand or something, and then doesn't.

"It was nice to meet you," Lorelei says. "Seriously. Even if it was a little weird."

"You too," Paul says. "Maybe I'll see you around?"

"Maybe," Lorelei says.

"I would like that," Paul tells her.

Lorelei smiles, and slips into the shop.

Inside House of Spirits, the curtains are drawn against the afternoon's glare, and the air smells like sage and lavender. It's cozy but not claustrophobic. Lorelei likes it immediately.

In the main room there's a cash register, staffed by a very normal-looking girl reading a paperback. The walls are lined with bookshelves, and small tables are stocked with colorful scarves and bundles of dried herbs. To her left is an open doorway, and something bright just beyond it catches the corner of her eye. Lorelei smiles hello at the shopgirl and then turns to follow the brightness.

The smaller room is filled with crystals. There's no curtain here, so the late-afternoon sun cuts in brightly, slipping through the slender pillars of selenite in the window and tinting them pale gold. Lorelei only knows they're selenite because of the hand-lettered signs that say so: *A very good psychic stone, meant for healing and cleansing—clarifies your aura and purifies the energy around you—will help other stones work to their full potential—beautiful and a little fragile!!!! Please ask for assistance.*

The rest of the room is just tables and cases and stacks of loose stones. Some of them have been shaped and most of them have been polished, but a few are rough-hewn. Lorelei runs her fingers across quartz, turquoise, lapis, and jade, whose names she knows, and then the ridges and curves of the stones she doesn't recognize. There are tiny barbed spurs of red coral laid carefully in boxes, on pillows of gauze.

The coral is blood-bright in the sunshine, lively even in the stark white beds. *Creativity, passion, energy, and love—red coral can be used to stimulate the body and mind and make your whole life sing!* the sign says. It seems like a stupid thing to trust, but Lorelei picks up one of the little boxes, anyway. It's only three dollars. She might as well.

The girl at the counter has clearly been stuck inside all day without company. "Ooooh," she says. "I love these! *So* pretty. My boyfriend is a scuba diver—I mean, not, like, professionally, but anyway, he went on a trip last year and I really wanted him to get me some coral—stuff is so much more powerful when it's hand-harvested, you know, when it's something that's *yours* and not, just, like, an object of commerce—but, duh, coral is protected, which I kind of knew, actually. Because it's alive. So he didn't get me any."

Lorelei doesn't know what to say to this speech. "That's nice," she tries, and winces at herself. "I mean, it's nice that it's alive. It's cool that things aren't always what they look like."

"Everything in the world has its own energy," the girl says seriously. "Which sounds super hippie-dippy, but if you think about it, it actually is kind of true. Since we're all made up of the same stuff—atoms and molecules—and they all vibrate, in some way? Like, the little tiny things that are me now will be dirt, someday, and then maybe part of grass that a bird eats, and whatever. And they'll still be vibrating! So they have their own lives, you know? Everything is everything, basically." She giggles at herself, and repeats the phrase in an exaggeration of her loose surfer accent: "Everything is, like, eeeeverythiiiiing."

It's a much more physical explanation of reality than Lorelei expected from someone reading *Know Your Stars, Know Your Soul*. "So do you believe in, like"—Lorelei can't help dropping her voice on the word—"magic?"

The girl looks at Lorelei, and Lorelei watches the gears turning in her head. She's at work; of course she's trying to figure out what will help her make a sale.

"Sort of," she says finally. "Energy again. If coral is alive when it looks like rock, and the molecules that are in me will someday be in coral, or seaweed, or sand—that's like magic, in its way."

"So what's all of this stuff good for? If everything is everything, and it's all . . . already . . . there?" Lorelei can't tell if she sounds stupid or the conversation does.

"We can use what's in these crystals, and our herbs, and oils, to help change how our energy flows. It's not about turning one thing into another, or pulling rabbits out of hats or whatever. You focus on the stuff you want, and that brings it into your life. Y'know, like, people tell you to think positive? *The Secret*? This is just that plus some. That's how I explain it, anyway."

Lorelei sags with disappointment. She wanted so badly for the girl to just say *Yes*, and then she could say *Have you ever heard of*, and the girl would say *Yes, of course, absolutely*, and tell her what to buy or wear or rub on her temples. But even this deep in California pseudospiritualism there's no record of a curse or a spell or a creature like her, or room for one to exist.

"Well, hopefully this will get me started," Lorelei says. She puts the coral into her bag and heads out again, onto the empty street. So she wasted fifteen minutes, and probably three dollars. So what?

Walking back toward the school to meet Nik, Lorelei pulls the Wikipedia page for red coral up on her phone. It's mostly boring and technical—information on habitats, and a history of how it was used in trade, and for gifts.

The Coral in Culture tab is the only part she ends up caring about: It says that in Greek myth, Perseus slew Medusa, with her hair of spitting snakes, and then put her head on the riverbank while he washed his hands of her blood. The blood in the river petrified its seaweed and turned it into hard red coral.

Lorelei loved myths when she was younger: the way ancient people had made the entire world into a series of metaphors, giving each natural phenomenon a narrative to make sense of it. They saw seaweed waving green and soft underwater, and coral that looked almost the same except that it was crimson and still. They imagined what could have turned the living into stone, and came up with a woman's face and a woman's blood. You couldn't even look at Medusa, so of course she had to die. Even in dying, she cursed everything around her with her fury and rage.

And maybe that's what Hannah's email will say, if or when she writes back: that the women in Lorelei's family are just women, singing. A fact of the natural world. *Maybe we're just what we are*, Lorelei thinks, *like coral, or selenite, or window glass with light passing through it*. Maybe they're like the women in *The Odyssey:* just because they're part of one story doesn't mean they have a narrative of their own.

She arrives back at school a few minutes early, so instead of heading for their appointed meeting spot out front, she goes straight to the soccer field to see if she can catch Nik's last few minutes of practice. The boys are already rounding up stray balls, though, and shoving their things into sports bags. Nik is nowhere in sight.

"Never showed up," one of the boys says when she asks. "I don't know, I haven't seen him."

Lorelei does a slow turn, taking in the empty field and the deepening dusk in the sky above her. The air is too cold for her thin jacket.

She walks toward the school building, which is unevenly lit from inside. The windows where students are still sitting, singing, or rehearsing for plays—or where teachers are finishing up grading before they head out for the day—are bright against the oncoming night. Everything else is blank, and dark.

Lorelei settles on the school's front steps, shivering at the cold concrete under her butt, and fishes out her phone. She's just thumbing through for Nik's number when he appears, flushed and grinning. He's wearing loose shorts and a hoodie, cleats slung over one shoulder. For a second her mind reels, trying to make sense of the image in front of her, and what the boys told her when she went looking for him.

Then she notices how the flush is low on his cheeks, at his neck, and how swollen his mouth is, and she understands where he was, and why he isn't saying anything.

"You ready?" Nik asks.

Lorelei nods, and follows him to the car.

She wonders what stories he tells himself to make sense of what's happening to him. If he has words for it, yet, or if he just lets his body take over and doesn't worry about it too much until he has to. She wonders when he'll have to worry about it, and how bad it will be when he does.

27

HANNAH'S REPLY IS IN her inbox when she checks her
email at home. No magic, no fireworks, no thunder to her-
ald its arrival. Just Inbox (1). Oh.

Thankfully, it's in English.

Dear Lorelei,

I'm so glad to hear from you! And I am sorry I haven't written to
you before. Your grandmother made a rule about it: no letters,
no contact, no word from the homeland. I think she would have
been that strict with herself if she could have borne it, but even
Silke missed her sister.

I don't know if you were old enough to have figured it out, but
even she was human after all. And I suppose if you hadn't yet
you will have, now. There's nothing like when someone we think
of as being a constant up and disappears on us.

But I'm sure you have enough grief of your own to keep you
busy. I'm not writing to share mine. You asked questions; I
believe you deserve answers. So. Here they are.

No one remembers when it was that our ancestors first found

their way out of the sea. It seems now that all human life might have begun there, and that makes sense to me: that the womb of the world is water and salt. But I am speaking more specifically about a kind of ancestor that not everyone on this earth shares. And of course that makes sense to me too. How could a world so vast produce only one kind of human being?

They used to call us sirens.

Lorelei's front teeth close over her bottom lip. She sucks in a long breath.

So this is the truth. Not a myth. Reality.

We have become storybook creatures over the years, villainesses who lure men to certain death. And I am not saying there has not been death—very real death. The ocean has its own call, and sometimes men's bodies hear it and respond. So it happened. Sometimes, it had nothing to do with us.

Sometimes, of course, it did.

This is the story that Silke and I were told as children:

At some point a creature crawled out of the sea and onto an island in the Mediterranean.

She was hungry and she was lonely.

She learned to call out to the birds.

She learned to make them come to her.

In time she taught herself all of her world's sounds: how to mimic them, and how to use them to entice.

She didn't know how to escape her island.

She knew only how to bring the world to her while she was stranded there.

Her voice became her tool, her weapon, her companion and friend.

Still, like all of us, she wanted more than that.

So she learned how to tempt sailors off their ships by throwing her voice into the wind, and then how to swim out and save them from rocky shoals and narrow channels. The boats were lost but the men survived. Some of their sons would be born with powerful voices, but their daughters always, always were.

You are one of us, Lorelei. You are my sister's daughter's daughter, and the same strong blood is in all of our veins.

I can trace our family's line back three generations, though why we chose as cold a place as Germany to settle in I will never understand. Silke and I grew up on the North Sea coast, near the water, near others just like us. It was many things, but it was never lonely.

Or it wasn't lonely for me, anyway. It was easy for me to fit in there: to gossip with the women, to cook and clean, to live in warm houses at the edge of a cold shore. Silke wanted the city as soon as she learned what a city was, and how many more people there were in the world.

She wanted to sing not just in private, with our community, but for everyone. She wanted to use her voice to make art, and share it. She loved music in a way none of the rest of us did— not because it was necessary, but because it was beautiful. Losing it broke her heart.

I'm not sure she ever recovered from that heartbreak.

She wanted to keep Petra, and then you, from ever having your heart broken like that. She thought if you never fell in love with your voice, and its power, and its beauty, it would never hurt you. I don't think she considered that there's more to it than that. That your voice might find you even if you didn't know how to look for it.

Our ancestors didn't have many choices—women rarely do. Working on human will is a dark kind of magic, but it was what they had.

Lorelei stops reading. There are a scant few lines left, and she almost can't bear to know what they have to say. It seems bleaker than she could have imagined. It's just—in her, whatever this power is. She can't cut it out or burn it up. She's stuck inside herself, with this voice she's not supposed to use—a voice that will hurt people if she lets it out. It broke her grandmother's heart, and her mother's, and her father's, and now, slowly, surely, certainly, it is breaking hers.

She hurries through the last few sentences.

You do have choices, though. You know the truth: what you are, and what you can do. If you use your voice, use it carefully: never sing for anyone you need something from, someone you want to summon or bend or change. Sing for yourself, Lorelei, and you will always find happiness in it. I hope this letter gives you answers, and maybe comfort; I hope it gives you a path to find joy.

It goes on just a little while longer, Hannah saying that Lorelei should write or visit. Lorelei closes the email and archives it, as if by hiding it she can unread it. If her brain was overfull before, beset by fantastic creatures and impossible ideas, now it's just the ocean crashing, and the same word whispering at her every time.

Siren.

Siren.

Creature, myth, temptress, killer: that warning sound cutting hard through quiet nights. Lorelei is a siren.

At least. At last.

28

LORELEI DOESN'T COME DOWNSTAIRS for dinner. Evening has arrived and brought a storm with it. Black clouds crowd the sky and make the air electric with tension. She sits and watches it happen distantly from her perch on her bed.

She used to think that she could hear the ocean calling to her when she was younger. That was when she made up her first songs. Now all of the melody inside her is too loud. It's too huge to contain in the quiet of her room and too dangerous to unleash anywhere else.

Hannah's letter doesn't change anything, not really. Her voice is still her voice. But it feels different to know that her kind has a name and a history. She thinks about what the girl at the shop said earlier, about energy and the way molecules keep vibrating as they move from body to body. Something that's been moving in women's throats for thousands of years is still moving in hers.

The ocean is still calling, and Lorelei knows it's time for her to go.

She gets up and gets dressed. She can slip out the back

door. The shore is less than half a mile away. *I'll just put my toes in*, she thinks.

When she gets to the beach, she slips off her shoes. The sand is cold and rough against the soles of her feet as she makes her way.

The world looks like it's been turned upside down: the sea is inky dark, and the sky is so light with clouds that she can see where it dips down toward the horizon. Stiff breezes whip through her hair and tangle it up, knotting the loose ends.

Lorelei opens her mouth, but she can't seem to find the song, or her song, or any song. Whatever it is that makes her voice powerful has such a long, dark history. She was born to two people still in the grip of its magic, and she's lived all of her life in the cool black of its shadow. Maybe she shouldn't. Too bad she already has.

Her voice is trapped in her throat.

A wild panic rises. This is fear with teeth and claws: rank, animal, and instinctive. She can't keep all of this inside her. She has to be able to sing.

Lightning flashes out over the ocean.

The sea rushes to her, waves breaking hard and then murmuring forward. Lorelei can't resist its pull. She walks across the first damp patches of sand, eyes fixed on the horizon. She doesn't know where she's going, but she doesn't know how to stop. When the water touches her toes, it's so cold she screams.

The sound is nothing like singing, but it comes from the same high, pure place. She uses the feel of it to find a longer note, and then a lower one, coming down like descending the rungs of a rickety ladder. The notes blend into melodies. It's so consuming that the rest of her body holds itself still while she does it. Her feet get numb and her fingers clench into fists. Lorelei is so cold she's shaking. She doesn't care as long as it's working.

Lorelei lets herself be like the storm, gathering slowly, wind and air pulling water and electricity from all around her. She thinks about Chris's hands, and Oma's, her mother's soft touch and angry mouth. She thinks about Zoe's sweet, serious eyes, and all of the things she wants. All of them. The crackle that she felt in her chest in Chris's sunroom, weeks ago, now, has nothing on this sensation, which threatens to overwhelm her. It will not be quieted.

She sings the thing that's been haunting her all the time in between, the song she started and never finished. The song they were supposed to sing together.

The first notes, furious with tenderness and ache, collide with the boom of a thunderclap. The sky sets a slow, rolling beat. Lightning comes across the water, closer and closer. When she finishes, she's so empty that she just wants to lie down and sleep in the sand until morning.

She doesn't, though. At the end of her songs, she's just a body again, and her body knows the way back home.

29

THE SCHOOL DAY FLOATS by like she's watching it happen to someone else. Lorelei just keeps thinking: *a siren,* and every time she slides right out of her skin. Everyone else is living in the same world they've always known. Only she can see how it's been shifted.

She wants to sing again but can't figure out how to do it. She doesn't want to be like those communities of women wherever her family comes from, keeping their power private the way women always do. For the first time Lorelei really understands what Oma wanted when she climbed onstage and looked out at a crowd. She was tired of hiding, and of being isolated, and lonely. She wanted her strange, lovely voice to join with everyone else's.

She wanted to act. To act out.

The knowledge simmers in her all day. By the time school ends, her skin feels tight and hot. Lorelei walks through the halls like she's stalking something, head turning, eyes scanning. She doesn't know what she's looking for until she finds him.

Jackson. Of course.

He's primed for her voice, and almost too easy to persuade.

"Yeah," he says. "That would be amazing. I kept trying to get you to sing for me again, but you wouldn't, you ignored me, and Nik said—"

"Don't talk about Nik." Hearing her brother's name reminds Lorelei of all the reasons she shouldn't be doing this. She can't be sure she knows what Nik wants or needs, or that she'll be able to deliver Jackson safely through the storm of her voice.

Oma would have counseled discipline, and restraint. But Oma also lied to her, telling her she couldn't sing when she can. She *can*. And Hannah said she could.

Kind of.

Which is why she needs to figure out what she can do. She would gladly use her power on herself if she could, but the thing about being a siren is that it only matters when someone else is around to hear it, and bear whatever it is you give them to carry.

Jackson doesn't ask questions. He puts them in his car, and drives.

At first he heads toward the practice space, but Lorelei isn't ready to be back there yet. His mom is at his house, he says, so that's out. Lorelei thinks about taking him to the beach before it occurs to her that her own house will be empty: Nik has practice, Jens is writing a history paper at the library, and her parents are still at work.

Lorelei hums along with the radio and watches Jackson's shoulders relax fractionally, and then some more.

"What changed your mind?" he asks.

Lorelei doesn't say anything.

"I'm good at keeping secrets," he says. "I think that's why you both picked me."

Nik again.

"Does he want to keep it a secret?" Lorelei asks. If it really is Nik's choice, she shouldn't get herself in the middle of it.

"He did when we started," Jackson says. "Now I guess it's my secret, because, you know. Angela."

"So you guys are still hooking up."

Jackson darts a glance at her, startled and wild.

"He didn't tell me," she says.

"If I tell you, I won't be keeping the secret."

This is it. This is how she's supposed to test him: to draw out what he doesn't want to say. It's not changing him, Lorelei reasons. It's just leaning a little harder on him than she would be able to, normally. It's just trying to learn the truth behind one more well-kept secret.

They pull up in front of her house before she knows whether she should go through with it or not. Adrenaline snakes down her spine. Her stomach flips. Her voice shakes with nerves when she opens the door and says, "We're here."

"I've been here before," Jackson observes. "Nik snuck me in a couple of times."

"Oh," Lorelei says. She remembers him driving her home from practice that first night, and how easily he took the turns. Of course. "Well. Come in again."

Jackson drops his bag in the hall while Lorelei checks her email, one last time, for anything from Hannah, a note that says *Just kidding!* Or *Never mind.* It's all spam, though, and ads, and she either has to do this or get Jackson the hell out.

"Are you thinking about singing with us?" Jackson asks her.

"What?" Lorelei says. "What? No."

"I just assumed." He starts to wander away from her, down the hallway to the living room. "I mean, I figured you were going to try to get back together with him somehow. Chris. And it seemed like a pretty easy way to do it. You know: give him what he wants."

Lorelei has been trying not to think like that—not yet, anyway. Not until she understands how this works. No need to get her hopes up. "Maybe," she says. "I wanted to try it out, first, though. Get a more objective opinion from you."

"I always want to hear you," Jackson says. It comes out automatically, the idea she planted that first time, when she didn't know what she was doing. *Listen to me.*

Be careful, Lorelei reminds herself.

She follows him into the living room, where he's already sitting on the couch. Lorelei just stands there, looking at him.

"Go ahead," he says. He tilts his head up and levels his gaze with hers, almost arrogant, almost like the old Jackson, and then it's easier to remember how infuriating he was, and is. Then somehow it's easy to open her mouth and let the song spill out.

He slumps gratefully into the embrace of the sound. She's not even doing anything, not trying anything, just singing mindlessly, the song that was on the radio, but he's completely surrendered to it. His head falls back as his eyes fall shut. His mouth goes slack.

Lorelei decides to start with something easy, as an experiment: not love, which is all undertow, but something physical and concrete. As she sings out, she thinks of waking up the morning after Oma went into the hospital. She'd missed dinner and slept late, and her stomach was an empty, angry knot. She imagines it so strongly that one hand comes to rest there, and Jackson, wide-eyed, mirrors the movement.

Lorelei cuts off the song, breathing hard. "You okay?" she asks him.

"Starving," Jackson whispers. His voice has gone hoarse. "You're starving."

"I'm not," she says.

"You are." He leaps up from the couch. "Where's the kitchen? I can get you something, I can fix you—"

"Jackson!" Her voice stops him in his tracks. Lorelei starts to sing again, mindless again, the tune that lulled him before. Jackson subsides back onto the couch, but he keeps tracking her. Lorelei lets the song drift while what she's just done washes over her: Holy shit.

Holy shit!

It worked.

It keeps working. She slips through variations on a theme: exhaustion, and then elation, because it seems unfair to keep giving him sadness that isn't his. It isn't fair to be doing this at all, really, but Lorelei is strung out on the sensation, almost stoned with the power of freedom and release. He made so many assumptions about her, and they were mostly mean ones. Now he can't help knowing all of her painful, complicated truth. He has to feel all of it like it's his.

She doesn't want to stop, but at some point the angle of the sun reminds her that Jens and Nik will be home soon, and she can't keep messing around. She's been lazy, playing with sensation, stuff that's instinctive and easy. Being specific is trickier: she remembers how she sang to him that first time, outside the practice space, but she's not sure she can do it again. Lorelei hums the song from the radio. Jackson calms and stills.

"I'm ready," he says. "Go ahead."

"For what?" she asks.

"Chris's song," Jackson says. "Your song."

"Sure," Lorelei says.

She imagines herself running the melody through with a delicate vein of a question, and a command. This was the song she used to think meant that Chris loved her; now she can use it to find out if Jackson loves Nik.

"I don't know," Jackson says when she's done. His words overlap the last echo of her last note, so there's no silence in between. His voice isn't powerful like hers, but she knows he's telling the raw truth, anyway. "I feel awful about it, but I don't know how to stop. I don't know if that means I love him, or if I'm just selfish. I mean, I am selfish, so it's probably that. But it's not like he hates it. I keep thinking, if we loved each other, we would be sure, but we're not. So. I don't know."

Lorelei wishes the answer was easy. That if you were in

love, you knew it, and knew what to do about it. She can make him say anything, but he can't tell a truth he doesn't know.

What she can do is make it easier on all of them.

So she tells him, "Stop, then. If you don't love him. Leave him alone."

"Okay." Jackson looks up at her, wounded, but he doesn't flinch.

"And leave me alone, until I tell you not to."

"Okay."

Lorelei can't resist one more question.

"If I did want to sing with you guys," she says. "Would Chris— Do you think he would let me?"

"Chris loves you," Jackson says. "You don't have to worry about that."

30

LORELEI DOESN'T LET HERSELF think about singing to Chris like a plan. It's not— She's not plotting anything. It's in her back pocket if things get unbearable. But there has to be another way out of what she's feeling.

Every day she walks around school and keeps her eyes fixed on the ground, trying not to see Chris, trying not to see who he's with. Her blood is always wild with adrenaline, anyway. Going from class to class becomes a game of roulette. The idea that she did this herself—to herself—takes on a raw, ugly edge. So what if she had the power, if all she used it for was to make a mess of her life?

She gets a text from an unknown number. *Hey it's paul,* it reads. *U comin 2 Daniel's tmrw?*

"Oh shit," Zoe says when Lorelei asks her. "Yeah. His birthday party. I was going to invite you, and then he said he'd asked The Trouble to play, like we talked about, and it seemed weird to ask him to cancel that, so I—I don't know. I figured you wouldn't want to go."

"I don't," Lorelei says. "Don't worry about it."

"No, but I do want you to be there," Zoe says.

"I wouldn't know anyone. You'd just have to entertain me."

"I don't really know anyone, either, honestly. His guy friends aren't interested in me—obviously—and the girls always ignore me when I'm around."

"Zoe. It's fine."

"It's not fine! And I think you should come, actually. Especially if Paul's inviting you. If he wants to see you. Might be good to remind Chris that you can move on if you want to."

Lorelei tries to pretend the thought hasn't occurred to her.

"C'mon," Zoe continues. "I'll dress you up. Carina's coming, and she said she'd drive. And we can all have a sleepover afterward! It'll be so fun, L. Fuck Chris and Daniel and Paul. We'll have ourselves a good old-fashioned laaadies' night."

Lorelei likes the idea of showing up somewhere with her best friend, and an older girl. It'll be like that night at the Whiskey, except she'll know what she's doing this time. She won't go up to Chris at all. He can watch her from across the room, and wonder who she's talking to, and why. She can dance with Paul, and kiss him, even, if she wants to.

The meanness of this plan curdles in her stomach. It doesn't feel good, but it feels better than blankness, and nothing. Lorelei remembers how scared she was before she sang to Jackson, and how good she felt after. She woke up in the morning and her hair was soft and her cheeks were pink. She wants to feel that way again: bright and fresh and clean.

She'll kiss someone for the first time at this party. She'll leave her tired, sad self behind and find a way to become someone brand-new.

∾ઉ৩৬

Lorelei checks in with Angela on their way to sixth period. She asks, "Are you coming to the show tomorrow?"

"The one at your friend's boyfriend's house? Probably. I don't know. You're going?" Angela seems to weigh something before she continues. "I'm not really sure it's a good idea."

"I'm fine," Lorelei says.

"Oh." Angela slants a funny look her way. "Yeah, no, I meant—Chris is, like, super broken up about this whole thing, you know."

"I didn't know that." Jackson said he still loved her, but he's seemed fine whenever she's seen him.

"He's incredibly bummed. He feels like shit about what happened between the two of you."

"Breakups suck."

"He misses you."

Lorelei doesn't know that she's been waiting for this particular set of words until she hears them. Hope blooms in her chest before she can name it. It's different from Jackson trying to placate her after she sang him into mindlessness. Angela says it like everyone knows it's a fact.

Lorelei says, "I miss him too."

"So it might be good to see him," Angela prompts. "You guys could work things out, maybe."

"That would be nice."

"Yeah. Is your brother coming?"

"Jens or Nik?"

"Nik," Angela says. And then, in a rush, "Look, I know he and Jackson used to—"

"Wait, what?"

"Whatever, Lorelei, okay, everyone totally knows that."

"They do?"

"I know, anyway," Angela says. "And I'm just wondering, because he was hanging around for a while, and then he wasn't, and if you're going to be there."

There's no question about where her loyalties lie, but Lorelei feels awful for not telling Angela the whole truth. And besides, it's over now. She made it be over, for all of them.

"I haven't seen Nik all that much recently," she says. "I can't imagine why he'd come to the party."

"Okay."

They're just in front of Lorelei's stop when she works up the nerve to ask a question of her own. "Chris said something the first time we hung out," she starts. "About your parents? Being pretty religious?"

"Yeah," Angela says.

She doesn't sound like she's about to shut down the conversation, so Lorelei presses on. "So you must have to lie to them. About what you do. Sometimes."

"Yeah," Angela says again.

"I just. I don't know. I don't understand why Chris can't do that. Won't do that. For me."

Angela looks up and down the hallway, as if preparing to share a secret—which, Lorelei supposes, she is.

"I don't agree with my parents," she says. Her smile is surprisingly kind. "I don't think Chris feels that way about his mom, and her reasons for keeping you apart." She's a few steps away before she turns to add one last thought. "I didn't say I liked it, either," Angela tells her, before disappearing down the hallway to class.

31

DANIEL'S PARENTS' HOUSE IS enormous, a supermodern fortress spiked high on one of the bluffs in the Pacific Palisades. The driveway is already full, so they have to park blocks away and then hike up in their high-heeled shoes.

Carina stops them at the top to brush some of Lorelei's hair from her face and hand around a compact for a quick makeup check. Zoe is nervous and twitchy. She glances at her phone over and over again, even though they're basically at Daniel's front door.

It's a cold night but they're all wearing dresses anyway, bare-legged and shivering in thin jackets. The wind is raw with chill and dank with brine blowing in from the ocean below. The air smells like her last conversation with Chris, and those last little hopeful moments. Lorelei wonders if he's already here.

Zoe punches in the gate code and turns around to link her arm through Lorelei's. Together they step over the low metal track as the gate pulls back. Lorelei spots Chris's battered Mercedes up the drive.

"You ready?" Zoe asks. She doesn't slow her pace.

"Ready enough, I guess," Lorelei says.

Inside, the band is setting up on an enclosed patio at the far end of the living room. The glass reflects the interior lights, making the boys look like miniature figures in a crystal jewel box. The house is very stark, all concrete and glass. Sound echoes wincingly off every surface. Bean and Jackson appear to be talking about hanging rugs before they perform. Jackson turns to gesture at the space, and for a second his gaze locks with Lorelei's. He looks down, frowning. Chris has his back to her and he doesn't turn. Lorelei forces herself to look away. The room is punctuated by cactus plants with flowers blooming at the end of their twisted, spiky arms.

The girls are shedding their jackets, still shivering even though it's warm inside, when Daniel and Paul swoop down on them. Now Lorelei recognizes how handsome Daniel is, in his proper context, with his sharp jaw and careful stubble. He's wearing black pants and a white button-down with a skinny black tie and a gold tie clip. Zoe's dress is a Goodwill find, short and tight and covered in gold sequins. Her skin is tawny and her lips and cheeks are sweet, glossy pink. She looks so lively next to him: very fresh, very young. He wraps an arm around her waist and kisses the top of her head. It's a move that says to everyone in the room: *We belong together,* or maybe, *She belongs to me.*

Paul hugs Lorelei and Carina hello. Does he hug Lorelei for a second longer? She isn't sure, and she isn't sure how much she cares.

"You made it," Daniel says. "And you brought decorations, as requested."

Zoe shoots Lorelei a private little look. She knows he's being lame. She doesn't call him on it, though.

"Does that mean you brought the drinks?" she asks instead.

As they make their way across the room, Lorelei becomes more self-conscious about her appearance with every step. Her hair is loose and wild around her face, and Carina daubed her mouth with hot-pink lipstick, something bright and a little harsh to roughen up her flowy white dress. The house is so stark and sophisticated, and all of Daniel's friends seem to match.

She allows herself one more glance in Chris's direction, and immediately loses track of whatever Paul is saying to her. Chris is shaking a curl out of his eyes, adjusting the microphone stand, and her entire body aches like a poked bruise with the desire to be close to him again. He sees her too, and freezes. Lorelei makes herself look away before he can.

The bar top is littered with bottles: big cheap plastic handles of vodka and whiskey, plus a random assortment of stuff that looks like it was pulled from a half-dozen liquor cabinets. There are liqueurs and fancy bitters and sodas, elegant in glass but dusty with age.

"What do you want?" Paul asks. Lorelei wonders if this is what dating is like when you're not in love: boys asking you what you want, and buying you drinks, or making you drinks, and then you talk until the drink runs out, and it's time to kiss, or leave.

She wonders when the music is going to start.

"Whatever is fine," she says, to cover the fact that she doesn't know the answer to his question.

Daniel pours himself whiskey on ice and makes Zoe something pale and clear and fizzy. He doesn't ask her what she wants. She kisses his cheek and takes a long, slow sip. Paul reaches for the whiskey after Daniel puts it down.

Carina is eyeing the array of bottles like she has plans for them. "This is a pretty fancy setup," she says.

"It's my parents'," Daniel says. "All of it."

"And they don't care—"

"They really don't."

"Great." Carina pulls down a couple of glasses. "Paul, quit that, she does not want a Jack and Coke. Lorelei, you trust me?"

"Yeah?"

"That's fine with me," Paul says. He dumps her drink into his cup and takes a long, deep swallow.

Daniel and Zoe round up their drinks and wander away from the group, looking casual, even though Lorelei is pretty sure they're heading for a dark corner to make out in. Carina looks back and forth from Lorelei to Paul. "So," she says. "Paul. Did someone tell you that Lorelei's ex is here?"

"Carina!" Lorelei expects Paul to be embarrassed, or angry, but he just laughs.

"Yeah," he says. "Daniel warned me. Don't worry. I'm not looking to get my ass kicked tonight."

"I don't think Chris is the ass-kicking type," Lorelei says.

"Oh." Paul misunderstands her. He slings an arm around her shoulders. "In that case."

Carina hands her a drink. She says, "Lorelei, if I leave you alone with this dude, will you stay out of trouble for, like, ten minutes? My friend Jamie is over there and I want to go say hi."

"I'll be good," Lorelei says. Paul's arm tightens.

She sneaks another helpless glance at Chris. His guitar is strung from its strap around his neck, but his hands are at his sides. He's looking down at the floor, at nothing. Bean jostles him and he almost trips, dazed, before he starts to tune the strings again.

I did that, Lorelei thinks. She doesn't know how to feel about the idea that she has some power over him, still.

"Can you believe this place?" Paul asks.

Lorelei wriggles out from under his arm. It's too weird trying to talk to someone whose face she can't see.

"It's something," she says.

"Daniel's parents bought it during the crash in '09," Paul says. "Some zillionaire had it built, and then he lost all of his money, couldn't make the mortgage—" The story drifts out of focus as the music starts up again. It sounds like idle chords, just Chris strumming, but the notes start to hang together and Lorelei recognizes the curl of the song calling her, Chris reaching out across the room and speaking in a language only the two of them know.

Paul sways in closer to her. His breath is sharp with whiskey, and he's telling her a story about ruin with a smile on his face. Lorelei wonders about the man who built this palace, who picked out the hilltop and the stones and the glass. She wonders if he ever got to live here, and look out over the ocean at storms rolling in and snarling against the shore below. He probably thought they would never reach him. She imagines the betrayal he felt when they did.

She doesn't want power that comes from jealousy or anger. She doesn't want Chris's mouth to look hard and flat, and his fingers to trip over the strings when he tries to play. Lorelei looks at Paul and doesn't recognize him. She couldn't pick him out in a crowd.

All this time, she's been telling herself that it was singing and then not singing that ruined her mother, and her grandmother. But maybe it was loving, and not loving. Lorelei can imagine all too well how it would be if she stayed here, and made polite conversation, and let this stranger kiss her. It would be fine. She wouldn't hate it. But it would dull down the best parts of her, sanding away her brightness and her edges until she was too tired to know the difference.

"I'm sorry," Lorelei says. She cuts Paul off in the middle of a sentence. "I think I have to go talk to Chris. My ex. For a minute."

"You sure that's a good idea? Sometimes booze makes things—"

"Yeah. I'm sure. I'm good. Thank you."

Paul heaves a tired sigh. "You'll regret it," he says.

"Excuse me?"

"You can get back together with him," he says. "But you'll just end up splitting again."

"You don't know him. You don't know me!"

"I know how it is," Paul says. "I'm in the middle of this shit too, remember? That was supposed to be the point of us. That we'd keep each other from making these kinds of stupid decisions."

"I don't want to be a distraction," Lorelei says. "I don't want to pretend not to want something anymore."

"Even if it's just going to break your heart all over again?"

Lorelei walked out on Chris so that he wouldn't break her heart, and she wouldn't take control of his. But they deserve a chance to run it all the way into the ground together—or to find a way to make it work. She knows what she is, at least. Her mother never did.

"Yeah," Lorelei says. "Sorry. Don't be mad at Zoe, or Daniel."

"I just think you're being stupid," Paul says.

Lorelei shrugs him off.

Letting herself be stupid feels like a privilege. Where have smartness and self-control ever gotten her?

Chris sees her coming, and comes to meet her.

"Hey," she says. "I just, um, I just wanted to say hi. Since we're both here. Or whatever."

"Yeah," he says. "Hey. Hi. How, um, how are you, I guess?"

"Fine." Lorelei has said the word so many times in the last few months that it's lost any meaning it ever had. *Fine* means lost and sad and grieving, and falling in and out of love, and singing at the seashore, and the glimmer of Zoe's dress tonight, bright against all the dark things in Lorelei's head. Being with Chris called out her lightness and all the best parts of her. He was the answer then, and he's the answer now. He always has been. "How are you?"

"Fine," he says. The catch of his gaze on hers makes her think that he means it exactly the way she does: fine and not fine. They're both too full with feeling to try to put it into words. "Do you, um—we could—talk, a little bit, if you want, upstairs."

"Sure."

He walks behind her on the staircase and across the landing at the top, one hand hovering lightly just above the small of her back to guide her. They head to a guest room littered with the band's stuff, guitar cases and stray pieces of sheet music and a three-quarters-full bottle of vodka on the bed.

Chris closes the door behind them. He looks at her for a long, searching moment and then seizes her face and kisses her, too hard, too much teeth and pressure and desperation. Lorelei clings to him all the same, though, winding her arms around him fiercely.

"I can't do this," he whispers against the skin of her neck. "I thought I could stop but I can't, I can't stop thinking about you. It's like you're stuck in my *head* or something, Lorelei. Oh my god, what am I doing?"

She strokes his hair and holds him, his long body bent down to encircle hers.

"Does that mean—" she asks, and doesn't finish the sentence.

Chris lets go of her and slumps down onto the bed. Lorelei doesn't join him. The wave of her joy starts to fall away.

"Where's your mom?" she asks. "I thought she always came to see you play."

"I didn't invite her to the house party that's paying us in booze," Chris says. "I'm pretty good, but I'm not *that* honest."

"So there are some things you'll lie about. Just not me."

"It's not only the lying," Chris says. "Trust me, I don't want to put you through . . . anything."

"Nik told me about Lisa."

"Of course he did. I mean, it sucked for her too, you know. Lying and sneaking around and—"

"I'm not her, though."

"Of course you're not." Chris sits up and gestures to Lorelei. "Come here," he says.

"No."

"I can't abandon her," he says. "I can't—"

"So don't abandon her. Make time for both of us. You could do it if she knew."

"I can't tell her."

"What do you think she'll do to you? Kick you out of the house? If she loves you, she'll give in eventually."

"I don't want her to give in, though," Chris says. "I don't want to hurt her and I don't want to hurt you. And I love you too much to lie about you, but I love you too much to just forget about you. Can you see, Lorelei, how much this sucks for me?"

Oma knew what she was when she made her choice to keep silent. Petra didn't when she sang to Henry and pulled him down with her, to live under her spell. Lorelei knows who she is, and what she's capable of. She's not going to keep quiet and she's not going to walk away, or let Chris walk away. Not without a fight.

"Do you believe that I love you?" she asks.

Chris nods.

"I want us to sing together," she says. "Just once. The

duet. Like we talked about." She'll tell him how she feels—really tell him—and let him make up his own mind.

"God, I would love that," Chris says, and kisses her again.

Lorelei marches downstairs and makes herself another drink before she can think better of what she's just put into motion.

The alcohol keeps agreeing with her decision. It's a very rough approximation of whatever Carina mixed her earlier—too sweet, almost sticky—but it doesn't matter, really. Zoe is hanging on Daniel's arm in the center of a small, sparkling group, and Carina is sitting on a low couch, smoking out an open window. Angela and Jackson are wrapped around one another in the kitchen, laughing.

Paul is sitting in the center of a group of guys, and even though she's never cared about him, not really, the way he avoids looking at her stings.

Lorelei knows she doesn't belong anywhere in this sharp-cornered room. When she tries to look outside, she just sees her own face reflected back and forth in the windows, superimposed over the dark stretch of ocean below. She'll get Chris back and they'll leave the minute his set ends. They'll get in a car and drive somewhere together, singing along to the radio, holding hands the whole way home.

Chris comes back downstairs a few minutes after she

does, and The Trouble starts tuning up in earnest. Zoe sees Lorelei and breaks away from Daniel to come stand with her. "Sorry," she says. Her breath is astringent with citrus and vodka. Lorelei watches her pour herself another drink, the shine of the liquid mixing sluggishly with the quarter inch of melted ice in the bottom of the glass. "Did I totally abandon you?"

"Nah." Lorelei regrets the second drink; she wishes one of them was clear-headed. "I went to talk to Chris, actually."

"Talk," Zoe says. She runs her fingers through Lorelei's tousled curls. "I'm so sure."

"We're going to sing together. Like we talked about before we broke up."

"Oh, I'm so excited!" Tipsiness makes Zoe's face mobile and childlike. "I've never heard you sing before!"

"I mean, it probably won't be that great."

"It will, though." Zoe regards Lorelei very seriously. "It will be great, because you are so great. The greatest, really."

"I'm not sure about that," Lorelei says, trying to make it a joke. "I'm pretty sure Paul doesn't think so."

Zoe will not be swayed. "Whatever to Paul. Seriously, Lorelei. You are the greatest and best, and I'm just . . . I wanted to say, all I want is for you to be happy. I think it's amazing that we're friends."

"I think so too," Lorelei says.

"I love you," Zoe tells her.

"I love you too," Lorelei says.

Zoe wouldn't love her if she knew, maybe, but then, she doesn't have to. No one does. If it works right, all it's going to do is open a door. Lorelei's family is good at singing, but better at keeping secrets, and she's her mother's daughter, and her grandmother's too.

By the time she's called on to perform, she's had plenty of opportunity to get nervous again. The Trouble seems to blow through their set with unusually polished ease, and Daniel's drunk hipster friends dance around happily, whooping and hollering between songs. Lorelei sees some of the girls eye Chris with interest, watching his shaggy hair and full, bright smile, the way he gets close to the mic and cups it in one long-fingered hand as he sings.

When it's time, he invites her up with a nod of his head. "This is Lorelei," he says to the crowd. "Everyone say, 'Hi, Lorelei.'"

"Hi, Lorelei!" Zoe's voice is loudest of all.

Chris puts his arm around her. He's warm and solid, the surest thing.

I love you, Lorelei thinks. *I love you, and I need you to be brave for me.*

Her nerves disappear the minute the beat kicks in. It's the same slow, driving build that caught her that day in their practice space. Chris takes the first verse slower than she's ever heard it and he looks at her while he sings. It's so clear, in that moment: Whatever there is between the two of them is palpable, and powerful. It's too big for Lorelei to deny any longer.

She comes in on the chorus. She meant to sing it a little on the low side, the safe side. She knew what she was doing with Jackson, but she's never tried singing in front of a crowd before—not on purpose, anyway—and she's not sure whether her siren powers will work on just Chris or if there will be collateral damage. So she looks at him. She thinks only of him.

When she starts to sing, though, sound pours out of her. It's like opening a valve or tapping a vein: Lorelei wails under the pressure of so much at once, sound and feeling exploding from behind a broken dam. The spaces within her that seemed to be hollow were in fact full of longing. Now months of desperate craving are laid bare for the world to hear. *I love you* becomes *I need you,* and *I need you to be brave* becomes *I need you, I need you, I need you to save me, I'm so scared of losing you, of being on my own, of having no one to take care of me. I need you. I need I need I need I need I need I need you.*

Lorelei's knees buckle as the chorus ends. She sways, almost stumbles, but keeps her feet.

Chris starts the second verse, but his voice is mechanical and flat. His eyes are locked on hers; if she didn't need the song to keep going, he would cut it off and let it drop. On the second chorus he steps away from the microphone, handing it over to her.

Lorelei thinks she should be scared but she isn't. The first chorus was a little messy, but she'll clean it up now. The second time is like the second drink: so much easier to swallow. She sings out as sweet and serious as she can, the same words again, again.

She hears someone calling her name faintly. Zoe is saying

Lorelei, waving and smiling, dancing in Daniel's arms. Even Paul is dancing, not frowning or avoiding her anymore.

Lorelei looks out at Zoe and loves her. She looks at Carina and loves her. She loves Daniel for making this happen, and she loves all of his dumb, rich friends.

Lorelei wants to stay like this forever. She never wants it to end.

The bond between her and Chris has been twisting and fraying, sparking like electrical wire. Lorelei feels the moment when she loses control, and it snaps and then spreads: she can feel herself catching them up in turn, everybody in the room coming under some version of the spell, and it's not love, that's not it, they're just—dancing, and smiling, glassy-eyed, like they can't stop. Lorelei surges forward, trying to rush her way to the end of the song.

But even she is caught up now. The floodgates are open, and the sound she's kept locked in the back of her throat is unleashed. It roars through her, a force all its own. There is no stopping it until it's done with her. Jackson and Bean and Chris keep playing. She makes it through the chorus once more, just once. All of the room's attention is focused on her. She's at the center of everything.

Lorelei closes her eyes and wrenches herself out of the song with all the strength she has. The boys keep playing.

"Come on," someone calls out. "Keep singing!"

"Keep singing," Chris says. He leans against her too heavily. "Please, Lorelei—"

"I'm done," she says to Bean and Jackson. "I'm done," she says again. "The song is over, let's—"

"Keep singing," Bean calls over the frantic beat. Everyone keeps moving in time with it. They're caught up in a crazy, synced unison. No one can break away from it. There's a compulsive regularity to their movements.

"Stop," Lorelei cries out. "Stop, stop, *stop*." The last *stop* comes out as a piercing shriek, high and thin and awful.

Bean drops his drumsticks. It takes a moment for the fuzz of the guitar and bass to fade from the amps.

The whole house descends into sudden, total silence.

No one moves. Everyone watches her. Lorelei is frozen to the spot, rigid with terror.

"Lorelei?" Zoe asks, soft and sweet.

It's her voice that breaks the spell. Lorelei is shot through with adrenaline, and she turns and runs back up the stairs, to the room where she and Chris kissed—an hour ago, maybe, or in some other lifetime. She slams the door behind her and locks it for good measure. She thinks to herself over and over: *What just happened?*

And then: *Oh my god, what have I done?*

❧ ☙

They come knocking. First it's Jackson. "I told you," he says. "I told you to just— Please, look, come back, okay? Everyone wants you to, Lorelei, please."

Then it's Bean, who she's never known to plead. "I want to— Can we do that again, please, please, let's, Lorelei—"

Then it's Daniel, and then Carina. "Come on," they all say. "Once more, just once more. I want to hear that again." She ignores them, and presses her face into the soft mound of pillows. The guest room is as stark as the rest of the house. There's nothing as human as a box of tissues to blow her nose with.

Zoe comes and sighs a little bit. "I don't understand what's going on," she says. "I wish you would come out and have fun with everyone. You were amazing, L. Everyone wants you to come back and sing more. The party might go all night if you would just come out again." It's terrifying to hear her own words in each of their mouths. *I don't want this to ever end.*

Chris comes last. He leans his body against the door and doesn't say anything, and for a while she can't be quite sure it's him. Finally he speaks. "Hey, baby," he says. He doesn't sound so strange. He sounds almost normal, she tells herself. "I brought you some water."

Lorelei is thirsty and tired. The first wave of adrenalized fear is gone, replaced by shaky numbness. She's tired of trembling, and waiting.

She gets herself up, courage in hand. *We were always already in love,* she tells herself before she opens the door.

He doesn't look like a zombie. Not at first, anyway. But when she gets closer, the signs are all there, unmistakable: his smile is a little too wide and his pupils are a little too large. He sits on the bed and lets her sniffle and sip the water for a while before he starts kissing her temples, her cheeks, the corners of her mouth.

"Hey," Lorelei says, "hey, hey," but he keeps kissing her, running his hands over her fretfully, like he just can't quite get enough contact.

"You sounded amazing," he murmurs. The words are so sweet and intimate, whispered close against her skin. They turn Lorelei's blood to ice. Glaciers form in her stomach, their edges jagged. "Why don't you sing like that all the time?"

"I don't know," she says, forcing a laugh. "I'm not sure I liked it that much, actually."

"You're so good, though." Chris pulls away enough to look at her. "You made me feel things, Lorelei. It was like, all of a sudden everything got very clear, you know? I listened to you and thought, okay, okay, this girl is— *I love you.* I can take care of you. I can make sure you aren't ever lonely, or alone."

Lorelei closes her eyes. *This is what I wanted,* she reminds herself. It doesn't feel like a victory, though. Instead, it seems tainted and ugly. She thought she could work it subtly. She was wrong. Her voice is a sledgehammer, and now she's sitting in a room full of what it shattered.

"Are you sure about that?" she asks. She wonders if she could use her voice to undo it, but that seems like an obviously bad idea, using magic she doesn't understand to fix magic she doesn't understand.

"Of course I'm sure," he says. He cups a hand against her cheek. His skin is rough with calluses. Lorelei takes his hand between her own palms and skims her fingertips over the raised patches. These are marks he's made on himself over the course of hours and years. He's worked his hands into shape so that they can bend strings to make music, so he can make the music he loves without the music causing him pain.

Chris says, "I was never sure before. That's why— I'm so sorry that I lied."

"You lied." Time stands very, very still. "About what?"

"About my mom." Chris is reckless with the need to confess to her. Lorelei wishes she could make him stop. "She's never made a rule about dating, really. But I always felt so awful. And it was easier to explain it if it was her fault. It was easier to let you believe that—but it doesn't matter, because I love you too much for it to matter, and I know that now."

"She said she never wanted to see me again."

Chris cocks his head and looks at her. "She was pissed that she'd talked to you like that," he says. "Gotten emotional. Told you those stories. And I mean, I wouldn't have made up the rule if she wasn't so lonely. If she didn't need me to stay around."

"But it was never her rule." Reality is a slow, cold thing. "You made it up, because it was *easier*."

"Because I love her," Chris says. "I didn't know how to be there for the two of you at once." He grabs her hands and holds them in his own. "I was so confused," he goes on. "I didn't know what I wanted, and I felt horrible, Lorelei, about you, and about Mom. About everything. But it's so clear now. It's like—like everything that wasn't you just faded away from me. That's how I felt when I met you, when I heard you sing the first time. It was like you woke me up, like you—"

"When did I sing to you?" The cold in Lorelei's belly seeps softly outward, wrapping tendrils around her shoulders, elbows, and knees. It locks her joints into place. "When, Chris, when—"

"You finished my song," he says. "You don't remember?

That night at the show, on the street, you sang that last line, and I—"

Oh lord, won't you buy me a Mercedes Benz? Of course she sang to him, that one little phrase, that tossed-off nothing. She didn't even realize he heard her; she certainly didn't think he could have caught anything from it if she did. She wasn't thinking about anything at all in the moment.

But he found her at school on Monday and walked too close, asked too insistently. She thought it was just her. She thought maybe he just saw her, maybe he just loved her, and that was all. But he didn't. He wouldn't have. He didn't love her enough not to lie to her: she gave him a taste, and it was too much and not enough.

The room spins. Lorelei is sick and shaking and everything is moving around her, so much color, so much light, Chris touching her, touching her, saying things, she can't, she can't, he's been under her spell every minute, and she can't—

"I have to go," Lorelei says. "Can you find Zoe and Carina for me? Can you tell them we have to go right now?"

32

ZOE AND CARINA DON'T understand. "Could you just—" Carina starts as they're buckling themselves into the car. Zoe socks her in the arm to keep her from finishing the question. Lorelei is in the backseat by herself, still shivering.

"I'm sorry," Zoe says. Lorelei asked them not to talk about it, and they're trying. "But, like, I almost can't even believe that was you, Lorelei. I can't believe you don't, like, sing all the time."

Carina says, "You just sounded great, that's all. I was only going to say if you *wanted* to, you could. You should. I don't know. Yeah. Okay, Zoe?"

"I'm sorry you're feeling weird, L," Zoe says. She reaches back to touch Lorelei's knee. "But it might make you feel better? To sing a little more?"

Lorelei wants to scream. *Stop talking about it,* she wants to yell, but it's useless, clearly: they're trying, and they can't seem to let it go. Her phone buzzes again and again in her purse, with texts from Jackson, Paul, Angela, Chris. *Come back.* She imagines all of them milling around uselessly, in that beautiful house so high above the city, trying to find the rhythm they're looking for. Something to hold them all in place again.

She can feel it, now, in the beat of her heart, the steady pulse that powers her. She could unravel herself and tie them all up again. *I won't do it,* Lorelei promises, and then remembers all of the promises she's made and broken since school started in September. She's not nearly as good as she's always thought she was. Oma and her mother were both right about one thing: She didn't want to know. Not really.

The rest of the ride back to Venice is quiet. As they pull up in front of Lorelei's house, Zoe asks, "You're sure you don't want to sleep over?"

"Nah," Lorelei says. "Thanks, no, I'm cool. I'll call you tomorrow—"

"You should," Zoe says. "I want you to—" But the rest of the sentence is lost.

Lorelei slams the car door behind her and almost runs up the steps to the house. She closes the door and slumps against it, breathing hard. She should feel safe, now, but she doesn't, really. She carries her own danger around with her. Destruction is always lying in wait, under her skin and at the back of her throat. Her own breath is ready and waiting to take her world apart.

33

LORELEI WAKES UP HUNGRY. Her stomach is clenched against emptiness, and her head hurts. With her eyes still closed, she thinks, *I want chicken soup*. Oma's is thick and rich and garlicky, and perfect for when she's feeling a little bit off. She thinks, *When was the last time Oma made soup, anyway?* before she remembers that Oma hasn't made soup in a while now, and loss comes crashing through her all over again.

When it's done with her, the coldness in her bones tightens and resolves itself, and she remembers the night before.

Her first sleepy desire for something warm and comforting curdles in her stomach. Her sheets are twisted, looped and knotted around an ankle, a wrist. She kicks herself free and sits up, pushing the tangle of hair off her face. She went to bed in last night's makeup, and her pillowcase is smeared with it, black and pink. What a mess.

Nik is downstairs, sitting at the dining room table with a textbook in front of him and a bowl of half-eaten oatmeal at his side. "Hey," he says when she passes by. He barely looks up from his work. "We're on our own this morning—Mom and Dad took Jens on a tour of UCLA."

"How'd you get out of that one?"

"Didn't apply. I'm not staying in California for college," Nik says. "They know that."

"You think Jens will?"

"I think Jens finds a lot of ways to avoid saying no to stuff."

In the kitchen, Lorelei opens the fridge and the freezer, but there's no magical leftover soup to be had. Nik is saying something in the other room, but his voice is muffled and she can't quite make it out. She slams both doors closed again and roots through the cabinets for a while before giving up.

She goes back into the dining room and asks Nik, "What did you say?"

"I asked what you were up to."

"Um. Nothing. I wanted soup but there isn't any. I might go out and get some in a minute."

"How was the thing last night?" Nik asks.

Lorelei freezes. He doesn't seem to notice.

"Jackson texted me something—I think he was drunk. Anyway, he said you sang?"

She nods.

"He wasn't making any sense," Nik says. "But he was superexcited about whatever you did."

Lorelei can't quite get her face to look normal. This time Nik does notice; he frowns, shuts his book, and turns his full attention to her.

"Meanwhile, I was here making myself miserable," he says. His smile is crooked. "Breakups suck."

They do, of course. Lorelei hopes she didn't do the wrong thing, interfering with Nik and Jackson. She doesn't want to add another name to the list of lives she's screwed up this year. Considering all of them—going through them one by one—slices through the flimsy barricades she's been trying to keep up between herself and what she did last night. There's no denying that she screwed up then.

Nik sits while she thinks, open and patient. His tenderness is sandpaper against her skin. It's unbearable to think of him loving her when she's so recently learned how to hate herself.

The crying happens so suddenly and thoroughly that it takes her by surprise. Lorelei puts her head in her hands and cries dry, ugly sobs that wrack her chest and make her shoulders heave and her lungs spasm. There are so many kinds of crying, she has discovered in these last few months. This feels compulsive, almost physically necessary, like vomiting: a way to get something poisonous out of her body.

After a little while Nik puts a tentative hand on her back. "C'mon," he says. "Whatever happened can't have been *that* bad."

Lorelei lifts her head enough to shake it once, hard.

"You think it's worse than anything I've seen?"

She can leave her head on the table and shrug.

"Seriously, L, do you really need to hear it? About what I did?"

Lorelei doesn't say anything.

"Yeah," Nik says. "Okay. I can tell you that story, if that's

236

what it will take for you to believe me. But you have to sit up and look at me while I do it."

Curiosity needles her into obeying. Her face is streaked with salt and snot, and she feels ugly and puffy. She wipes her nose defiantly on the back of one hand.

"It's Chris's fault, actually," Nik says. "When he disappeared, when his dad got sick, Jackson started driving me home after soccer and stuff, you know? That's when we started talking, really talking, and I—"

"Are you gay?" Lorelei asks. Her nose is stuffed up, and her voice is flat and nasally. "I mean, have you, like, always been gay, or whatever? It's fine, I don't care either way. I just wanted to understand. I guess."

Nik shrugs uncomfortably. "I don't know about all of that," he says. "I'm not sure."

"But have you always? With guys?"

"Jackson was the first," Nik says. "Not the first one I thought about, but the first one anything happened with."

"Before Angela?"

"Before Angela." Something tightens around his eyes and mouth as he says the name. Lorelei feels awful all over again. She definitely shouldn't be in the middle of any of this.

"Jackson told me about it, kind of," she says. "After I saw you guys. That you used to hook up, and you stopped, and then, you know. Halloween." She won't let on yet that she knows that it kept on happening after.

"And then Halloween," Nik agrees. "That part is your fault."

"How is it my fault?"

"Well, I can't bear it being my fault," Nik says cheerfully. "And you make sense, in a way."

"Did you ever think he was going to break up with Angela?"

"No."

"So you just—"

"I didn't think about it at all," Nik says. "I just *wanted*. I missed him. It was so much easier to say yes, when he asked."

"Love is a trap," Lorelei says, recalling that conversation in the kitchen and the hundreds of complicated things she didn't know when they had it. She ignored what he was saying, then, because ignoring it was easy when she didn't know it was true.

"Love's a goddamn mess," Nik says. "I fucked it up pretty good, anyway."

Lorelei sighs. Nik gives her the corner of a smile.

"He wanted to go public. Before Angela. He wanted us to be together for real, and I was scared. I was the one who said no." He shakes his head. "It's, um, it's something I decided, and that's taken me a long time to admit even to myself. We could have been together. And I could have said no, when he asked, when he was with someone else. So really, L, whatever happened, whatever you did or think you did—it's not the worst thing in the world, I promise. Everyone has their own personal catastrophe story."

Lorelei starts to shake all over, like the first rumblings of a big, bad quake. Nik hurt Jackson and Angela, but mostly he went after himself. Her mistakes were aimed outward, at everyone around her. That is different. It's worse. "You got scared," she repeats.

"Yeah," he says. "Now are you ready to tell me what this is all about?"

"I did something to Chris. I put him under a love spell, kind of," Lorelei says, all in a rush.

Nik has the courtesy not to laugh.

"Oma told me not to sing when I was little," Lorelei starts. "And again, recently. And then after she died, Mom told me it was because of a curse, which seemed crazy, but I got in touch with Hannah—our great-aunt—and she said— look, I know this is insane—she said we're all sirens. Me and Mom and Oma and her. I'm a siren. And last night I sang to Chris."

"Lorelei." Nik reaches out for her. She puts her hands on the table, but they won't stop shaking. Her nails clatter frantically against the glossy wood.

"I know it sounds crazy. I don't know how to prove it to you, okay, but it's true. It's totally true."

"I believe that you believe it," Nik says carefully. "Is that enough? For now?"

"You should have seen them last night, Nik. It really— It was like they were possessed."

"And you're sure you weren't seeing stuff? You know, confirmation bias, just because Oma and Mom told you to expect it?"

"Read me Jackson's texts," Lorelei says.

Nik fishes out his phone and scrolls to find what he wants.

"*Lorelei sang tonight and totally killed it,*" he reads. "I mean, there are some autocorrect mishaps, but it's close. Anyway, then there's another one that says, *She went home but she should come back. Tell Lorelei to come back.*" He pauses. "I just kind of, um, assumed he was drunk."

"That's it?"

"There's another one," Nik admits. He frowns down at the phone. "It just says your name, Lorelei. He just, uh, he just sent me your name. A couple of times. Um."

"I can go get mine," Lorelei says. "I'm sure I've got weirder stuff than that."

"What, so you put some kind of whammy on everyone at this weird birthday party by singing to them?"

"Everyone."

"And now they're all in love with you? Are Chris and Jackson gonna come beat down our doors and fight each other to the death if they can't have you?"

"It's not like that," Lorelei says.

"I'm sorry. I'm sorry. I won't make fun."

"I thought I could focus on him," Lorelei explains. "On Chris. And just let him know how I felt. That's all I was trying to do: to make sure he knew that I wanted to be with him. And then it got away from me. I wanted it to go on all night. I was having so much fun."

"And then they wanted it to go on all night too." Nik sighs and rubs his hands together. "I mean, you have to admit, L, it sounds kind of crazy. It's hard to believe."

"You think I want to believe it?"

"I see you've got yourself tied up in knots about it, that's for sure," Nik says.

Lorelei's voice sounds so small when she says, "I wish Oma was here."

"Even though she was a siren, and she never told you?"

"Yeah. I mean, maybe she could—I don't know, maybe she would have been able to tell me how to undo it, or fix it. Or something."

Nik stands, and Lorelei stands too. He wraps her up in a hug, fitting his arms tightly across her back. Her head rests in the hollow of his shoulder, and his chin butts gently against the top of her head. The last time she hugged one of her brothers it was Jens in Oma's hospital room. Nik is just as tall. "I miss her too, you know," he says. "I miss her cooking like crazy."

"I wanted her soup this morning," Lorelei admits. "And I miss her knitting me terrible hats to wear to school too."

Nik laughs. "I know, right? It's LA, it's sixty-five in the depths of December, and we have wool caps coming out of our *ears*."

Lorelei lets herself laugh too. "I miss thinking someone else was in charge," she says. Nik pulls her in tighter, closer. "I really fucked up, Nik," she says. "Whatever else you believe, trust me on that, okay."

"Oh, baby." Nik squeezes her once, hard, and then lets her go. "I can't do anything about that," he says. "But let's get some breakfast in you before we try to take anything else on, okay? I don't know what I can do about sirens, but I feel like between the two of us we can figure out how to make some chicken soup."

34

WHEN THEY OPEN THE front door to leave, Chris is sitting on the porch. He hasn't changed his clothes since last night. He's blank-eyed and exhausted. His gaze is unfocused until Nik moves aside and Lorelei steps into view. Then he snaps to attention.

"I'm here," he says. "I didn't know if you would want me to come in, but I thought I should be close by."

I need you I need you I need you I need you.

He moves to stand and come toward her. Nik shifts himself between them again. "What are you doing here?" he asks.

"Lorelei, please," Chris says. "Tell him. We love each other. You need me. I have to keep you safe."

Nik turns around to look at Lorelei. It's awful to watch his face change as he begins to believe—*really* believe—in what she's done. "This is what you were talking about," he says. "But they're not all like this, right?"

"No one else is on the porch, anyway," Lorelei says. "I got Chris worst of all."

"You've got me, baby," Chris says. He moves toward

her like a puppet on strings. She wanted Chris to choose her; instead, she made him need her. She got love and desire mixed up. His body has become the staging ground for her battle against herself. "You got me, I promise. I'm here. We'll never be apart again."

"That's not what she wants," Nik says.

"Hey," Lorelei tells him. She touches the back of his shoulder. She can't fix it, but she can at least offer Chris a little temporary relief. "He won't hurt me, okay, Nik. Just give us a minute, yeah?"

Nik steps aside. Chris's face lights up. He rushes into her arms and sags against her, melting with relief. Lorelei holds herself rigid so she won't shiver at the wrongness of his touch.

After a minute, though, her body adjusts. Having Chris in her arms is still familiar, even after everything. She brings one hand up to stroke his hair. "Have you tried thinking about other things?" she asks gently.

Chris shakes his head. "My whole brain is you," he says. "It was never like this before. I don't understand how I thought about anything else."

"It was different before," she says.

He nods happily.

"No, I mean I did something to you, Chris, something not good."

"I'm sure you had a reason."

Yeah, she had a reason. Everyone has a reason. Except now all of his reasons are hers.

"Never mind," she says. "Nik and I are going to the store, okay? You want to come with us?"

Of course Chris says yes.

At the grocery store, Chris hovers at Lorelei's back, glaring protectively over her shoulder when anyone looks at her. He keeps touching the knobs of her spine where they rise above the neck of her sweater, as if to make sure that she's really there. His spell-struck eyes under the store's fluorescent lights are bright and empty.

Before all of this, Lorelei always thought that magic was real or it wasn't. If she was a creature or a witch, she would get swept up into some parallel universe, to ride dragons and conquer evil sorcerers. She's never read a story about someone being enchanted into going to the produce aisle to pick up onions, garlic, and potatoes for soup.

When they get home, they convince Chris to watch some television, at least, to keep him out of Lorelei's hair. "I'll be right here," she tells him. He nods. He doesn't seem to care what they pick out for him to watch.

"You weren't kidding," Nik says under his breath when they're finally alone. "Jesus, Lorelei, what did you *do*?"

"I didn't know," she says. "Or I thought I did, but I told you, okay, I fucked up."

"It's gonna take a lot more than chicken soup to fix this." Nik's mouth is set and grim. He chops vegetables fiercely.

"Do you think you would have done it, if you could, though? To Jackson?"

"Jesus, Lorelei!"

"Sorry."

"That's a really messed-up question."

"It is. I'm so sorry. You don't have to—"

"I wouldn't do it now," Nik says. "Like, having seen Chris. Obviously I wouldn't do that. And it's not like I want to— I don't know. He's not right for me. We're not good for each other. I want it to be over."

"So no."

"I've done a lot of dumb things to make it stop hurting," Nik says. "There are times when I would have done it. Absolutely. Anything. I would have done anything." He finishes chopping his onion with a flourish and sweeps the pieces into a pile. "Okay?"

"I wasn't trying to prove a point." Lorelei doesn't know whether she has to tell Nik about what she did to Jackson. Probably. Probably she should. Everyone tried to warn her, and she had to make her own mistakes. Nik deserves the same. But she can't do it yet—not with Chris still broken in the next room. One problem at a time.

The front door opens and then slams shut again. Lorelei and Nik exchange a guilty look. Chris is in the den with the TV on; as long as he doesn't move, and her parents go straight upstairs, they might get away with it.

Lorelei listens to her mother's footsteps tap-tap-tapping up the stairs; her father finishes a conversation with Jens and then follows. She exhales most of the breath she's been holding. Then she hears Jens coming toward the kitchen.

"Did you think we'd abandoned you?" he asks. "Did you go into survival mode in the four hours you were left to your own devices?"

"Just making soup," Nik says. "There's gonna be plenty when we're done." His voice is deliberately mild. Lorelei has never seen one twin try to fool the other. She's never had a secret with either of her brothers before. Somehow it seems like the first time she's earned her own little place in the family.

Jens says, "I'm not sure I trust either of you in the kitchen."

"Does that mean you're going to help?"

"That means I'm going to supervise," Jens says. "First of all, Lorelei, stop hacking at the garlic, you don't need it that small."

"The recipe said minced."

"What recipe?"

Nik points to his phone where it's propped between the counter and the wall.

Jens laughs. "Didn't anyone ever tell you not to trust what you read on the internet?"

"You have a better idea?"

Jens answers by pulling one of Oma's binders off the shelf where they've been sitting, mostly untouched, for as long as Lorelei can remember. There are three of them, thick and inelegant, stuffed with handwritten notations and pieces cut from newspapers and index cards brought over from the old country. Oma only ever referred to the recipes in passing—they were mostly there to jog her memory, as part of an ongoing conversation with herself.

"You read German now?" Nik asks.

"I've been teaching myself," Jens says easily. "Kitchen vocabulary, anyway. Seemed like a shame to just let her work all disappear."

He sounds dispassionate, like he's talking about studying for a test or writing a paper: *might as well, really*. But Lorelei knows what it means to sit and struggle with a language that won't unfurl itself for you, and to reckon with the memories and the headaches that it stirs up when you start making your own work from a dead woman's papers. She's been tugging on the knots of one kind of family legacy while Jens untangled another downstairs. Only one of them has been keeping the family fed with his work.

"That's really cool," she says.

"I haven't gotten to the chicken soup one yet," Jens tells her. "But I can rough it out for you right now if you want."

"Please," Lorelei says.

"Put that garlic in a Tupperware; I'll use it for something later."

Lorelei doesn't know what passes between her brothers while she's finding the container and making space in the fridge, but when she's done, Jens is looking at her softly, like he knows just how badly she needs the distraction of something to do right now.

"If I translate, can you take notes?" he asks.

Lorelei says, "Yes."

35

LORELEI CAN'T BEAR TO make Chris leave. Every time she brings it up he just *looks* at her and she finds herself saying, "Later, then, I guess, that's fine." He can stay for dinner, she tells herself. Her dad might not even notice that he's been enchanted. Her mom probably won't come down at all.

She's not that lucky, though, and she hasn't been in a while. She and Nik are setting the table when Petra walks into the dining room.

"You really cooked," she says.

"Soup is easy," Nik says.

"And who did you invite over?"

"I'm Chris," Chris says. "Lorelei's boyfriend."

Lorelei is watching Petra, so she sees her mother see Chris's spell-blank eyes. She sees Petra's face go slack with disbelief, and then pull up and in, again, tight tight tight, to protect herself.

Petra leaves the room without another word.

Henry was behind her. He sees the same thing: Chris

smiling and nodding, Lorelei wretched, Nik looking around at all of them, trying to figure out what to say.

"Oh," Henry says. "Did you make enough for all of us?"

"Of course." Jens brings the last bowl in from the kitchen and sets it in front of Henry's place.

"I'm Lorelei's boyfriend," Chris repeats.

Jens does his best to make dinner bearable. He talks to Chris about the precalc class they're both taking. He nudges Nik into saying some things about soccer. This kind of exchange used to drive her crazy when he and Oma did it, but now Lorelei appreciates Jens's commitment to normalcy at all costs. He fills up the silence so she won't have to, so she won't just start spilling out apologies.

Nik even rallies after a little while, and the two of them do the same dance they perfected years ago at this same silent table. The twins' banter doesn't need anything to sustain it except the threat of awkward silence. Nik barely breaks stride when he turns to Lorelei and says, "You should go see if Mom is hungry. We can get the dishes."

Chris takes the hand that's been resting heavily on Lorelei's thigh and cradles it against his chest. He watches her climb the stairs, and settles himself at the bottom to wait.

Lorelei gets to the top, turns a corner, and leans against the wall to breathe a long sigh of relief. She hadn't really understood what it meant to have Chris watching her until she escaped his gaze. Now she's impossibly loose and light: just herself again. She wishes she could keep that feeling.

Instead, she goes to her mother's study.

This is where Petra told her version of their family's story: the tale of an evil mother who silenced her daughter, and how the daughter, in turn, cursed her own daughter and granddaughter, out of spite or maybe because she thought she knew what was best.

Petra was wrong, though. Their legacy isn't a fairy tale, in which true love or a witch's death can break a spell; it's myth, full of shape-shifters and dark corners, bad middles, messy endings. No moral.

Lorelei hasn't had the courage or energy to tell her mother that she knows the truth, now, and that it's better and worse than either of them could have imagined.

"Don't," Petra says when Lorelei pushes her closed door open. "Leave me alone, please."

"Mom. I need to talk to you."

"Don't you think you've done *enough*?" Petra's eyes are dry now, but her face shows the signs of recent tears.

"You don't understand."

"What am I not understanding? Oma told you not to sing. I told you not to sing. I told you what happened when I tried it with your father. And still you went ahead and—"

"I got in touch with Oma's sister, Hannah, a few weeks ago."

"And she told you to ignore us?"

"She told me what I was," Lorelei says defiantly. "What we are."

"Cursed? Miserable?"

"Sirens," Lorelei says.

Petra's laugh is almost hysterical.

"Oh, sweetheart," she says. "I wish it was that simple."

"It is," Lorelei says. "Or, it's not simple, but it's— That's what Hannah said. Why would she lie?"

"How could that possibly be true?"

Lorelei lifts her empty hands and spreads them out wide in front of her. "How could any of it be true?" she asks. "But you know it is."

"Whatever we are, you still broke that boy," Petra says. "I hope you're ready to live with that."

"I didn't—break him. I didn't mean to."

Petra doesn't say anything.

"I'm sorry," Lorelei says. "I thought I was doing it differently."

"Everyone always does," Petra says.

36

IN THE MORNING SHE wakes early. She forwards the email from Hannah to Petra, typing at the top: *See? I'm not making this up.*

Downstairs, Chris is asleep on the couch, tucked under one of Oma's knitted blankets and snoring softly. So Nik couldn't get him to leave last night. She wonders what Jens thinks, and how her father feels, before she shuts off that train of thought. It's too murky and painful, and she has to keep moving forward.

Outside, the usual marine layer is thick and cold, piled underneath something darker, something that looks like it won't burn off by noon. She shivers in her sweatshirt but doesn't turn back. Her feet keep her moving forward. Her body is finally giving in to instinct, and going home.

When she arrives, the beach is deserted, just blank sand and rolling spume as far as the eye can see. The waves move back and forth. Their rhythm is the same as the rush of blood in her veins.

The gulls cry out from their throats.

It isn't like she decides to go in, exactly, but she's already cold and shaking.

Lorelei pulls off her sweatshirt and her jeans, her underwear. She kicks off her shoes. She leaves them in a pile in the sand. Her body is naked against the air that's full of seawater, salty on her skin and her tongue. It feels good and right and not enough, not yet. She walks into the water slowly and deliberately.

The first wave laps up against her ankles and calves, stinging and then numbing. She closes her eyes and keeps her arms at her sides as she advances, her body going quiet at the knees, the waist. An electric shock trembles through her when the water reaches her lungs. By the time she ducks her head under, she's burning up with the cold.

Lorelei tries to swim out but her arms are weak and tired. The tide has its own ideas. It keeps tangling her up and spitting her back toward the land. Still, she presses forward, toward the horizon and the deepness she's never allowed herself to know before.

Waves crest up and up, over and over. Every time she emerges, gasping, there's another one curving over her head. She struggles helplessly, spitting and coughing, her hair knotting itself around her neck and in her eyes. She loses her way.

Finally she comes up to a moment of relative calm. The waves have turned into swells, rolling without breaking. The adrenaline that's been protecting her is starting to wear off, and she's shaking so hard it feels like her bones are rattling.

Her lips and the tips of her fingers are blue. A huge wave is gathering itself off in the distance. *I should go back in,* she thinks.

They've lived near the beach for almost her entire life, but Lorelei can barely remember the last time they came here as a family. She would have been six, maybe. The memory is dim and fuzzy, faded at the edges, nonsensical in the way childhood recollections are. She spent most of the afternoon on the towel at Oma's side, sitting under an umbrella. After lunch the boys dragged her out with them. She loved to swim but was wary about giving herself to the ocean, which was so big and so strong.

"Come on," Nik said. He was serious even then, hands on hips. "We have to teach you how."

At first there was just too much of it. The mass of water overwhelmed her. But their father came out with them and held her in his arms when the twins tried to take her out too deep. When she was ready, he carried her toward the horizon. It wasn't so scary after they got past the breakers. Once she'd adjusted, they brought her in a little ways so that Nik and Jens could teach her how to slam up against the waves and how to swim under them, letting them pass right over her head.

It seemed crazy, then, to face down that enormous oncoming rush and throw yourself *into* it, under it. It seemed like you'd never be able to come up again once you went down. It took Lorelei the whole afternoon to train herself to do it, and to believe that she too would surface behind the wave, sitting on its back, her hair slicked against her skull from the water's rushing force.

It's the best way to take on the big ones, Nik told her then. So now she faces down the wave that's coming, the one that looks like it will envelop and destroy her. The water rolls over itself, speeding forward to swallow her whole. *I am your daughter, your daughter's daughter's daughter,* she thinks. She closes her eyes and dives as far down as she can go.

37

LORELEI COMES HOME A WRECK. Nik has finally gotten rid of Chris, or at least he's not in the living room. She makes her way up the stairs with leaden legs. She's so, so tired. Her brain is fuzzy and weak. She has to crawl the last few feet to the bathroom, slumping against the door as she pulls it shut behind her.

Her skin is still wet and her clothes are damp and clinging. She runs a hot bath and lies on the floor to undress, then hoists herself over the lip and into the tub.

She's covered in sand and flecks of seaweed. The bathwater cools quickly against her icy skin, getting grainy and dark as everything she picked up flakes off. It doesn't feel like the ocean did, limitless and purifying, but it's nice, anyway. Lorelei is half human, after all. Her skin craves warmth and quiet just as often as it wants to be rushed upon and overrun.

In the stillness of the bathroom there's nothing to distract her from the situation with Chris, and from what and who she is. A siren: a scream that rings out across water, through dark, at night. What she can do is ugly, or difficult, but it's also hers. It's her.

Some families keep darker secrets, Lorelei knows. Some run to violence or madness or other kinds of ruin. Hers ran to singing and then to silence. They were magic but never the right kind, the kind that can fix things. Just the kind that's good for cracking them open to show you exactly what's inside.

Even though she couldn't have fixed it, Lorelei wishes that Oma was here to talk to. She didn't have spells, but she could have told stories. *Here is how I screwed up; here is how I kept living.* And then Lorelei would know that she was allowed to keep living too.

It would have been a grown-up conversation, she thinks now. She and Oma would have leveled out with each other over time, maybe.

Instead, Oma will only ever have known her as a child.

And trying to stay a child won't bring Oma back. This is Lorelei's after. Now there's nothing to do but live with it. It seems unbearable. Lorelei counts the seconds passing and wonders when she'll stop being surprised to make it through this one—and that one—and the next one—and the next.

Floating in warm, soft water, naked and scraped clean by knowledge, she hears her great-aunt's sentences clear as a ringing bell: *If you use your voice, use it carefully: never sing for anyone you need something from, someone you want to summon or bend or change. Sing for yourself, Lorelei, and you will always find happiness in it.*

Lorelei has only ever allowed herself to sing in desperation and confusion, in moods dark with fear and need. She wonders if doing it just because she wanted to—for herself—would make a difference. Part of her thinks it's too late to care either way; part of her, the part that pulled her body into the ocean, under the waves, and then all the way out again, understands that sometimes *too late* is as soon as you can start.

38

WHEN SHE'S DRY AND WARM, Lorelei takes the bus to Chris's house. He's still spell-wreathed, with big, blank pupils and a smile that unfolds itself for her. "Your mother told me I had to go home," he says. "But I knew you would come."

Lorelei's voice feels like something swollen inside of her, creating a nauseating pressure against the rim of her throat. "Is your mom here?" she asks. Chris shakes his head. "Did you tell her?" Lorelei asks. "About us?"

"I did," he says. He reaches for her. "I told you. She doesn't care. She wants me to be happy. And I want to be with you. To give you what you want."

Lorelei feels the words like her own knife turned back on her, needling against her breastbone: *what you want.* "How did that go?" she asks. "When you told her."

"Not as badly as I would have thought. She doesn't hate *you*, you know. She said you have a beautiful voice."

"Yeah," Lorelei says. Everything is too big and too heavy. She's too tired to keep on.

"Come in," Chris says. "Come upstairs."

Despite herself, Lorelei does.

They curl up in his bed together. Lorelei shelters herself in the cove of Chris's body. If she closes her eyes and holds very still, it seems peaceful to pretend with him. He runs his fingers through her hair and kisses the top of her head. "Finally," he murmurs, drowsy. The draw of his breath lengthens and evens. Lorelei doesn't stir. They both need to rest, she tells herself. She's too wrung out to be useful. She drifts off without meaning to, floating away from herself so slowly that she doesn't even realize that it's happening.

When she wakes again, the angle of the light has changed, and there's something about the stillness of their bodies, the bed and the room, that makes her think: *It's like a grave in here.*

Chris's chest rises and falls in rhythm, but the blank slackness of his body reminds her of Oma's when she was lying in that hospital bed. Lorelei envies him for a moment. She wishes she could put herself under her own spell, and stop caring what happens next. But that's not living. That's what the living give up in order to move on. And it's not what Chris wanted, or would have chosen for himself.

When Oma died, it seemed for a little while like there were no more rules left to break. Lorelei could unravel however she wanted, and it wouldn't matter at all. But just because there wasn't a punishment doesn't mean there wouldn't be consequences. Now it's up to her to figure out how to deal with them.

⁓

In the end there's only one thing for it: "Do you want me to sing for you again?" Lorelei asks. Maybe she can soothe him with her voice, and convince him not to need her so much, though that's just another kind of compulsion. He'll never be the same as he was before he knew her. Everyone leaves marks, but these are scars. Chris might never recover himself from the force of her greed, or her love.

"Yeah," Chris says. His face is lit up with what Lorelei can no longer mistake for genuine feeling. "Of course I do."

They go down to the sunroom together. Lorelei moves carefully, afraid of jostling their fragile peace. Her body feels like it's held together by wet glue. Chris slides into place on the piano bench, fingers poised eagerly over the keys. "Tell me what to play."

"Play me something you love," she says. "Play me what your dad used to like." Maybe she can call him back to something older than her selfish magic.

"You won't know the words," he says.

"I'll make them up."

He plays and she sings. It's the first time they've really done this together, standing apart from each other, making something new. *I release you,* Lorelei thinks, like the words will be enough.

She tries to think of him and him alone, but that's not

how she's known him, so he appears in her imagination as he always does: his dark head bobbing through the hallways or haloed in stage lights, just in front of her or at her side. The air in the room shifts while she sings, rustling like the warm, dry breath of the night they met and the cold, damp spray of the afternoon they broke up. She remembers his hands on her, tender, searching, in his upstairs bedroom, and how badly she wanted him to love her, how the raw edges of her longed for him to reshape her into someone else.

She was looking for love that would save her, which doesn't exist; if love could anchor you in place, Oma would still be here, and so would Chris's father. Lorelei was looking for lightness that didn't balance itself with dark, love without consequence, desire cut free from obligation. She wanted the impossible, and she got it, and now she has to find a way to give it back.

She sings herself into the blank empty center of sound, the part of it that is just sound, and nothing more. The music becomes a wave, and her voice is the energy that moves through water, racing under the ocean's glassy top to throw it forward. Deeper, though, in the very deepest parts, all is calm and still and whole. Lorelei imagines Chris floating up out of it, dazed as he stumbles onto dry, sandy land.

He stops playing abruptly. His hands still and he looks at her, confused. "What was that?" His voice is rusty. "What did you do?"

"I let you go," Lorelei says.

"Did you have me?"

"I did," Lorelei says. Her legs are watery. She drops down next to him on the piano bench. He scoots over as if to make room for her, but he makes a little too much room. She can feel the air between them, stirring the fine hair on her arms.

"I don't understand."

"I put a spell on you," Lorelei says, because that's the simplest way to explain it. "I know how crazy it sounds."

"It does sound crazy," Chris agrees. His tone is less skeptical than it is puzzled. "But it feels like it might be true."

"I never meant to do it. I never wanted to hurt you. Or make you do anything that you didn't want to do."

Chris looks down at his feet and swings them back and forth, back and forth, their arc stunted so he doesn't kick the piano's base. There's a long, uncomfortable pause. "You're still beautiful," he says. "You look the same to me. Mostly. Is your voice—"

"That's really what I sound like," she says. "I'm not— That's not how it works. I'm not a witch or anything. It's just . . . more powerful than some people's."

"I've felt crazy, the last few days," Chris says. He almost reaches out a hand to touch her face, and then pulls it back. "God, did I really show up at your house? What a lunatic."

"It's fine."

"It's messed up."

"It was what I wanted. For you to, you know, want me. To want me enough."

"It was more than enough."

"Too much." Lorelei ducks her head. "I got greedy."

"You broke up with me!"

"I wanted to make you realize what you were missing," Lorelei says. "I tried that, I tried Paul, this guy, it doesn't matter, anyway, I just—I don't know. All I wanted to do was show you that I loved you. I thought if you really knew that, you wouldn't be afraid to love me back. And I'm sorry." Lorelei's voice breaks. "I'm sorry. I hate what I did. I hate that I—that I'll never know if you could have loved me for real, if I'm even—if anyone could have loved me like that."

Chris closes the piano's lid over its keys and rests his elbows on the slick, lacquered wood, shoving the heels of his hands against his eyes. "I don't know what to tell you," he says. "I don't know how I feel. How I've felt."

"Okay."

"I think I almost knew," he says. "I've had girlfriends before, and you—after that night at the Roxy I couldn't stop thinking about you. I wondered. About how sometimes it felt normal, and sometimes—not so much."

"So there were times when it felt normal. Like. Okay."

"I think so." Chris frowns down at the piano. "Hard to tell. I'd never been under a spell before." His laugh is ironic, and short. "I'm sorry. I just—I need some time to think about this. To figure it out."

Which means it's time for her to go. Lorelei stands up and tugs at the hem of her sweatshirt. It's Zoe's, and a little bit baggy on her, but she's glad she wore it. The pool of fabric around her makes Zoe feel present, somehow. It reminds her that there are other people left in the world. She doesn't let herself remember that she hasn't heard from Zoe since the party.

Chris walks her to the front door. He doesn't move to hug her goodbye.

"I'm sorry," Lorelei says again, like it matters.

"Me too," Chris says.

He closes the door carefully. Lorelei listens to the lock clicking into place. There are other people in the world, of course, and there are people who love her, but staring at the blank wood and listening to the silence behind it, she finds it's hard to make herself care.

39

ON MONDAY LORELEI SKIPS SCHOOL. She rides with Jens and Nik, but the minute they get onto campus she starts to feel sick to her stomach. She loses herself in the crowd of students when they near the buildings, and slips back toward the parking lot as soon as she can. She steps off campus, and disappears.

At first she just walks around and watches cars on the street and all the other people who are also wandering around. What is it, exactly, that everyone else does all day?

She distracts herself with the usual things: catching up on homework, pretending to go shopping, thumbing through Facebook on her phone. She visits a coffee shop, and then a juice shop, and then the library. The world is the same as it's always been: boring, and too busy for her. By four p.m. she's unbearably lonely.

Happy hour is just getting started when she ducks into a restaurant filled with drunks saying good morning to each other at the bar. Lorelei takes a little two-seater along the wall and orders a sandwich. She pulls her English book out to read while she eats.

As she's finishing up, one of the men at the bar makes his way over. He's not stumbling, not yet, but his big hand grips a double shot of whiskey so cheap Lorelei can smell the fumes from across the table. He's well-kept but his eyes are bloodshot and there's a soft tremble to him, an unsteadiness that lives under his skin.

He says, "You look like you could use company."

"Not really." Lorelei doesn't have to fake indifference. She just doesn't care anymore. Let him try to talk to her.

"Shouldn't you be in school?"

"If I should, shouldn't you be leaving me alone?" Lorelei is proud of herself for channeling Zoe so effectively. She looks pointedly at the glass in his hand.

"There are a lot of creeps in this place. I should know. I spend a lot of time here."

"I'm sure."

He leans across the table. "You're a very pretty girl," he says. "You should be careful."

Something ugly rushes up in Lorelei. She is a pretty girl, with a pretty voice, and she's never allowed to use it again. She's going to have to put away the most beautiful and un-usual part of herself because she doesn't know how to wield it, because she let it get the best of her. And no one will ever know it. No one will ever know *her*.

No one should want to.

"Maybe you should be careful," Lorelei says. She smiles. There's a song playing at midvolume through the bar's speakers. Deliberately, she starts to hum along. She weaves the melody through with the thinnest strand of compulsion, pulling him to her and braiding him up. His eyes get glassier and his pupils swell. "Don't you think?"

"Very pretty," he repeats. Lorelei doesn't even know what she's doing with him, only that she's doing it, siphoning off the dark feelings inside her because they're too much to contain anymore.

"I'm ugly," Lorelei says. "I'm horrible."

"Okay." He puts the glass down on the table, finally. Her pull is stronger than its thrall. Lorelei's fingers twitch toward it but she doesn't pick it up. She doesn't need it now.

"Tell me how awful I am," she says.

"You're awful," he says. "Like that?" When he says it, she can hear the nastiness in her tune reflected back at her, cruel and delicious. "Like that?" he asks, again. Lorelei hums a little more.

"Awful," he repeats. "No one's ever going to love you, you know. No one could ever love a girl like you. What are you?" He leans forward across the table. "Do you even know?"

A server catches sight of what's going on: the pretty little girl and the big drunk man. He hurries over to stop it. "Everything all right here?" he asks. His eyes dart frantically between Lorelei and the man, and Lorelei and the glass of whiskey on the table. "Can I get you guys anything else?"

Lorelei hums and hums, until his jaw slackens too. "I'm leaving now," she says. "You'll cover my meal, right?" They both nod dumbly. "And forget me," she says. "Like I was never even here." She sings along to the words of the song as she leaves, and watches in the long mirror at the bar as every head turns to follow her out.

It's a little weird, singing her way into places, but it works. There's a row of open-air bars along the beach that Lorelei can slip into from the sidewalk, and if anyone notices her, she has ways of dealing with that.

She's as young and vulnerable as she's ever been, but now she's untouchable too, surrounded by an invisible column of song. The freedom and power lick up her spine. The feeling is intoxicating.

Lorelei embraces the corrosiveness inside herself, and for the first time she understands all the bone-thin girls at school with sallow skin and peeling cuticles, the ones with long sleeves pulled down to hide their wrists and arms. Those girls looked their own darkness in the face and then descended into it. They ate themselves up instead of letting the world do it for them.

Lorelei wants to go on and on, through the night and across the city, into her own black depths.

"Lorelei," someone says. She has to look at Carina for a minute before her brain puts a name to the face.

"Leave me alone." She's too surprised to say it convincingly.

"You shouldn't be here," Carina says. "What are you doing here?"

Lorelei should just sing her into submission and keep going, but Carina looks too much like Zoe, and Lorelei's not quite that ruthless. "I'm serious," she says instead. "I'm fine, okay. Just let me go."

"Where are you going?"

The lie doesn't come quickly enough. Carina reaches down and clamps her hand onto Lorelei's arm. "I know trouble when I see it," she says. "C'mon, sweetheart. I'm getting you the hell out of here."

❦

Carina drives her home in silence, and parks a block away so she can crack the window and smoke a clove. She doesn't ask about the party, which is a relief. If Carina has recovered, she might not be the only one.

She does have some questions, though. "All right," she starts. "I'm gonna need at least a partial explanation for what you were doing in a bar at five-thirty on a weekday."

"What about you?" Lorelei asks.

"I'm in college." Carina waves her hand dismissively. "Different story. Out with it. Is this about that asshole, still?"

"Yeah."

"Breakups suck," Carina says.

Lorelei cracks a smile. "That's what Nik said," she agrees. "That's what everyone says."

"So what makes you think this one is special?" Carina asks. "Why is he worth . . . There's a lot of trouble you can find if you go looking, Lorelei."

"I guess you know from experience."

Carina refuses to take the bait. "That doesn't give you a license to make my mistakes."

"I wasn't in any trouble."

Carina raises a skeptical eyebrow and smokes in silence. Lorelei doesn't know what to say, so she doesn't say anything. The inside of her head is too loud. She misses how quiet it got when she was singing.

"Anyway, he's the asshole," Carina says. She grinds her cigarette butt into the grimy mug jammed into one of the car's cupholders. "I know he's cute and he's older, but if he broke your heart, he's the asshole."

Lorelei shakes her head grimly. She does know this answer. "No," she says. "It was my fault."

"Did he ask you to—"

"No," Lorelei says. "No. Nothing like that." Chris never asked her for anything. That was part of the problem.

"How could it possibly be your fault?"

"I tricked him," Lorelei says. "It's hard to explain, okay, but I did."

Carina laughs. "Oh, honey," she says. "It always feels like that."

"It's not the—"

"Sure, yeah, okay." Carina lights another clove and settles herself into her seat again. "I know you think you've reinvented heartbreak, but trust me, it's always— You have this thing, and it's so beautiful and great and fun. And then it's over, and you've never had anything end like this before, right?"

"Not really, no."

"The trick is to remember that however it ended—

whatever you did and whatever he said—it doesn't erase the stuff that came before it, you know? You don't get to write off the relationship because of a bad breakup. Every relationship ends in a breakup, except maybe one, if you're lucky. But that's your *life*, Lorelei. You can't just, you know, every time some dude ends a thing, you can't be like, well, that was a waste, and I was wrong, and I'm the worst."

"But the stuff that came before is the problem," Lorelei says. "I lied to him. He never knew me at all. So he can't have loved me. Not really."

Carina considers this. "So next time don't lie," she says. "I mean, trust me, there will be a next time."

Lorelei shakes her head helplessly. Not lying will never really be possible for her. She'll always be hiding a part of herself and her family's history.

"I see this is a problem that a quick chat won't begin to solve," Carina says. "C'mon, come over for dinner. Zoe will be happy to see you."

Lorelei shakes her head harder. She isn't ready to face Zoe yet, or the Soroushes' house, where she's always been happy, and welcome.

"You sure?" Carina's phone lights up with a text. "Think about it while I answer this," she says. She drops her cigarette into the coffee cup while she texts. The lit end smolders but doesn't go out.

There's a drag, probably two, left on it. Lorelei picks it up gingerly. The filter is honey-sweet and the smoke burns, unexpectedly, in her lungs. She wonders whether she could smoke it out of herself, scratching up her voice until its power vanishes entirely. Then there would be nothing left to tempt her. And nothing left to lose.

"I should go home," Lorelei says.

Carina looks up. "Oh, give that back," she says. She plucks the clove from between Lorelei's fingers. "C'mon, Lorelei, buck up. You'll survive it, but you have to want to, you know."

40

LORELEI TRIES TO TAKE Carina's advice. She eats dinner and does her homework. She behaves like everything is normal, like she wants it to be. It's helpful. It doesn't solve anything, but it helps her get through the night, and most of school the next day. She wears the idea of normalcy like armor, something that will protect her from her messed-up world.

The fantasy she's cocooned herself in falls apart when she sees Jackson sitting slumped against her locker at the end of the day. He looks underslept and miserable, dark circles blooming like bruises below each eye. Lorelei has never been into Jackson but she's always understood why other girls were—why Nik was, or is. Now his handsomeness is sanded down by sleeplessness and worry. The bones in his face stand out sharply. He doesn't look well.

"Fuck," she says.

"You have to help me," Jackson says. "Please. Lorelei. You have to."

Guilt keeps her from responding for a moment. She's

been so wrapped up in herself that she forgot all about Jackson.

"I can," she says. "I'm sorry. I will."

"Chris told me about you." Jackson won't look her in the eye, but he keeps darting glances at her. "I don't— You did something to me. Those times when you were singing. Right?" Lorelei nods. "So. He says you can undo it too."

"I can," she says. "But we should probably go somewhere. Somewhere else."

"No one's in the practice space this afternoon." He gets up and starts to walk without waiting to see if she's coming. "You'll understand if I don't want to go back to your house. Or take you home to meet my mom."

❦

They pass Zoe on their way to the car. She looks at Lorelei like she doesn't recognize her for a second, and when she does, she looks down, and away.

❦

Lorelei keeps waiting for Jackson to ask her how it can be true, or to prove herself, or something. But he's long past wanting an explanation of his symptoms. All he's interested in is a cure.

"How's Chris doing?" she asks.

"None of your business." Jackson sounds almost cheerful. "I always knew you were bad news."

"You were just jealous."

275

It's mean, and a lie. Jackson doesn't deserve it but she can't take it back.

"Ha. Tell yourself that, though."

He doesn't say anything else until he's letting them into the practice space building. In the hallway between the front door and their studio, he speaks again. "You forget, I met your brother first," he says. "So I always knew your family was a catastrophe."

"Nik's stuff is—"

"It's all the same stuff. You want people all to yourselves, on your own terms. He didn't want to come out, fine. I got a girlfriend. I moved on."

"But you didn't."

"What?"

"You didn't, though. Move on."

"Don't tell me—"

"Listen. I've done everything wrong," Lorelei says. "I mean, just. Everything. You *know* that. But I'm not wrong about this. You still wanted him. You *asked* him. He messed up but you messed up too." It feels so good to accuse someone else. "You were in that one together."

"So get me out of it, please. I asked for that, maybe, but I never asked for this."

Lorelei can't imagine what it's been like: while she's been picking apart the idea of a cursed family, Jackson has had questions with no answers, and her name in his head, and no relief. She acted like part of him belonged to her. She's sick with herself for having done it.

Jackson unlocks the studio with a flourish. Lorelei walks in and the familiarity of the space overwhelms her. She wishes she didn't know this is the last time she'll be here. Her life has felt too full of lasts, lately.

Jackson cracks a window and pulls a long, thin joint out of his backpack. He lights it up and inhales. "You gonna do this or not?" he asks.

"Do you have to do that while I do?"

"How do you think I've gotten through the last few weeks? When I wanted—and then after you—" Jackson takes another hit and holds it until he coughs. "You have no idea what it's been like."

"It's about to be over."

"Humor me."

Lorelei sings. She isn't sure it will work again until it does, and then it's just like it always is: like the teeth of a key clicking against lock pins, and everything opening up all at once.

When she did it for Chris, it felt sad and awful and necessary. The thing between them was a complicated snarl of her feelings and his, what he had on his own and what she made in him. She swept everything up, all together, and then she let him let it go.

Singing for Jackson doesn't feel like anything. She slices through the strings she knotted them together with, and takes back all of her influence. She washes him clean of her compulsion. When she's done, all she can sense in him is faint, resonant relief.

In the quiet that follows, Jackson says, "Thank you."

"Do you feel better?" Lorelei asks.

He says, "No."

He doesn't sound surprised.

Jackson fumbles the keys when he locks up the studio, and when he tries to unlock the car. He drops them twice getting them into the ignition.

"Yeah," Lorelei says. "This isn't happening."

"I can drive," Jackson says.

"No, you can't."

Lorelei pulls out her phone to call someone, and draws a blank. Nik has an away game, and Jens took the car to see him. Chris won't come. She doesn't have Carina's number.

Her dad picks up on the first ring and says, "Are you okay?"

"I'm fine, Dad. I just kind of need a ride."

"Tell me where you are. I'll come right away."

Lorelei can guess what he's imagining: something awful, something to do with Chris. She lets herself sound as tired as she feels when she says, "I promise, you do not have to hurry."

❧❧

The drive to Jackson's happens in complete and total silence.

Lorelei feels so shitty about the situation that she turns to her dad as soon as they're alone and says, "Just so you know, he was stoned. That's all."

Her dad blinks at her.

"I'm not stoned," she says.

"Okay," he says. "Well. Good."

He puts the car in gear and turns them toward home. "I'm not worried about him," he says. "Or Chris." It's strange to hear her dad say his name. "I'm worried about you."

"Why? I'm the one who screwed up."

"I know I haven't been around much since Oma died. Or before that, even."

Lorelei nods cautiously.

"I wish I hadn't let myself disappear on you like that."

Lorelei wants to say: *That has nothing to do with what happened.* Having a different kind of dad wouldn't have saved her from herself.

"It's just that you should know: if you ever want to talk about anything, I'm here for you. I don't know what you know about . . . what happened. But your mother and I, we went through—"

Lorelei cuts him off. "I don't want to talk about it, actually," she tells him. "But thanks for the offer, I guess."

◦⌒◦

At home, Lorelei tries to tally up what she broke and what she's fixed. Chris is fine, but they're over forever, this time, and there's nothing she can do about it. Jackson is fine, but he's probably never going near Nik again.

She owes Nik the truth of what she did to him.

She owes her mother and her father something much, much bigger.

Because if she can undo the effects of her song, it means

her mother probably could too. She could let Henry go. Lorelei could give them what they need to dismantle her family for good.

She's just not ready to do it, yet, is all.

❧

After dinner there's more homework. There's always more homework. Lorelei wants to text Zoe a question about the math, but they haven't spoken since the party, and after their non-encounter at school she's pretty sure there's no pretending it didn't happen and just moving on. There's a very real possibility that Carina told Zoe about seeing Lorelei at the bar, and their conversation after.

There's also a possibility that Zoe is too freaked out to want to be friends anymore. Lorelei can't even let herself consider that one, although she wouldn't blame Zoe for bailing.

She emails one of the other girls in her class the question instead.

Of all of them, this is the smallest and stupidest betrayal. It stings her like a pinprick, sharp and insistent. The smallness somehow doesn't make it hurt any less.

41

LORELEI EATS LUNCH ALONE on Wednesday, sitting in the bleachers like every high school movie cliché. It's lonely, but it's also quiet. She thinks she could learn to appreciate the austerity of her days without Chris, or the band, or her friends. At least everything gets done.

Carina texts her, *are you not speaking to Zoe or something?* Lorelei is tempted not to respond. It's none of Carina's business. It's probably unfixable, anyway. But then there's the little part of her that knows she's being self-indulgent. She owes Zoe a last explanation and apology, at least.

Kind of? she sends back. *Not sure she wants to talk to me.*

Don't be dumb, Carina says. *I thought we talked about this.*

Are you sure? Lorelei wishes she could take it back the minute she sends it. It's too vulnerable. Carina knows how much she loves Zoe, but it feels like rolling over and exposing the thinnest skin, the softest part of her belly. What if Zoe sees it, and knows?

Lorelei. Seriously. Talk to her.

Mrs. Soroush comes to the door. "Hey, Lorelei," she says. "It's been a while."

Lorelei is surprised that she hasn't heard, somehow. She half expected that they wouldn't even let her in.

"Yeah," Lorelei says. "I've been, you know. Busy."

"Is Zoe expecting you? She didn't say . . ."

"She isn't. I'm, um, I'm surprising her. You know. Since it's been a while."

"Aren't you sweet! Zoe's just in the den." Mrs. Soroush stands back to let Lorelei pass. "I hope you two are planning on getting some work done," she calls down the hallway after her.

Lorelei pauses at the mouth of the den. The sliding door has been pushed most of the way open, and the TV is on with the sound off, which means Zoe's halfway between pretending to get work done and buckling down to actually do it. Right now she's gotten as far as opening a book she doesn't seem to be reading. When she sees Lorelei, she sits up too straight. "Hey," she says. "Uh."

Lorelei stands in front of her, feeling like she's going to faint. Her hands are empty and heavy at her sides.

"I—" Lorelei starts at the same time Zoe says, "I really—" and they both laugh a little, but it doesn't break the tension.

"You first," Lorelei says. At least she'll know what she's getting herself into.

"Sorry about being weird at Daniel's party," Zoe says.

"You weren't that weird." Lorelei's reply is automatic. It takes her another few seconds to register that it wasn't anything—that Zoe doesn't seem mad at her. At all. Somehow.

"Yeah, I was." Zoe closes the book without bothering to mark her page and scrubs a hand through her long hair. "God, I woke up in the morning and I was just like—what was that, you know? I never drink like that. Or I haven't, before. And then we were all being weird. No wonder you wanted to leave."

"Yeah. I mean, no. I get it! You were excited."

"I just did not want that night to end," Zoe says. "But then it did, and it was like—I don't know, it was weird. Like the world snapped back into focus or something. In the morning. I still wanted you to sing again, but it wasn't, like, urgent? Anyway, I'm sorry."

"Me too." Lorelei carefully sits down on the couch. "And I'm sorry about the last few days. I just needed to figure some stuff out. You know?"

"Yeah," Zoe says. "Of course."

She looks down at her hands. There's a vulnerability in the movement that makes Lorelei just a little bit brave.

"I missed you," she says.

Zoe says, "Me too."

Then, finally, it feels normal in the room. It's like the air Lorelei sucked out by coming in rushes back, and they can both breathe.

Zoe remembers something with a start. "Oh shit," she says. "Come upstairs. I have a secret to tell you."

In Zoe's room they take their usual spots on the bed.

Lorelei has her head on the pillows, and Zoe props herself up against the footboard, so they can face each other. Their feet meet in the middle.

"So we went back to the party after we dropped you off," Zoe starts.

"Oh. Good." Lorelei doesn't really want to hear about what the party became in her wake. "Was it fun?"

"Yeah. Because. I, um. I totally did it with him. With Daniel. That night."

"Holy shit." Lorelei sits straight up, all of her misery knocked right out of her head. "Whoa, Zoe, that's, like, *huge.*"

"I know!" Zoe wails. She hides her face in the covers. "I had thought about it before, and we'd kind of talked about it, and I just felt like, I don't know, there he was, there the house was. Why not, you know?"

An awful thought occurs to Lorelei. "Did you decide after you dropped me off?" she asks carefully. "Did you— Did it have anything to do with my singing?"

"No," Zoe says. She laughs. "Don't get me wrong, L, you were good, and we were excited, but, uh, not that kind of excited."

"Okay. Yeah. That probably sounds crazy. I'm about to sound crazy. I have to tell you something," Lorelei says. She's lost Chris, and if she's going to lose Zoe—better to get it over with. In a second more she'll lose her nerve. "I sort of accidentally influenced you. And everyone there."

Zoe gives her the look everybody gives her at first: like she's crazy.

Lorelei tells it as quickly as she can: Oma's rule against

singing, and her mother's idea that it was a curse, and Hannah's email, which gave it a name. She tells Zoe about her single-minded desire to win Chris back, even if it was risky to try. And about Chris showing up at the house, and singing to him on Sunday. She leaves out the parts with Carina and Jackson.

When she's done, Zoe says, "That's really a lot. Are you— You said your mother believes all of this too? And Nik and Chris?"

"They know it."

"You understand why I'm having trouble swallowing it, though, right?"

Lorelei doesn't know what to say. She doesn't *want* Zoe to believe her. She doesn't want it to be true. But offering proof means singing, and she's done with doing that, now that there's no more to undo.

"I know you were good," Zoe says again. "But. Lorelei. Magic? Sirens?"

"Why would I make this up?"

"I don't know!" Zoe throws her hands in the air. "Are you— Could it be a sad-about-Chris thing? Are you mad at me for losing my virginity first? I just don't—"

"It's not about anyone else. It's about me," Lorelei says.

Zoe relents. "Okay. Sorry."

They fall into silence, and even though they're in Zoe's familiar bed in her warm house, it's uncomfortable between them all over again.

"Can you sing to me?" Zoe asks. "If you can influence people with your voice—I don't know, if you could just show me."

"It's unpredictable," Lorelei says. "I'm not really sure I have enough of a handle on it."

"You did it with Chris, though, and it kind of worked. Right? You cured him, or whatever."

"I think so. But I had to. Leaving him that way was worse. If you're okay, I just—I don't want to. Don't ask me to."

"It seems like it matters," Zoe says curiously after a while. "Who you sing to. What you want. What you're thinking about."

"Yeah," Lorelei says. "Exactly. The letter said never to sing to anyone I needed anything from."

"Do you need anything from me?" Zoe asks.

"I don't want to lose you."

"Oh, Lorelei." Zoe crawls over so they're facing the same direction, and butts herself up against Lorelei's side like a cat. "I don't want to lose you, either."

"Some things we just can't share, though. You and Daniel. Me and this."

"I trust you," Zoe says. "I do."

"I don't trust me."

Lorelei decides to change the subject.

"Did you know?" she asks. "That you were ready?"

Zoe laughs. "I thought so, I guess," she says. "Enough so that I did it, anyway."

"Have you changed your mind since you did?"

"I just didn't know what it was," Zoe says. "I thought I did, and so I thought I was ready, and it wasn't— I wasn't wrong, exactly. It's just different. I couldn't have known until I did it. What it would be like. I'm not sure there is such a thing as ready, when it's that big. When it's a before-and-after question. When you can't know what you're trying to be ready for until you've already done it." She rolls onto her back and stares up at the ceiling. "It's funny. I think I was more scared after, actually."

The last light of day is coming in through the windows, heavy all around them, making the room glow gold. Days of rain have cleared the air so that it's desert-bright, fine and clean. The sunset will be neon clouds and a pastel sky. In the morning Lorelei will be able to see the mountains again.

"I didn't know what I was doing," Lorelei says. "I'm not sure I ever will."

"Who does?" Zoe says. "I mean, seriously, I don't. Carina sure as shit doesn't."

"That's awful."

"Yeah." Zoe sits up so that the sunlight silhouettes her, black against the gold.

Lorelei closes her eyes and opens them again. "Okay," she says.

"Okay?"

"Sure."

Lorelei waits for a melody to come to her. It arrives from somewhere deep in the back of her brain, something she thinks she might remember from a long time ago. She hums it until the words come to join in. They aren't English. They're sounds she must have picked up in childhood, her mother or grandmother bending over her crib to whisper her a song. She tries to remember which it was, but their faces blend together and it's impossible to know what she actually remembers and what she's just inventing.

It would be too easy to sing Zoe to her. She could reinforce their friendship into something steel-boned and enduring. Lorelei knows how to do that. She's familiar now with the seeking tendrils of her own desire, and the way they can warp when they tangle up with somebody else's. But that's not what she wants, actually. She wants Zoe to be able to keep choosing her because that's what she wants too.

So instead, for the first time, Lorelei sings about herself.

She sings out the quiet years, and the recent months, the things she never said to Oma and can't say to her mother and won't get to say to Chris. She sings about the cold silence she spent so much time cultivating, and how good it felt to abandon it, and how scary it is to feel it growing inside her again. Lorelei sings about Chris's hands on her skin, and the ocean all around her, and the fear that she's too much, and not enough, and that nobody will ever love her, or that someone will, and that will be worse.

"Oh," Zoe says when she's finished. "Oh, Lorelei." She wraps her up in her arms and holds her there. "I'm sorry," she says against the cotton of Lorelei's T-shirt. "I'm so sorry. You're right. I didn't know."

⟡

Lorelei stays at the Soroushes' for dinner. Zoe insists that she sleep over, even though it's a school night. It's a relief to be at their dinner table, among a close, chattering family. After dinner they watch television, a luxury Mrs. Soroush allows only because Zoe tells her Lorelei got dumped.

("Thanks," Lorelei says. Zoe gives her a pointed look and says, "Hey, it worked, right?") They don't talk about it again until they're tucked up in bed together, each of them co-cooned in her covers.

"I think the last time I slept over was the first night we went to one of Chris's shows," Lorelei says. "When we snuck out to go to the Roxy."

"That feels like a million billion years ago," Zoe says. "I was right, though. He did totally fall in love with you."

"Kind of."

"What do you mean, kind of? You said you only sang to him that one time, at the party."

"I sang him a line outside the Roxy that night," Lorelei reminds her. "And again the night his mom caught us in their house. It was only a little bit, but he said— Anyway. I think it was enough to make a difference."

"Isn't that kind of like falling in love with you, though?" Zoe muses. "Like, I've been thinking about it, and I had talked to Daniel about—you know, doing it, that night. And your singing probably pushed me further in that direction, but so did the drinks I had, and, like, I don't know, the stupid text messages he sent me earlier in the day, and pheromones or something. It's not like falling in love is a streamlined process, you know? People fall in love for all kinds of dumb reasons."

"But this is *magic*," Lorelei protests. "This was against his will."

"You sang to him, what, three times? Over the course of two months? And you didn't know what you were doing."

"I knew it wasn't right to do it."

"And the first time you really talked, you were wearing lipstick and a cute dress, and when I went out with Daniel, I put on high heels and talked about stuff he would think was funny. We're always trying to show our best sides to people. You're not the first wily seductress in the world, Lorelei."

"It's an unfair advantage."

"And you won't ever do it again," Zoe says. "But I'm not sure it invalidates your entire relationship with Chris. It makes it complicated, for sure. But it doesn't ruin it. And it doesn't mean you'll ruin the next one. Your life isn't over yet, you know."

"Not 'til the fat lady sings," Lorelei mumbles nonsensically. It's late and she's so, so tired.

"Pork up, buddy," Zoe says. She pokes Lorelei in the ribs and then rolls over to wrap her in a lazy embrace. "I love you no matter what, though, right? Okay?"

"Okay," Lorelei says. It's a relief to find, finally, that one thing can be simple and true.

42

LORELEI'S INSTINCT IS TO be alone, still, but she fights it: no more quiet. On Thursday she actually convinces Jens to let her help in the kitchen a little bit, and then she does homework with Nik. She finishes before he does, and curls herself up on his bed. He lets her.

He opens up a math book and turns on music, low in the background. It's the first time Lorelei has heard music in her own house, a song played casually, just to keep time. The sound is sort of crappy, actually, coming from his laptop's tinny speakers.

"You need anything?" Nik asks her.

"Nah," she says. "Just company."

❧

Nik finishes up and goes to bed around eleven, or he shoos her out of the room, anyway, and Lorelei doesn't ask why. He deserves some of his own secrets, though she's hoping he and Jackson are really done. Angela doesn't deserve it, but neither does Jackson, and neither does Nik.

She passes Petra's office on her way down the hall. Her mother has been there or at work every minute since Lorelei sent her the email. There's more to tell her—more, still, always more—but she seems too dazed to take anything else in yet. Lorelei trails her fingertips against Petra's doorjamb as she walks by, and then along the walls past her own room, to Oma's.

She sits on the bed. She's excruciatingly aware of her weight wrinkling the comforter. Oma made this bed every morning: she pulled the sheets tight and made sure her corners were neat. It's been waiting for her return for months now, and even if Lorelei gets up and strips it herself and remakes it, even if the bed looks correct again, it won't be the one Oma made. It won't ever be Oma's room again, either.

There's no good reason for the family to keep waiting to turn it into something else.

On the other hand, it's not like they need another room in the house. The family as it is won't last that long, anyway: the twins will leave for college, and then Lorelei, and when Lorelei tells Petra what she's learned . . . Lorelei tries not to think about it. As soon as she tells her mother, Petra will have to try to free her father. And the great relief of Lorelei's life might end up being the undoing of her parents'.

But maybe that won't be the end. Maybe her parents will move out and find somewhere smaller and more suited to them. They'll have to figure out how to be happy together, then, and how to fill a different kind of silence.

It should make Lorelei sad to imagine all of this, but

the image lightens her: The rugs on every floor being lifted, dusted and beaten, and rolled up and sold or put into storage. Her parents finding a place just for the two of them, and some young family filling this space up with laughter and sound.

Lorelei flops onto her belly. The sheets twist underneath her when she does. It's a deliberate action. Then she jumps up and starts pulling books from the shelves.

There are no boxes, but she makes piles: to keep, to ask someone else in the family about, to give away. She does the same with her grandmother's clothes, which are mostly sensible polyester things, cheap and well cared for. She saves the few funny little luxuries, mothballed furs left over from Germany's frigid winters and a few favorite pieces of Oma's knit wool. She sorts knickknacks and tchotchkes, rearranging the space so that it's very clear that no one lives here anymore.

Only then does she turn off the lights and take off her clothes and lie naked between Oma's crisp, cool sheets. Sometimes when she was little and sick, Oma would put out a cot for Lorelei at the foot of her bed, but she's never actually slept here before. It doesn't feel magical, particularly. It just feels like a bed. Lorelei lies still and watches the darkness. When she wakes up, it's morning.

43

ON FRIDAY LORELEI COMES home from school with the afternoon stretching out emptily. It's the first day of winter break. She's too exhausted to believe it yet.

Her father is there when she arrives, sitting on the living room couch.

"There you are," he says, and closes his laptop with a click.

"Yeah." Lorelei shifts from foot to foot and considers the likelihood that he'll let her escape this conversation twice.

"I noticed Chris hasn't been back here since the weekend," Henry says.

Lorelei winces. "No."

"He seems nice."

"He is."

"I wish you had told us you were dating someone." Henry nods his head to the space next to him on the couch.

"Dad, I've really got to—"

"Come sit," he says, and it's not a question.

Lorelei does.

"I'm not dating him anymore," she says. She crosses her

arms and pulls her knees to her chest. "Anyway, what, am I not allowed?"

"No, no, you're allowed. I just . . . We do need to talk about this, Lorelei. Because I could have told you more about your voice."

"I *asked*," Lorelei says. "I asked Oma, and she told me not to sing and not to worry about why. And then Mom told me your whole messed-up story, okay, so— I just wanted one thing to be normal for a little while. One thing. Which obviously didn't really work out for me, so."

"I'm sorry." Her father scrubs the heels of his hands against his eyes and runs his fingers through his thick gray hair. Lorelei bites down on the tenderness that rises in her. "I didn't think it would end up like this."

"How did you think it would end up, then? You heard me, that afternoon. You knew."

"I thought Oma told you. I should have known she wouldn't."

"Because she didn't *trust* me."

"Your grandmother was very proud," he says. "She believed in keeping up appearances. She wanted things to be normal too, after her fashion. I don't think she realized this wasn't going to go away."

"And then Mom told me I was cursed."

"Your mother has her own way of taking things."

"So what would you have told me, if I had asked? That the women in my family enchant people by singing to them? That you've been under a spell my whole life?"

"Is that— Is that what she told you? Oh, Lorelei. That's not true."

"Please. I've seen how you look at her. She told me what happened." Lorelei's stomach tightens and twists sharply when she thinks of how he'll look if he loses Petra, or loses the part of him that loves her.

"It was bad for a few years," Henry says. "And it's— I don't know. I'm inside of it. I don't know what it would be like without it. You're right that I probably wouldn't have stayed with your mother for long enough to find out.

"But it's been— We've been together for a lot of years now. It's kind of impossible to know how much of it was mine to begin with." Henry scoots in a little bit closer. He doesn't touch her but he's close enough that she can reach out, if she wants. "You and your brothers, though," he says. "That's not complicated. I love you because I love you. I always have and I always will."

"Would you leave her?" Lorelei asks. "If you could."

Henry heaves a huge sigh. "It would depend," he says. "I was very angry for a long time. As angry as I could be, under the circumstances. That might come back. And you know, she might want me to leave. We both remind each other of a lot of tough stuff. But grown-up relationships are always full of tough stuff. That doesn't make them broken. And I promise you, it doesn't have anything to do with you."

"I'm *just like her,*" Lorelei spits out. "I did exactly the same thing."

"No one ever told her, either, what the consequences were," Henry says. "And she was so sad, and so lonely. You know why I forgave her?"

"Why?"

"After Oma told her, she never sang to me again. I begged her. For years. I still—" He doesn't have to tell her. Lorelei remembers his face when he thought the song might be for him. "But she never would, once she knew for sure. That's how I've been able to stay with her, and to trust her. Everyone screws up. The question is only really what you do afterward. Whether you're brave enough to face up to what you've done."

There it is again, the grown-up question she wanted to ask Oma, about the possibility of survival and transformation. Carina started to answer it, saying: *You'll survive it, but you have to want to.* Now her dad is amending the answer: *It's not enough to want it. You have to go ahead and try.*

It's not much, but it's something. Hope starts to glimmer at the horizon of Lorelei's mind. Maybe she's right about something, finally: that growing up leaves traces on you—a scar, a tear, a glue-mended crack—to mark the violence of the change that made it. You don't get to become someone else without letting go of the person you used to be.

Lorelei isn't certain she trusts him, but then, there's no power in his voice, nothing that could pull her under or bend her will. He's just her human father, sitting with his palms up in his lap, trying to convince her because he wants to fix some small part of things. She's grateful for the animal comfort of his body next to hers: the pulse of his heart beating, the tidal hush of the blood in his veins. He reaches out and puts an arm around her shoulders.

Maybe whatever happens between her parents has

nothing to do with her. Maybe she can tell her mother the truth, and let them figure it out. They have before. They might be able to again.

"Be brave," he says against her hair. "Be brave, do better. That's all anyone is asking of you, Lorelei."

44

IT'S LIKE SHE RECOGNIZES the guitar, the first time she sees it: it's small and sweet, honey-blond in the sunlight, worn in from years of being played. "This one," Lorelei tells her father.

"Are you sure?" he asks. "We can look at the new ones. You can—"

"This one," Lorelei says. "I'm sure."

Lessons won't start until break ends. Everything is on hold for the holidays. Lorelei teaches herself chords and songs in her room. Her fingers bruise. Her wrists hurt. She takes the guitar with her to the beach and sits and plays in the sand. Sometimes a tourist passing by will toss her a dollar, like a joke.

She's out there, sitting on the low cement wall that marks the edge of the paved pedestrian path, when Chris materializes in the corner of one eye, at first just as a far-off blur.

They haven't spoken since that day at his house. He hasn't called, and she hasn't texted. Lorelei's body knows him just before her brain does, her heartbeat ratcheting up an instant before she can explain why it's pounding.

He's walking alone, wearing a navy sweatshirt she doesn't recognize. His curls have been trimmed short again. He moves to flick them away from his face, before remembering they aren't there. Those funny, reflexive gestures that stay after the use for them is long gone.

He sees her too. She watches him startle, and freeze, and decide something. He keeps walking toward her. He stops when he gets there.

"Hey," Lorelei says.

"Hey." Chris rocks back on his heels and looks at her. "What's all this? I thought you said you weren't going to sing anymore."

"I'm not!" Lorelei puts the guitar down on its soft case. "I'm not. I'm just trying to figure out if there's another way for me to make music. You know."

"You really love it, huh?"

Lorelei nods. "I really do," she says. "I don't think I could live without it."

"Good. I mean. Good."

"It is," Lorelei says. "It seemed like—maybe if I had something for myself—I wouldn't want to . . ." She can't find a way to say what she means without bringing too much of it up. "Anyway. Um. How are you?"

"I'm okay. I'm actually fine, really."

"Are things with your mom . . . How are they?"

"None of your business." Chris sighs, and then relents. "Also fine, though."

"I'm really—"

"I know you are. And it had to happen eventually. I just wish—"

"Yeah," Lorelei says. "Me too."

"So you're teaching yourself?" he asks, looking down at the guitar.

"I'm trying. It's hard."

"Yeah, well," Chris says. "Good luck, okay?"

He smiles at her. He's still beautiful. Lorelei's heart twists. Something dark stirs in her, that old blind longing. But he isn't hers to want anymore.

She picks up the guitar and strums. It hums in her arms, low and sweet.

45

LORELEI KEEPS CLEANING OUT Oma's room, one day at a time. She leaves boxes of giveaways in the front hall, and her brothers drive them out to Goodwill. Her progress is slow and steady. It's the weekend again before it's empty. On Sunday morning she starts to put it back together: sheets on the bed, a few books on the shelves.

Petra comes in to watch her work. She doesn't say anything.

"I was thinking it could be a guest room," Lorelei tells her. "It seemed like it was time."

Petra stays silent. She walks across the room and trails her fingertips over every blank, shining surface, like she can't decide whether the world is real or not.

At length, Lorelei asks, "Do you miss her?"

Petra looks up. "Why—" she starts, but her voice cracks and she has to start over again. "I guess I've missed her for a long time," she says.

Lorelei puts the last pillow in its case on the bed. She

says, "I was thinking of going for a walk. You, um. Do you want to come with me?"

She can't tell which of them is more surprised when her mother says, "Yes."

❧

Petra blinks sharply at the daylight outside. She's not one for walks: she goes to work at eight a.m. and returns each day at seven. She usually stays in on weekends.

"I'm glad I got to read the letter," Petra says. "Did you— You wrote to her?"

"Yeah. I had been reading Oma's old letters, trying to figure out what was going on, and it seemed like maybe Hannah was the one who would know."

"Are you sorry you found out?"

"I don't think so," Lorelei says. "No, you know. I'm not."

They arrive at the beach where Lorelei threw herself under, and found her way beneath the roll of the tide. Petra steps into the sand without hesitating. She kicks off her shoes, and picks up the long hem of her skirt to keep it from trailing while they walk. Lorelei stumbles as she bends down to untie her sneakers.

There's nothing more to wait for. Lorelei has been resolved to tell her mother for days. The opportunity is handing itself to her.

"I think it's different if you know how to use it," she says. The sand is damp and gritty from the rain but the sky is lightening above them, a hundred different layers of white and pearl and gray.

"*Use* it?" Petra's calm turns furious.

"You read the letter," Lorelei says. She refuses to back down. She's weathered enough of her mother's storms to know what the dangerous ones look like. "It didn't say not to sing. It said to be careful. It said—"

"Not to sing to anyone you needed anything from. But I didn't think you would be stupid enough to test out a theory on some—on someone—"

"I was stupid enough to sing to people in the first place," Lorelei says. "I had to see if I could undo it."

"Undo it?"

"Yes."

"You could?"

"I did."

The words are small and stark against the world's tuneless humming, the crash of water and the rush of wind. Petra's body sags hard, like her strings have been cut. Her shoulders fall toward one another and her spine goes liquid. Her knees give up as she sinks to sit in the sand.

Lorelei sits next to her. "You could—with Dad," she offers. "I think you could—" But she can't say it, *let him go.*

Petra hears the unspoken words, and her chest heaves once as she sucks in a long, gasping breath, and then another.

"Do you want to?" Lorelei asks.

Petra puts her head down on her knees. Lorelei only barely hears her when she whispers, "No."

Lorelei frowns down at her feet where they're burrowing into the wet sand. She's always thought of her mother as hopelessly, hideously selfish. She's wanted to revise her opinion, these last few weeks, at first because she thought Petra was spellbound, and now because she knows that the spell was only ever something Petra put on herself.

She can see now that Petra never trusted her own mother or her own desire, her marriage or her children: anyone or anything. She locked herself up in offices and spare rooms because she couldn't stop herself from wanting things, but she could stop herself from getting them, at least.

Petra lifts her head. "I have to," she says. She's dry-eyed and sober. "I know I have to. I will. And he'll leave me."

"He might not." Henry can tell her the rest of it himself. Lorelei offers what she can: the truth, some hope.

"How did you do it?" Petra asks. "Did you just sing?"

"That's the trick, pretty much."

"But how do you keep yourself from—from wanting—"

"I don't think it's possible not to want things," Lorelei cuts in. "That's not it, exactly. You just have to want for them to be themselves when it's all over. You have to want to be yourself too. It isn't easy. I screwed it up the first few times. Clearly."

"What if I don't love *him*?" Petra says. Her laugh is bitter and brittle. "What if he does, and it's me who can't?"

"Only one way to find out."

The two of them sit for a little while longer.

"The letter said the women used to gather at the shore and sing sometimes," Lorelei says. "After they stopped needing things. To keep in practice. It sounds like you have to use it, one way or the other."

"Or it wears you out," Petra says. "Dries you up. I know."

"You know?"

"Every couple of years, I would get too tired. I would see myself in the mirror and I would be so hideous. I would sneak out and come here, where no one could hear me. Where it would be safe."

Lorelei finds her mother's hand and curls her fingers around it. They're both white-knuckled with cold. "Now we can do that together," she says.

"We don't know any of the same songs."

"Teach me yours," Lorelei offers. "I can teach you mine."

"I've heard what your brothers call music," Petra sniffs. "I'm not sure that even counts."

Lorelei laughs and tightens her grip on her mother's hand. "Come on," she says. "I've never heard your voice before."

Petra gives her a long, thoughtful look, and stands up, pulling Lorelei with her. They walk until their toes are at the edge of the frigid, foaming sea, until it's lapping at them, begging them to come back. Petra opens her mouth and lets out a long, wild wail.

The sound is raw and awful, like thunder ripping the sky open, like lightning hitting water. Lorelei's voice buzzes against the back of her throat when she hears it. She opens her mouth and lets it out.

The song is about needing and wanting, about getting and having: giving back, giving up, and all the long days they've both lived.

Afterward Lorelei feels an emptiness that's peaceful. Waves recede from the shore, leaving smooth sand in their wake. Her mother turns to her, smiling and radiant. Her lips are parted. Lorelei takes another deep breath, filling emptiness so sound can billow back out.

ACKNOWLEDGMENTS

THANK YOU:

Logan Garrison, who plucked me from the slush pile.

Katherine Harrison, who saw this book in the draft we sent her.

For too many things over too many years to even begin to name: Abram, Alex, Alex, Alex, Amanda, Charlie, Chrissie, Emma, Gina, Henry, Julia, Logan, Lydia, Mia, Nozlee, Sparrow, Tori, Verity, Zoey.

Thank you especially to Gina Delvac, for naming this and every band, and to Andrea Schlosser, who translated all of the German so that I could get a feel for what Lorelei was reading in the letters.

Miranda: f'evz and always my first reader, my very favorite, and my best friend.

For being my extended family, to the communities of the chavurah and the Rosspack. (That's Allison, Alysha, Annie, Becky, Jen, Kate, Raphaela, Sami, and Shira, plus Celo, Gregor, Jarren, Jay, Magpie, Rachel, Sam, Sharifa, Tallevi, Terk, Terri, Thom, Trower . . . and Al.)

For giving me all the time I needed, thank you so much, Ayana, and all of the East Side Jews.

To everyone who taught me how to write, but especially Temple Israel Day School, Jeremy Michaelson, Margaret Wappler, and Adam Cushman. (Extra thanks to the Thursday-night Writing Workshop Los Angeles crew, who read the first draft five messy pages at a time.)

To Rachel Fershleiser, who got excited about a Tumblr post about this book when it was still—and seemed like it might always be—just a Word document in search of an agent.

To my very tall family, for supporting me in my work, and working so deliberately on making your own. Everything I could possibly say about you sounds sentimental and stupid, which is to say: you are too good for words.

Finally, to everyone who ever read something I had written on the internet and asked if I was going to write a book someday—truly, this one is for you.